SINFUL CURSES

THE SHADOW REALMS
BOOK 8

BRENDA K DAVIES

CHAPTER ONE

"Look out!" Elsa cried when something erupted from the sand.

Sahira threw her hands over her head and ducked as it took flight and sand rained down on them. Blinking against the grainy bits clinging to her face and lashes, she tried to clear her vision while craning her head back to take it in.

She lifted her spear as the beast's arms, wings, or whatever they were, spread like a phoenix rising into the sky, but this monstrosity was no beautiful phoenix. The thing was made entirely of sand; pieces of it speckled them before it plunged back into the loose, red earth beneath their feet.

Jumping to the side, Sahira darted out of the way as sand plowed up like a giant earthworm raced toward her. When she kept moving, the thing turned in the sand to track her.

Refusing to run anymore, Sahira lifted her spear, planted her feet, and prepared for battle. They'd survived three days in the Barren Lands; she wouldn't die at the hands of this *thing* or... not hands, but sandy bits all grouped together to become a killing machine. And Sahira was sure this creature was lethal, even if it was only dirt.

As the thing burst free of the sand and flew toward her face, she thrust her spear up to stab it in what would be the belly of a normal creature. It was impossible to tell where she stabbed it, but the sand monster erupted into millions of tiny particles that pelted her.

Her skin turned red, and welts formed beneath the onslaught of the sandblast. When it finally stopped, Sahira attempted to wipe the sand from her eyes, but it was almost impossible since it coated her fingers too.

Eventually, Sahira saw well enough to know the threat was gone and lowered her spear. She wanted to ask what that thing was, but so much sand coated her lips she didn't dare open her mouth to speak.

Over the past three days, she'd probably inhaled and eaten a gallon's worth of sand; she didn't need any more in her system. Refusing to let go, the tiny particles clung to *every* part of her.

"Are you okay?" Zeth inquired.

Sahira could only nod as Orin walked over to study the ground around her. When he lifted his black eyes to hers, they shone with a steely light, but she didn't think it was because the thing had attacked her. It was most likely because he was still infuriated with her.

Ever since he'd accused her—*wrongly*—of sleeping with Zeth, he'd been distant toward her. After they had sex, he'd happily returned to his womanizing ways with who knew how many more sexual partners.

He hadn't shown any care to her or given her anything more than a passing wave in all that time, but because he now believed she had sex with Zeth when she fed from him, Orin was pissed at *her*. The hypocrisy of his attitude wasn't lost on her... or appreciated.

She could *never* deny her intense attraction to the dark fae, which lingered as her dislike for him grew. She never would have believed it possible to hate him more than she used to, but Orin, and his shitty attitude, had proven she could.

"What was that?" Elsa whispered.

Sahira's gaze flicked to the pretty witch whose chestnut brown eyes were wide as her gaze ran over Sahira. Elsa had pulled her chocolate brown hair into a braid she'd coiled like a crown around her head. The red sand coating it had turned her hair a different shade, but strands of its pretty color peeked through.

"I have no idea," Zeth answered. "I've never encountered anything like it during my travels into the Barren Lands, but I rarely encountered the same creature twice, and it always felt like this place was changing around me."

Wonderful, one more thing to worry about in this endless hell of sand and sun.

CHAPTER TWO

WITH A SIGH, Sahira tried wiping away more of the sand, but only spread it further. The tiny particles had gotten into crevices where they should *never* be and refused to come free. It covered every part of her.

It hurt to walk as it rubbed against her skin and made between her thighs and ass raw. She never could have imagined sand making life so miserable, but it had.

She'd always loved the beach and ocean but hoped never to see sand again after this. Eventually, she succeeded in freeing her lips enough to speak.

Waving her fingers in front of her face, she whispered, "Air in front of me, mote it be, mote it be. Air protect me, mote it be, mote it be."

Though she couldn't see it, a small wall formed before her eyes to keep the sand from blowing into them. From experience, she knew this reprieve wouldn't last; the sand would find its way in again, but it gave her a little break, at least.

"Anyone else?" she asked as she wiggled her fingers.

"No, mine's still working from the spell you cast earlier," Zeth said.

"I have my own," Elsa replied.

As much she hated the idea of doing anything nice for Orin and knowing he would probably refuse, as he had the other times she'd offered, she shifted her gaze to him. He was almost always a complete asshole, but she wasn't like him, even if she would prefer to choke him.

He wasn't paying attention to her, and she wouldn't go out of her way to offer help. Lowering her hand, she watched as Orin surveyed the sand where pieces of the thing landed before turning to examine where it first emerged.

"What is it?" Elsa inquired.

When he shook his head, sand flew from his black hair. As his hair settled back into place, the tips of his pointed ears poked through it. He brushed a few strands away from his forehead.

With his narrow face, high cheekbones, slightly pointed chin, and hawkish nose, he was gorgeous even as he radiated an aura of menace. Unfortunately, his handsomeness also hid a cruel, soulless heart.

The only things Orin cared about were Orin and his family. Technically, once Lexi and Cole wed, Sahira would be related to him by marriage, but she was *not* on the list of things he cared about.

And she was fine with that.

Sure, she could admit his rejection of her after they had sex —which, despite everything, was still one of the best nights of her life—had cut deep, but she'd moved on since then.

Or at least that's what she told herself, all while his smell of cinnamon and clove caused yearning to clench at her heart. She would have to get used to being disappointed because, while she'd made the mistake of falling into his bed before, she wouldn't repeat it.

"What is it?" Elsa asked again.

Orin turned away from the horizon and focused on Elsa. Wearing his cloak, a long-sleeved shirt, and pants, she couldn't see the ciphers running across his upper chest and arms before ending at his wrists, but they were there.

During her night with him, she'd traced each of those marks until she memorized their ebb and flow. Each of those ciphers was like fire and water as they flowed like a river but possessed the sharp points of flames.

Ciphers indicated how much power a dark fae possessed, and while his older brother Cole had more than him, she hadn't seen any other dark fae with as many markings as Orin.

And those were only the ones he *allowed* her to see. Though she'd never seen them, and he kept them hidden, she was sure far more marks covered him.

"Nothing," Orin finally said. "We should keep moving."

Sahira would prefer not to encounter another one of those things, but at least, even if it was a weird, frightening creature, it wasn't deadly.

That wouldn't last long in these bleak, Barren Lands.

CHAPTER THREE

ORIN FOCUSED his attention ahead while he searched his surroundings for any hint of a threat. He didn't believe the thing that erupted from the sand earlier was as harmless as it seemed.

Nothing was harmless in these Barren Lands, not even the sand sticking between his ass cheeks and rubbing his skin raw with every step he took. He loathed the Cursed Realm and everything it had to offer.

He would do anything to escape this place but wasn't sure if traveling these Barren Lands was the answer or how they would get killed. *At least then, we'd finally escape the Cursed Realm.*

It was far from the ideal way to escape and *not* the route he planned to take. They had to kill anything they encountered in this land of endless sand and few possibilities.

Something wasn't right; whatever that thing was, it couldn't destroy them, so why reveal itself? Had they somehow scared it out of its hiding place, or was it meant to be a distraction for something else?

Was it a lookout for something bigger and worse?

In this hellhole, that was a good possibility. They'd encountered a few strange creatures since leaving Belda's town, but most kept their distance and remained distant, shadowy figures on the horizon.

They were deeper into the Barren Lands now; it would be much harder to turn back and flee whatever awaited them. Sand kicked up around them, swirling in the sun as the breeze spun it in circles.

It shifted across the desert, creating movement like the sea rippling with waves. He spotted motion in his peripheral vision, but when he looked, it vanished.

He couldn't tell if it had really been there and gone or if the sand was creating mirages. If something was out there, fucking with them, it should stop being a coward and make its presence known.

He preferred to face things head-on; this sneaky, spineless shit didn't sit well with him. It was like Radagast when he was tormenting Sahira, and he'd ensured the warlock paid for his cowardice.

Orin glanced over his shoulder to where Sahira stood with her spear clasped in both hands and held before her; she was ready to gut anything trying to attack her. Her baggy clothes and cloak mostly obscured her hourglass figure, but she could have a hundred layers on, and he'd still know every curve, dip, and hollow of her lush body.

Beneath the cover of her hood, she'd pulled her mahogany hair into its customary bun. Her hood and sand mostly covered it, but he glimpsed some of its striking color.

The chin of her heart-shaped face was set in determination, and her cupid's bow mouth was compressed into a firm line. Across the distance separating them, and over the earthy aroma of the desert, he detected her honeyed scent.

She kept herself as hidden from the sun as possible, but the tip of her nose had turned red. As a half vamp, she could expose herself to the sun without it killing her. However, it burned her more easily than them.

That reddened nose was cute, but it meant she was suffering through one more injustice in this bleak realm, and he didn't like it. *Why do you care if she's suffering?*

He had no idea, considering she'd gone and screwed the demon instead of coming back to him like he'd planned—a fact he'd make her pay for.

Few immortals ever did something he'd never seen coming, and she was one of them. She was supposed to have been pining for him; instead, she'd turned to the demon to fulfill her needs.

Despite deciding to play by a different set of rules with the demon and screwing up *his* game with her, he wouldn't let her die out here. He'd be the one to make her pay for her choices, not this realm.

His teeth ground together at the recollection of what she'd done with the demon. It wasn't jealousy that caused his body to thrum with anger; no, it was because she'd surprised him by turning to the demon, and he didn't like surprises.

Now, they would play a new game; this one would make her days a living nightmare. She'd regret turning to the demon and plotting with Zeth and the other witch to enter this land *without him*.

She'd plotted to leave him behind while she left with them to explore the Barren Lands. It was another betrayal he wouldn't allow to slide.

She had a *lot* to make up to him, and once she did, he'd happily toss her aside for the next woman to cross his path. He'd made the mistake of not moving on after her, as she had; he wouldn't repeat it. First, he had to get out of this realm so he could find a woman to bury his cock in.

Sensing his attention, her thick lashes lifted, and her amber-colored eyes met his. He rarely saw any apprehension in those beautiful eyes, but it was there now, and, for a change, it had nothing to do with him.

He didn't have to ask; he *knew* he wasn't the only one

thinking something wasn't right here. They were all waiting for the trap to spring.

When she looked away, Orin shifted his attention back to the endless, red, sandy landscape that had become a nightmare that haunted his waking moments. Even asleep, he dreamt of sand and creatures moving through it.

He'd fought in countless battles and wars, slept in some of the most uncomfortable and disgusting places in the realms, and experienced things he would far prefer to forget, but this place was hell. He'd rather go back to sleeping on muddy, bloody battlefields than spend one more night with sand creeping into every crevice of his body.

He now understood why so many who ventured into the Barren Lands returned without answers. The place was a psychological war zone with no respite in sight.

But he wouldn't turn back. There was nothing for him back there, and he wouldn't die out here either. He'd find answers; there were no other options.

The wind blew over the sand again to create waves that turned the landscape into a red sea, but there was no water here. There was only the sand, wind, and the sun above.

Thankfully, the sun was nowhere near as hot as their desolate surroundings suggested it should be. The temperature remained steady and pleasant; it was the only good thing about this forsaken land.

From the corner of his eye, he caught an unnatural shift in one of the waves. No breeze created it. Orin froze and held up his hand to halt the others. They stopped a few feet behind him.

He focused on where he'd seen that strange movement and waved a finger toward it as Sahira came to stand beside him. She gripped her spear in both hands while surveying the landscape.

"What is it?" she whispered.

"I'm not sure."

When the sand shifted again, something rolled beneath it

before dropping lower into the earth. Orin braced his feet apart as he pulled his sword from the scabbard on his back.

If this new threat was anything like the last creature, his sword wouldn't be much use against it, but he suspected this rolling, unnatural wave wasn't the same. Zeth came to stand beside Sahira while Elsa fell in at Orin's other side.

"What did you see?" Elsa asked.

"I don't know," Orin said, "but it's hunting us."

CHAPTER FOUR

ORIN'S WORDS caused the hair on Sahira's nape to rise. They'd mostly encountered sand, bones, and a few small critters since leaving Belda's town, but she didn't doubt Orin's words.

She glanced at Zeth, whose seven-foot-tall stature towered a good foot and a half above her. The red horns coming out of the sides of his bald head curved toward the middle of it.

His yellow eyes, clawed hands, and broad shoulders with their sharp, bony hooks coming out the top of them all combined to give him a menacing, intimidating aura, but the man was far kinder than his lethal facade suggested.

With his broad nose, strong cheekbones, chiseled jawline, and deep-black skin, he was handsome, but she felt no sexual attraction to him. And he felt none for her either as, outside of the Cursed Realm, he had a wife and child waiting for him.

To immortals, marriage was a sacred bond only death could sever. Zeth had become her friend, and as this new threat stalked them, she was glad.

Twenty feet away, the ground rolled as their hunter moved through the earth. Sahira ignored her sweaty palms as she shifted her hold on her spear and questioned what was beneath the ground.

Not being able to see their enemy had her heart thumping out a riotous beat as her imagination ran wild. She tried reminding herself that she'd come up against far worse than this before and would continue to do so, but the idea of something under the ground, coming at them, had her adrenaline spiking out of control.

The thing dove beneath the earth and vanished. Her heart beat out the seconds as she waited for it to reemerge or swallow them whole.

Sweat beaded her brow as the seconds ticked endlessly onward. She glanced at her feet, but no hole opened there, and she didn't dare look too long as she lifted her gaze to search the desert.

Another three beats passed before sand sprayed into the air like it was launched from a whale's blowhole. The grainy beads peppered her skin, creating more welts and bruises, but her spell kept her eyes protected.

She had no idea how he didn't flinch away from the sand pelting his face, but Orin didn't turn his head away. The ground quaked as something thudded against it, and dozens of snake-like appendages rose to wave through the air.

Like worms rising from the earth, they wiggled and swayed, but no birds would come to pluck these things from the ground. Instead, whatever this was would have devoured those birds as it sought to eradicate life from these lands.

The monstrous creature, with its awful appendages, flopped forward. When it did, Sahira saw that the things slithering from it weren't appendages but snakelike tongues sliding toward them.

At least a dozen of those tongues blurred with speed as they raced across the shifting red sand before some buried themselves beneath the earth again. Some of the others continued straight toward them, providing a distraction to their comrades who hunted below the ground.

Sahira studied the earth for any sign of the ones who'd gone under it, but she saw no indication of them in the shifting sand. Suddenly certain they were beneath her feet, racing up to eat her, she took a small step back.

The second she did, sand spouted from the ground as one lunged out of the earth at her. Razor-sharp teeth snapped inches from her face, and its rotten stench nearly gagged her.

Twisting the spear up, she batted the creature away before it could bite her. Beside her, black blood sprayed the air when Orin sliced the head off a different one before driving his blade through the head of another, pinning it to the ground.

The main creature, a massive, wormlike thing the color of bile, released an eerie screeching sound as parts of it died. Sahira stabbed another one zigzagging across the ground toward her before yanking her spear free.

Zeth seized a different appendage and jerked its head to the side before tearing it free. Elsa shrieked when one of them shot forward and sank its hundreds of needlelike teeth into her arm.

Orin hacked through the thing attached to Elsa before spinning. He plunged his sword through one that had launched into the air and headed straight toward Sahira. She gasped as she stared at the creature only inches from her face.

Its teeth clacked as it wiggled against Orin's blade until he yanked it up, slicing it in two. Sahira didn't get a chance to thank him before another one burst out of the sand at her feet, rapidly encircled her leg, and yanked.

Unprepared for the violent motion, it pulled her off her feet. Her back smashing onto the ground knocked the air from her. She didn't have a chance to draw another breath before the thing dragged her forward.

Its momentum hauled her across the ground so fast her cloak

sword down to slice through two of the appendages, freeing her legs. The one drinking her blood released its hold as it fell.

One of the other tongues whipped out at his head and sliced across Orin's temple to spill blood, but he didn't acknowledge it as he cut through two more. While he worked to destroy more of them, Elsa gripped her arms to help hold Sahira away from the monster that had shifted its attention to Orin.

One of the tongues that had retreated into its mouth surged out to snap at Orin. He ducked the thing and lifted his sword to spear the appendage.

With Elsa holding her, Zeth released his grip and seized one of the things cleaving to her arm. A crack echoed through the land as he broke it in half, and black blood spurted.

The thing loosened its grip on her before Zeth tore away what remained. When Orin severed the remaining one clinging to her arm, Elsa pulled her back as Sahira tried to get to her feet and scamper away from the monster.

Finally regaining her feet, she staggered back a few steps before nearly collapsing into the sand again. To stop herself from going down and becoming vulnerable to those things again, she locked her knees and planted her spear handle in the sand as the beast shrieked.

"Are you okay?" Elsa demanded.

"Yes," she whispered as blood dripped down her leg, but the flow wasn't lethal. "Thank you."

Closer to the creature, Orin and Zeth used their blades to carve through the remaining tongues. Some had retreated, but others still sought the meal they'd been denied.

Most of what remained outside the monster sprayed blood as they waved through the air. The creature, realizing it was taking more of a beating than it was unleashing, started sinking beneath the earth, dragging its appendages with it.

"No," Sahira breathed.

They couldn't let this thing get away to attack again. Lifting her spear from the ground, she raced forward as the monster continued its retreat.

With a yell, she leapt up as Orin hacked a tongue out of her way. Twisting it around, she gripped the spear and plunged the weapon into the creature's head.

The spear sank through the monster's spongy flesh before breaking out the other side and pinning the creature to the ground. With a violent shake, its entire body jerked upright; it tore from the earth to reveal the thirty-foot-long beast.

She pulled her spear free and jumped down as the creature lurched, and some of those appendages rolled out of its mouth again. Most of those awful things remained trapped inside as her spear kept the creature's orifice closed, but these flopped across the ground as they sought more food.

Orin chopped off the remaining tongues before walking closer to sink his sword into the creature's brain… if it had one. The thing lurched once more before going completely still.

The headless tongues, still searching for food, flopped to the ground. Silence descended as Orin stepped back and lowered his sword.

With the back of her arm, Sahira wiped away the black blood dripping from her forehead. It did little good as she looked down and realized it also coated her hands and arms.

She longed for a shower, bath, or anything she could use to clean herself, but they hadn't encountered something like that in this forsaken land. She was just happy not to have been devoured by this thing.

Orin's gaze flickered over her before settling on the wound on her thigh. "Are you okay?"

She bent to examine the bite that had already stopped bleeding. She poked at it for a second, wincing as she irritated the sore flesh, but it would heal soon.

"I'm fine," she assured him.

His head tilted to the side in that endearing yet maddening

way he had of examining her. Despite her bloody, battered condition and extreme dislike of him, her body reacted to those fathomless black eyes.

Clenching her jaw, she tried to control her impulses and kept her face impassive as he briskly nodded. When he turned away, her shoulders sagged a little as she was released from whatever strange hold he had over her.

She shifted her attention to the others to discover they were as bloody and tired looking as she felt. They'd only been out here for three days but were battered, exhausted, and filthy.

And this is just the beginning.

"We should keep moving," Orin said.

Everything inside her rebelled against moving. She'd prefer to sit and cry or sleep, but those damned to Hell didn't have time for sleep.

CHAPTER SIX

SAHIRA GLANCED NERVOUSLY around as Orin bent to peer inside the rocky formation that towered high into the sky. The thick black slabs of the structure created a cave at least fifty feet tall, but the opening was barely big enough to fit him.

He glanced back at them. "Candle."

Sahira set her spear down before removing the pack she'd created and stuffed full of supplies. They'd planned and saved so much, but she was beginning to realize they wouldn't have enough to get them through this place.

She sorted through her bag before locating a candle and some flint; she handed them to Orin. When his fingers brushed hers, a familiar thrill went through her as electricity crackled between them.

Gripped with the compulsion to clasp his hand, her fingers twitched as she resisted. If he'd felt the sizzle between them, he didn't show it, as his face remained impassive while he took the flint.

She'd never let him know he had any effect on her. He'd moved on, and so had she... or at least that's what he believed.

She much preferred that to the truth... where he stomped all over her heart while fucking his way through the women in the Cursed Realm. When his hand moved away from hers, an inexplicable feeling of emptiness descended over her, but she shoved it back into the deep, dark recesses where it belonged.

Trying to bury her longing for him and cursing herself for it, she kept her face set in stone while he finished with the flint, handed it back, and she stashed it away. Inwardly, her heart raced as her body yearned for more of him.

She had no idea how she could still be so attracted to him after everything he'd done and how heartless he could be. However, no matter how much she opposed it, she couldn't deny there was something between them... or at least there was on *her* end.

He'd already proven he could have sex with her and bounce on to the next woman without hesitation, like all the dark fae. She'd never expected him to be different, but she was disappointed when he proved her right.

Yet, he was enraged with her when he accused her of having sex with Zeth. Even now, days later and in the middle of this endless desert, she could still see his face, hovering only inches from hers as he confronted her in Belda's pub.

His black eyes had shone with fury while wrath twisted his handsome features into something malevolent. She hadn't worried he'd attack her, but she'd never seen him so incensed.

Until then, she hadn't believed he could exhibit so much emotion. He was pure dark fae, a species renowned for their control and lack of emotion. Orin had always been the perfect example of his kind until that morning in the pub.

And now she had no idea what to make of him. He'd been so emotional and angry that morning, and now he was nothing but the ice-cold man she'd always known. He was such a contradiction, and she hated him for it.

Or at least that's what she repeatedly told herself, but she couldn't fully buy the lie. And soon after, he'd returned to being the dark fae who kept her at a distance.

She still didn't understand what had upset him so much that morning. Yes, he believed she had sex with Zeth when she hadn't, but why would that bother him? Did he really expect her to sit around and pine for him?

He certainly hadn't expected it out of any of his other conquests. When she first arrived in the Cursed Realm, she'd walked in on him having sex with three other women. Those three women had traipsed through the pub with numerous other men, and Orin hadn't so much as blinked.

Why did he care what she did or *who* she did, especially when he'd hopped right into someone else's bed *the next day*? None of it made any sense to her.

Maybe he wouldn't be so distant if she told him the truth about what happened between her and Zeth, but she didn't owe it to him. She didn't owe him *anything*.

Still, she hated this strange distance between them. She never would have considered them friends, but they'd been *something*. A weird, messed-up something, but still something more than *this*.

She hadn't thought it possible, and Hecate knew she'd done everything to fight it, but they'd become allies. She couldn't trust him enough to consider him a friend, and Orin didn't have friends, but they'd worked together.

He'd been there when she needed him with Radagast and the scarog beetles, but now he'd erected a wall around himself, and she had no idea why. She was better off with things being like this between them, but she missed him, even if she hated admitting it and would only do so to herself.

CHAPTER SEVEN

ORIN HELD the candle before him as he crawled into the crevice the giant rocks had created. The flame flickering off the walls cast shadows around the space but didn't illuminate much.

With his excellent vision, he saw that the cave went ten feet back before ending in a rock wall. He didn't look back at the others as he crawled into the space.

They would either come inside or stay out there. He'd had enough of the sand and was glad to be out of it. Some of it had blown inside, creating a pile near the entrance, but the small cavern was refreshingly empty of the insidious debris.

Sahira followed him inside. He let some candle wax drip onto the rocks before sticking the candle into it and rising to wipe his hands together. Sand fell off and settled on the floor around him as he stomped his feet.

Elsa and the demon followed her into the cavern, making it feel smaller, but he couldn't do anything about that. They all removed their cloaks and outer layers of clothing before draping them over some rocks.

By the time they finished, he wore a loose-fitting pair of brown fae pants that hung low on his waist. He tried to stop it, but his gaze wandered to Sahira as she neatly folded her clothes and set them on the floor.

He couldn't see her legs under the green fae pants she wore, but the short sleeves of her tunic revealed the welts and bruises on her arms from where the creatures grabbed her. Blood and holes marred her pants, but from what he could see of her injury, it was mostly healed.

He buried his anger over those marks. *Nothing* should have marred her skin in such a way or hurt her like that, but those things had managed to get by him to *her*. In the process, they nearly killed her.

And what do you care if she dies? She was little more than another game for him to play and a way to pass the time. That's all she'd ever be.

But as he told himself this, he couldn't deny that a part of him rebelled against the idea of her dying. He told himself it was because she was practically family, and he had a duty to bring her home. He wasn't sure he bought that.

He also intended to get her in bed again and make her forget about the demon before making her pay for what she'd done. But those things still weren't enough to explain his rage over what that thing did to her.

Refusing to think about it anymore, Orin swept away some of the sand they'd dragged into the small space before sitting with his back against the wall. The others did the same while he removed some food and water from his pack.

He packed enough to last two weeks, but after these last three days in the Barren Lands, he'd started rationing his food. They said nothing, but he noticed the others doing the same after their first night here.

"I have a salve that could help with that," Elsa said as she waved at Sahira's leg.

Sahira turned her leg to examine the wound. "I'm good,

thanks. It had a lot of teeth, but the punctures weren't very deep. It's mostly healed already."

Orin broke off some bread before wrapping the rest and stashing it away. It was already becoming stale as he chewed while staring at the flickering shadows dancing across the wall.

"We can hunt some of these creatures, too," Zeth said as he chewed on a dried piece of meat. "That will get us through longer. We could have eaten that thing today."

"I'd prefer to starve," Sahira muttered.

"What about water?" Elsa asked.

"That could be harder to find, but at least we won't die without it or food," Zeth said.

"Maybe not, but we'll be exhausted, weak, and find it increasingly difficult to move if we go too long without either. And once we're like that, we'll be extremely vulnerable to everything out here," Sahira said.

"We have plenty left for now," Orin said, "and we could find something to eat and a river tomorrow."

They didn't respond while they ate their meager meals. When they finished, they spread their blankets on the ground.

Orin had been happy to leave the sand and desert behind, but the cave suddenly felt too confining. Sahira and Zeth didn't look at each other while they worked to set their blankets up at opposite ends of the cave.

Despite their distance, Orin was reminded that the demon knew what touching, kissing, and being inside her was like. His fingers clenched and unclenched as he contemplated beating the demon to death.

It would serve them both right if he made Sahira watch while he killed her lover. The idea brought a grim smile to his lips.

He was bored, and it would be fun, but he couldn't kill the demon... not yet. There were too many hazards in this realm, and as much as he would prefer the bastard dead, he wanted the demon's strength to help them get through this.

When they were finally free, he'd kill the demon, but not before then, or at least, that was the plan, but plans had a way of changing.

Unable to stand being in the cave with them anymore, he rose, pulled his cloak back on, and clasped it at his throat. "I'll take the first watch."

No one spoke as he left the cavern.

CHAPTER EIGHT

SAHIRA HAD no idea what time it was when she woke, but the candle had burned out and enshrouded the cave in darkness. She hadn't known the time since leaving Belda's town and the single clock in the pub behind. And she had no way of knowing if that clock was right.

In this realm, days revolved around sunrise and sunset. It was the only guarantee they had.

Twisting on her blanket, she stared into the darkness while listening to the faint breaths surrounding her. She couldn't see the others, but she was certain Orin wasn't one of those breaths, which meant he was still outside.

Pushing herself up, she ran her hand over the cool stone while searching for her pile of clothes. She finally located it against the wall, removed her cloak from the top, and pulled it on.

She would change out of her ruined pants tomorrow but was too exhausted to bother doing it tonight. With their limited supplies, she'd shove them into her pack and probably have to wear them again.

She started toward the gray light indicating the cave entrance before hesitating. The idea of dealing with Orin after everything they'd been through and on her limited amount of sleep was exhausting, but she couldn't leave him out there.

He didn't know she was awake, but they'd all agreed to take turns keeping watch while the others slept, and since she wouldn't be able to fall asleep anytime soon, he might as well get some rest. Still, she would have preferred if Zeth or Elsa had woken first and gone out for this.

Dreading her return to the land of sand, Sahira pulled the hood over her head. She kept her hand against the wall while shuffling through the darkness toward the patch of gray.

As she walked, she recalled Zeth and Elsa's locations in the cave. Elsa was further back in the crevice, and Zeth was on the opposite wall, so she wouldn't step on one of them.

Feeling over the cool, bumpy stone surrounding the opening, she ducked to slip outside. When she emerged on the other side, she rose to take in the moon and stars shining brightly in the velvety night.

For once, no breeze moved across the earth, and sand didn't pelt her. The three-quarters-full moon spilled across the red, sandy sea to illuminate a pathway across its pristine surface.

Her fingers twitched as she had the sudden idea she could cross that pathway and touch the low-hanging moon. Something would probably eat her before she arrived, but it was so inviting that she almost wanted to try it.

With the moon, serene sand, and stillness of the night, she could almost believe the desert was as beautiful as it appeared. It was only a trap meant to lure them into a false sense of security before jaws clamped shut on them.

"What are you doing out here?"

The low, gravelly question drew her attention to where Orin sat with his back against the rocks and one leg drawn up to his chest. He'd draped an arm over his knee.

Like the crows the dark fae used to send messages, he was

barely visible amongst the shadows created by the moon. Crows flew into the woods and vanished into them, and the dark fae disappeared into the shadows they used to cloak themselves.

When she edged closer, his onyx eyes came into view as they glistened in the night. His tussled black hair couldn't hide the tips of his pointed ears.

She recalled how he'd turned into her touch when she ran her fingers over those ears and how they felt beneath her hands while she'd grasped them to hold him between her thighs. The memories of the warmth of his kiss, the power in his chiseled, lean body, and the way every one of his touches made her come alive bombarded her.

Gulping, she glanced away as she licked her lips and tried to regain control while staring at the peaceful night. The reminder of that unending sand and the monsters it hid doused some of her rising lust, but still, her skin crackled with its awareness of *him*.

He'd managed to wedge his way inside her soul, and like a parasite she couldn't get rid of, he'd stuck with her. She feared he always would.

She never should have come out here, but now that she was here, she couldn't stand around and not say anything. Finally, she spoke. "I came to relieve you so you could get some sleep."

"I'm not tired. Go back into the cave; tomorrow will be a long day."

"It will be longer if you don't sleep."

"I'll get some rest in a few hours."

She should slip back inside and, even if it wouldn't happen, try to sleep some more, but her feet remained frozen as she studied the moon and stars. She didn't know any of these constellations, and this moon wasn't one she'd seen until arriving here, but they were all so similar to the ones she knew.

It was so beautiful and peaceful out here tonight; it reminded her of home. She hadn't thought much of her brother, Del, and niece, Lexi, since leaving Belda's town, but she couldn't help recalling all the nights they'd sat outside together, studying the stars while laughing, talking, and sharing some drinks.

The memory of their laughter rang in her ears, but after so much time away from them, it sounded duller than it used to.

Am I already forgetting things?

She hadn't believed it possible to forget after little more than a month away from them, but their laughter wasn't as loud as it once was in her mind. Closing her eyes, she fisted her hands against her anguish.

We'll get through this. We'll get out of here.

But her certainty of that grew smaller with every passing day. She wouldn't give in to her doubts; she couldn't. She didn't know if she could go on if she did.

When she opened them again, she focused on the stars as she recalled another memory. She didn't realize she intended to share it until the words were spilling from her.

"Before the Lord unleashed his war on the humans, I dreamed about going into space to see the stars, planets, and moon. I considered opening a portal to the moon but wasn't sure how the whole antigravity, lack-of-oxygen thing would work out if I did.

"Maybe one day I'll get up the courage to try it anyway and curse myself as I float away. Outer space has always fascinated me, and I used to envy the humans who got to explore it. Of course, the Lord destroyed all that, but maybe one day the humans will return to space, and I'll get to float amongst the moon and stars."

CHAPTER NINE

ORIN'S ATTENTION shifted back to Sahira as she stood outside the cave entrance. Bathed in the moon's silvery glow, its light danced across her mahogany hair and striking features.

She'd managed to clean the blood from her arms and face, but her hair still held the reddish hue of the sand adhering to it. Despite the sand and circumstances, she was exquisite.

His cock stirred, and it wasn't simply because he'd gone too long without feeding on sexual energy, like all dark fae did; it was also the woman herself. And he'd destroy her and the demon after he finished with her.

He half hoped they were in love with each other so her betrayal would hurt them both more; because demon or not, he *would* fuck her again. He couldn't do that if he didn't bury his anger and start playing the game… like he did last time.

He should start it now, but he *was* tired and should rest. He couldn't leave her out here by herself, though.

He'd have no problem leaving Zeth or Elsa alone, but he couldn't sleep without knowing she was safe. She was tough and could defend herself, but there were too many dangers out here.

He told himself he only hesitated because Lexi and Cole would be disappointed if he returned without Sahira, but a small part of his brain called him a liar. Whether it was the truth or not, he hated that part.

She slipped her hands into the sleeves of her tunic as she bowed her head. "I don't know why I said that."

He wasn't really in the mood to engage with her but found himself replying, "The universe beyond our worlds is a fascinating place."

"So are the realms."

"Except for this one."

She bit her lip before replying. "This one is fascinating too, even if it is a nightmare."

"That's the polite way of putting it."

She didn't speak again as she shifted her attention back to the sky. Orin's gaze fell to the blood on her pants. He couldn't see the bite from here, but he suspected it fully healed while she slept.

"Are you okay?" he asked, waving his hand at her leg.

Pulled from exploring the stars, she blinked at him before looking at the injury. "Yeah. I think that *thing* rattled me more than hurt me."

"I've never encountered anything like it before." And he hoped never to see one again.

"I wonder how many of them are out there."

"I don't want to find out."

She chuckled as she leaned against the rocks and crossed her legs before her. It was then he realized she had no intention of going anywhere, and if she stayed, the scent of her would drive him mad.

Unlike her, he only had two options to feed from while they were here. Elsa was a very pretty witch, but she wasn't the one he desired.

Rising, he stretched his back and legs as he lifted his arms over his head. He felt her eyes on him, but when he glanced at her, she was studying the desert again. She couldn't fool him; she was as aware of him as he was of her.

When he prowled closer, she folded her arms across her chest. Her head turned toward him.

He stopped beside her and rested his hand against the rocks next to her head. Her chin lifted as her defiant eyes clashed with his. He saw the wariness in her gaze but also curiosity.

Her scent was a breath of sweetness in this land filled with the earthy, crisp aroma of sand and the muskier odor of the creatures who hunted here. And she looked better than she smelled.

When he ran his fingers over the sleeves of her shirt, she stiffened but didn't pull away. Pushing back one of the sleeves, he saw her welts had healed and only reddened skin remained.

He relished the feel of her silken skin beneath his hand as her hands slid free from the sleeves of her shirt. It bothered him the demon had been with her after him, but he'd erase the memory of any enjoyment the encounter gave her from her mind.

In doing so, he'd ensure she never turned to the demon again, at least not while in this realm. By the time they were free of this place and back to their lives, he'd ruin her for all other men.

He could never turn her into one of the shadow kissed sex fiends the dark fae could leave in their wake; she was too strong-willed for that. But he could make it so she pined for him and found it impossible to turn to another while he was fucking his way through the realms.

First, he'd hear her screaming his name as she begged for more. Stepping closer, a bolt of desire ran through him when his chest brushed hers, and her breath caught.

When his gaze fell to her lush lips, she drew the bottom one into her mouth and nibbled it. He clearly recalled the taste of those lips and the fire of her kiss.

Her body had fit perfectly against his as they melded together and her fingers raked his back. While they were together, she was uninhibited in a way she never was, with her hair in a bun and her no-nonsense approach to life.

He'd enjoyed breaking down her barricades, stripping her bare, and her sweet curves. She'd been the greatest pleasure of his life, and he would have more of it.

His hand slipped down until it found hers. Lacing his fingers through hers, he grasped her hand. While his fingers tightened, her grip remained loose inside his, and her breath came faster, but she didn't stop him.

He held her eyes before turning her to face the wall. He expected her to pull away; instead, as if she could no more resist him than he could her, her fingers clenched around his.

Something more than excitement and lust pulsed through him as he gazed at her bent head and exposed nape. In this position, she was vulnerable, but she trusted him not to harm her while he plotted to stomp all over her heart.

He almost smiled with satisfaction but couldn't resist kissing her nape. She trembled as he ran his lips along her tender skin, savoring her taste.

When he stepped forward, his chest pressed against her back. With her hand still in his, he slid them between the valley of her breasts and down her flat stomach to the rounded hips of her hourglass figure.

He thought he'd recalled how good she felt in his arms, but he was wrong. Memories were nothing compared to the actual woman.

Lifting his lips from her neck, he rested them against her ear and whispered, "Do you remember how you begged me to fuck you, how you pleaded for me to go harder, faster, *deeper*?"

Her mouth parted as she turned her head toward him, and desire emanated from her. He felt the quickening of her body against his and knew she was already wet for him.

Oh yes,—he slid their joined hands between her thighs—*I will have her again.*

"Do you remember?" he demanded.

"Yes," she whispered.

CHAPTER TEN

SAHIRA COULDN'T THINK as her mind spun and her body clamored for release from the tension he so easily stoked within her. His breath against her, his erection prodding her back, and his hand guiding hers as he stroked her clit through the thin material of her pants were all she could think about.

She'd missed him. The realization screamed through her even as she tried to deny it, but she had. She'd missed his touch, the way his head tilted to the side when he looked at her, and his often obnoxious attitude.

Before coming out here, she'd been adamant she'd prefer never to see him again, but it would have been a lie. She'd done everything she could to forget him and to deny something different passed between them that night... or at least for her.

In all her life and different partners, she'd never had a man make her body come alive the way Orin did or make her come as hard as he did. Maybe it was a dark fae thing; maybe they had that effect on everyone they were with, but she didn't think so.

She knew plenty of men and women who had slept with a dark fae and easily moved on to their next bedmate. Yes, the dark fae were known for their sexual prowess, but none had raved about the experience, and they'd all moved on without a problem. If they'd experienced the same bliss and wild abandon she had with Orin, they would have at least hesitated.

As much as she hated him sometimes, she didn't think she could ever move completely on from Orin. It had taken nearly all of her four hundred and fifty-three years to be as uninhibited with a man as she was with him.

She'd keep that buried deep inside her; he could never know. He'd only use it as a weapon against her, which should make her pull away from him, but her legs wouldn't move. His mouth returned to her neck, and his kisses sent shivers down her spine.

"It was so good between us," he whispered before nipping her shoulder. "It will be better this time."

It *was* so good between them... until everything went horribly wrong.

An image of that nymph sitting on his lap, the night after they had sex, flashed through her mind. He'd smiled and waved at her from his stool while flaunting his newest conquest.

They were trapped in this desert, and she was one of only two women. He was probably hungry, but that wasn't her problem.

She hadn't asked him to join them on this trip; he'd forced his way onto it without the proper supplies and no way to feed his dark fae appetite. He would have to face the consequences of his shitty choices because she wouldn't be his food supply until they broke out of this realm or turned back.

Despite her body begging for release from the sexual tension he created, she jerked her hand, and his, away before slamming both their hands into the rock wall. The pain that flared through her hand was a welcome reprieve from the screaming ache of her body.

Head bowed, she resisted gasping for air while struggling to control herself. "No."

He'd frozen against her when she pulled her hand away, and

his lips lifted from her neck. He didn't move away as his mouth hovered near her ear.

"You're going to deny yourself this?" he demanded in a raspy voice.

"Yes." She said the word while her body wept over its denied release.

"You know how good it is between us."

"And I know how *bad* it goes afterward."

Regaining more control, she turned in his arms. She planted her palms against his chest to push him back a step. "I'm not your toy or the piece of ass you use to nourish you while you're here. I'm nothing to *you*, but I am something to *me*, and I won't do this again."

She went to push past him, but before she could, he rammed his hand into the stone. Bits of the fractured rock rained around her as his face twisted into a snarl.

"But you'd fuck the demon," he spat.

"I'm free to fuck whoever I choose, just as you are... just as you already *have*. I don't owe you anything."

"And you think I owe *you* something?"

"I never said that. And you made it clear you didn't when you left me in that room so you could cuddle up with a nymph and lick beer off her chest. We don't owe each other *anything*."

She didn't want to do it, she'd prefer to walk away with dignity, but he wouldn't move out of her way. Her refusal had annoyed him; he wouldn't yield to her, so she started to duck under his arm.

He lowered his hand to block her way. Her eyes slid to his as she rose to glower at him.

"If you want to keep that arm, I'd move it," she grated through her teeth.

"Do you think you could take me, little witchy witch?"

"Maybe not kill you, but I'd do some damage."

To her surprise, a smile curved the corners of his cruel

mouth. Goose bumps rose on her neck as that smile unnerved her more than his snarl.

"You won't fuck the demon while we're out here."

He was the only man she knew who could arouse her so completely and, less than a minute later, make her contemplate tearing his dick off so she could beat him to death with it.

"Let's get one thing perfectly straight." She poked his chest with her finger. "I'll fuck whoever I want, and I'll do it in *front* of you if I decide to. You have *no* say over my life."

His eyes glittered with malice. "That's true, but I'll kill him if you do, and you'll have *no* way to stop me."

Sahira blinked at his words and the certainty accompanying them. "What does it matter to you who I have sex with?"

CHAPTER ELEVEN

THAT WAS A VERY GOOD QUESTION; what did it matter to him? Why *did* he care? Why did the idea of the demon knowing her the same way as *him* make him itch to tear the bastard's horns from his head and shove them up his ass?

It was never an issue for all the other women he'd been with, but for her...

For her, the idea made him murderous. He didn't understand it, but he loathed it and the lack of control that came with this new development.

The woman was an enchantress who had worked her way under his skin, and he wanted to claw her out as badly as he wanted to screw her.

He was a dark fae, as cold and calculating as it got, but he didn't feel indifferent to her actions and thoughts. She kept telling him no and had turned to another when she should be craving *him* as badly as he did *her*.

She stared expectantly at him as she awaited an answer he didn't have. Finally, he shrugged. "I'm not done playing with you, and I won't let anyone get in my way of that."

Sadness flickered through her eyes, and her face briefly fell before she composed it again. Orin quirked an eyebrow over that development but didn't say anything as she shoved his hand out of the way.

He decided against stopping her. Her question still had him rattled, as did his lack of a true answer, and not the one he'd give her because, at heart, he didn't think it was true. She was still a game, and he would make her pay for her betrayal, but she was also more than that to him.

"So, I'm still a game to you. Got it," she said as she retreated toward the cave.

Orin restrained himself from following, but when she rested her hand on the wall above the crevice and bent to enter, he spoke again. "I'm not kidding, Sahira. If you don't want to cause his death, you'll stay away from him."

She froze for a minute before her hand fell from the wall. With graceful steps, she sauntered back to him. Stopping a few feet away, she lifted her chin to glare at him.

"Do you *really* think you could take him?" she asked.

"I know I can. Are you so eager to watch it happen? Because I'll gladly take your lover's head and hand it to you. If you'd like, I'll kill him now… for fun."

She didn't flinch, but something passed across her face and eyes. It wasn't sorrow or anger but more like… resignation.

"I don't want anyone to die," she said.

"Then stay away from him, because if you look at him the wrong way, he's dead."

"And just *what* is the wrong way, Orin?"

"I'll know when I see it."

"You're such an asshole. You don't see how hypocritical and cruel you are. You have no idea of the suffering you cause or the destruction you leave in your wake. We're not pawns in some twisted game of yours; we're living, breathing immortals with hearts and souls."

"He'll keep living if you stay away."

"There are times when I truly hate you."

He suppressed the hurt her words caused. She could hate him until the end of time if she was only with *him*; hate would make the sex more intense.

"As long as you don't fuck him again, I'm okay with that."

Her eyes flitted away before returning to him. "I'm not telling you this because I think you deserve any insight into my life, but since you're such a psychopathic douchebag, and Zeth is too good a man to be caught in your twisted, dark fae bullshit, then you should know. I would never forgive myself if you two fought over something that never happened."

Orin's head tilted to the side. "What didn't happen?"

CHAPTER TWELVE

"ZETH IS MARRIED. He has a wife and a son at home," she said. "*That's* why he's in this desert with us and why he tried to leave the town before; he's determined to break free so he can return home to them. We never had sex. He has *no* interest in me sexually because he's in love with someone else."

Orin kept his shock over this revelation concealed, but inwardly his mind spun as he tried to process what she was saying. "You're just saying that to protect him."

"No, I'm not. Ask him tomorrow; he'll tell you he's married, and if you think about it, you'll realize he was never with *any* of the women in Belda's town."

Orin contemplated this as he tried to recall the demon's actions. Yes, he came into the pub alone and left the same way, and he couldn't recall ever seeing the demon with anyone. Still, he was usually too focused on himself to pay much attention to anyone... other than Sahira.

He could have been there or left with other women without Orin knowing, but if Sahira was lying, he could easily confirm it by asking the demon. Marriage didn't automatically equate to faithfulness, he didn't know any immortals who ever ventured from their spouse, but the demon had been here for a while.

His father had sex with other women after the death of Cole's mother, but she'd died, and he was a dark fae who required sex to survive. He'd slept with those other women but never loved any of them.

Many immortals never moved on after the loss of a spouse. Zeth may not have seen his wife in thirty years, but he'd most likely remain faithful to her while he believed she was alive.

"But you fed from him," Orin said. "That can awaken bloodlust in a vamp."

"I did, and I've fed from plenty of others without being consumed by bloodlust. I'll feed from many in the future without losing myself to it too. Zeth offered me his wrist, and I took it; *nothing* else passed between us."

A smile tugged at the corners of his mouth. "So, you're saying I'm special?"

Her mouth dropped a second before she smashed her hands into his chest and pushed him backward. "You're my biggest mistake, the one that keeps kicking me in the ass—the one who *won't* go away. I always knew I'd regret sleeping with you, and you didn't disappoint, but you continue to make that mistake so much worse for me! You're the most selfish asshole I've ever had the misfortune of meeting, and I want you *out* of my life."

She turned on her heel and stomped back toward the entrance. She was ducking down again when he spoke.

"All those things are true, Sahira, but you're forgetting one thing."

She paused to look back at him. "And what is that?"

"You want me as badly as I do you."

She gave him a look that said she'd prefer to see him hanging by his balls before giving him the finger and disappearing into the cave.

Orin grinned as he crossed his arms over his chest and leaned against the wall. Despite his delight over her revelation, her words, while true, stung a little. He was sure plenty of others had considered him the same and worse, but it irritated him that she did.

He'd always enjoyed being a selfish asshole and saw no reason to change. Why would he change perfection?

But why would she feel any different? You've never given her a reason to.

It was true, but he still didn't like her thinking that. It's who he was, who he'd always been and always planned to be.

She should accept and embrace it instead of wanting him to change. He accepted her for who she was, a sometimes uptight pain in the ass who could infuriate him and make him mad with lust.

She fought him at every turn when it wasn't necessary. If she would stop and have sex with him again, they'd both be a lot happier.

Did she think he enjoyed her annoying combination? No, he didn't, but he accepted it.

He wouldn't change, and anyone who didn't like it could die for all he cared... except for her.

For some reason—and he didn't plan to figure out what it was—he didn't like her low opinion of him.

However, that didn't matter as much as what she'd revealed. She *hadn't* slept with the demon. She hadn't moved on to someone else.

Which meant he didn't owe her the punishment he'd planned to unleash on her. *She did plot with the demon and witch to leave you behind while they ventured into the Barren Lands together.*

That was true, and it still aggravated him, but he'd also sought to push her buttons with the nymph and other women he'd paraded in front of her after they had sex. She still should have returned to him to feed.

The fact she hadn't didn't bother him as much as it did when he believed she screwed the demon. He'd still make her pay in the most wonderful of ways for her betrayal when she caved and screwed him again—and she would—but he wouldn't seek to destroy her anymore.

Rubbing his hands together, his smile widened in anticipation of this more enjoyable game. Of course, he'd have to verify she was telling him the truth first.

Sahira wasn't a liar, but there were few he trusted to tell him the complete truth, and she wasn't one of them.

CHAPTER THIRTEEN

OVER THE NEXT THREE DAYS, they made their way deeper into the Barren Lands and toward whatever lay beyond, which Sahira was beginning to fear might be absolutely nothing.

She had no idea where they were anymore. They'd tried to stay straight so they could find Belda's town again if forced to turn back, but with all the shifting sand, it was impossible to know if they were heading straight anymore.

For all she knew, they could be going in circles in this forsaken land. Zeth remained confident they were heading the right way and could easily return if necessary. Sahira was glad he was so sure.

She trusted Zeth's judgment; he'd traversed the Barren Lands before and always managed to find his way back. She had to have faith that he could do so now too.

If he didn't, they would die out here. They'd all already lost weight.

Orin had lost the most as his high cheekbones were more pronounced. Even after only six days in this desert, the lack of sex and his inability to feed on it, along with their smaller food portions, was wearing on him, but that wasn't her problem.

Then why did she feel compassion for him when she shouldn't? He'd decided to come out here without someone to sate his needs. The obstinate jerk had assumed it would be her, but he'd been completely wrong.

That would not happen. Still, she didn't like seeing the toll it was taking on him, even if he would have flaunted his blood to get her into bed again if their roles were reversed. And she was thirsty for blood too, but she could make it a little longer; she wasn't sure about Orin.

She didn't worry he'd try to assault one of them to feed; he wouldn't. He was many things, but a rapist wasn't one of them.

But he might get so weak he couldn't defend himself against an attack. She shoved aside the annoying part of her rebelling against the possibility.

On their sixth day in the Barren Lands, Zeth announced he'd never made it this far. Apprehension churned in her belly as she tried not to think about what that could mean.

Turning back now meant certain failure, and she didn't want to turn back. She assumed they felt the same way since no one else suggested it.

They could only continue onward. It was what they'd planned when they started this, and they'd prepared for it to be bad, but she couldn't shake her growing anxiety.

At lunchtime, or at least it was probably lunch, as their stomachs rumbled, they halted their progression. They settled onto the sand to eat.

Orin leaned against a rock as he chewed a piece of bread. The son of a bitch had been in a better mood since her revelation to him.

"Do you have any family, Zeth?" Orin inquired as he picked at his bread.

Sahira's eyes narrowed on him. She'd expected him to ask Zeth, he didn't trust anyone outside his family, but it still irked her that he didn't take her word for it.

Zeth gazed distrustfully at him as he bit into a piece of dried meat. "Why do you ask?"

"Just trying to learn more about my fellow desert dwellers. What about you, Elsa? Any family?"

Sahira stiffened; she already knew the answer to this question, and it wasn't good. Orin was trying to make sure she'd told him the truth, but that didn't mean her friend had to suffer because of it. Orin's question would reopen deep wounds in Elsa's heart.

Elsa's family was killed by witches and warlocks when she was a girl. Though Elsa didn't respond to his question, Sahira rested her hand over her friend's and squeezed it.

"No," Elsa said flatly.

She knew Elsa had some family who might still be alive, but no one she would acknowledge. Sahira didn't blame her; they were all murderous assholes.

Orin turned his attention back to the demon. Zeth stared at the desert as his hand lowered to his knee, the piece of meat in his hand forgotten.

His questions hadn't just pulled the scabs off Elsa's barely healed heartbreak but also Zeth's. She silently cursed the man as she glared daggers into him.

"Yes," Zeth said, "or I did."

"Brothers, sisters, cousins?" Orin pressed.

"A mother and an uncle."

Zeth stopped speaking as his mouth quirked into a smile, and a sheen of water briefly filled his yellow eyes. Seeming to recall where he was, Zeth turned his head away, and when he faced forward again, the sheen was gone.

"And a wife and son." Zeth's features hardened into something that would have sent many running. "I *will* see them again."

Sahira stared pointedly at Orin as she waited for some sign he was satisfied with Zeth's response. Maybe the dark fae didn't see it because she doubted Orin saw anything he didn't want to, but Zeth clearly loved his family.

"I hope you get to see them again," Orin said with more kindness than she was used to from the man.

Maybe he did have a bit of a soul. It was doubtful, but maybe.

It still irked her that she'd told him about Zeth, but she wouldn't let Zeth get attacked because of Orin's overwhelming arrogance. The dark fae was a dickhead who considered himself a self-appointed God in bed and couldn't handle that she might have moved on to someone better than him.

Sure, he was fantastic at sex, but he wasn't a god, and while he'd completely blown her mind, she'd have orgasms with other men too. Until then, she would keep her friends safe from Orin's manipulations as much as possible.

She scowled at him as she chewed on her dried piece of meat. Orin didn't deserve any insights into her life, and she owed him nothing, but she'd done the right thing telling him about Zeth.

She couldn't let them fight over something that never happened. She didn't understand why, but for some reason, the idea of her sleeping with Zeth bothered him enough that he might have caused problems in their group.

And they had enough problems.

Orin was confident he could take Zeth, but Sahira wasn't sure. Yes, he was fast, powerful, and could cloak himself in shadows, but Zeth was physically stronger, and demons were notoriously good fighters. Zeth also had a family to fight for, and Orin had lost weight.

As much as she hated to admit it, she never would have forgiven herself if Orin or Zeth got hurt in an unnecessary fight. So, she'd given Orin information he hadn't known existed, and instead of listening to her, he'd poked at her friends.

She'd still done the right thing, even if it pissed her off.

Determined to ignore Orin, something he made nearly impossible, Sahira shifted her attention to the distant mountains. They were at least twenty miles away, but the terrain was changing.

Instead of endless sand, some rocks had started jutting up from the earth. Those large, black rocks also hid small creatures that scampered behind them. They'd tried hunting a couple of them, but they were too small for an easy kill and often fled under the sand when they approached.

She'd like to believe all this would improve when they reached the mountains but doubted it. This realm was determined to imprison or kill them, and it was doing a *fantastic* job.

CHAPTER FOURTEEN

"We should get moving," Orin said. "Maybe we can make it to the mountains before nightfall."

"It would be nice to leave the sand behind," Elsa murmured.

Sahira studied Orin as he rose. His skin didn't have its normal, healthy glow, and there was something off about his movements even as he glided forward with mesmerizing grace.

It had been a while since she'd satisfied her vampire's thirst for blood, yet she wasn't ready to ask Zeth or Elsa if she could drink from them. She'd already fed from Zeth, but it was such an intimate thing that it was difficult to ask others for it.

And she wasn't asking Orin.

She'd controlled the bloodlust that could occur when vampires fed while she was with Zeth and countless other men before him. She despised Orin and everything he represented but wasn't sure she could control herself if she fed from him again.

He tasted and smelled too damn good. Not to mention, it would evoke the barely suppressed memories of what passed between them the last time she drank his blood, and those memories could be dangerous if unleashed.

It wasn't a risk she was willing to take.

As if he was reading her mind, Zeth turned to her. "Do you have to feed?"

Orin stopped shoving his supplies into his bag and froze before lifting his head. From the corner of her eye, Sahira saw him watching her but didn't acknowledge him.

"You must have to," Elsa said. "It's been a while."

Sahira's stomach rumbled, but until Zeth offered, her hunger hadn't been a screaming, clawing thing. It was now.

With Orin's eyes burning into her, she remained focused on Zeth. If she fed from him now, she had no idea how Orin would react, and it wasn't something she wanted to deal with.

She could feed on Elsa or Zeth when they were alone again, but not now. "I'm still good."

"You can't get weak out here," Elsa said.

"I won't."

Elsa studied her before shrugging. "Okay. Let us know when you're hungry; we're here to help."

Sahira smiled at her as she finished her piece of meat. "I will."

Elsa wrapped up what remained of her bread and placed it in her bag. Unable to continue ignoring him, Sahira's attention shifted to Orin.

His face was inscrutable and his eyes colder than black ice. She held his gaze before wiping her hands off and placing the rest of her things back in her bag.

She didn't know what he would have done if she tried to feed on either of them, but it would eventually have to happen. It was only a matter of time before it became impossible to ignore her thirst and she started weakening.

Rising, she swung her pack onto her back and cinched it in place. Before she lifted her spear, she tried again to open a portal, something she did daily. And, like always, she failed.

She couldn't stop trying. Maybe one day, she would magically regain the ability to escape this place.

With a sigh, she lifted her bloodstained spear from the ground. She tried not to think about what else lurked out there for them as she started toward the mountains a few steps behind Zeth and Elsa.

Orin fell in beside her. "When you're ready, you'll feed from me."

Sahira didn't bother looking at him. "I'm not playing your games anymore, Orin. I'll feed from Zeth or Elsa; there's nothing you can do about it."

"Do you want to test me on that?"

"Do you want me to get to the point where I'm starved and weakened?"

"That would be your choice."

She stopped walking. He continued for a few more steps before turning to face her.

"I've made my choice," she told him, "and it's *them*. You have to accept it."

He smiled at her as he stepped closer and ran his fingers down her arm. Her skin came alive beneath his touch as all her nerve endings focused on *him*.

Sahira jerked away from him; she wouldn't give him the satisfaction of knowing how deeply he affected her. But it was too late. This man was a calculating asshole who knew exactly what he did.

Orin smiled at her before glancing at the others; they'd continued walking. "You'll feed from me."

Before she could respond, he turned and trudged away.

The fuck I will.

He was about to be in for a rude awakening, but she wouldn't argue with him anymore. They had deserts to cross and mountains to climb.

CHAPTER FIFTEEN

THEY WERE SURROUNDED by mountains when something slipped from behind the rocks and scampered into a crevice. Orin frowned after the creature, but it didn't reemerge and didn't bring a horde of friends out of the hole with it.

Zeth and Elsa exchanged a glance before continuing toward a rise in the craggy, black mountains. From a distance, the peaks looked like they rolled one on top of the other, but up close, they were separate peaks and valleys.

The valleys concerned him the most. From the peaks, they could see anything coming for them and the land for miles around. The valleys were confined spaces they couldn't easily escape.

"Has anyone made it this far before?" Elsa asked.

"I don't know. No one, who ventured into the Barren Lands and returned, spoke of mountains, or at least not anyone I know. There could have been other immortals who left, made it this far, and didn't return," Zeth responded.

"That's encouraging," Elsa murmured.

"Do you think there's a way around these mountains?" Sahira asked.

"There might be," Zeth said, "but it would take time to get around them, and we could lose our path."

"We don't have the water or food supply for that," Orin stated.

Sahira tipped her head back to take in the black rocks towering over them before focusing forward again. "Then it's onward and upward."

Orin wasn't thrilled about that, but he wouldn't try finding a path around these mountains. They'd come too far, and it would take too long.

And that was *if* there was a way around them. They might be impossible to avoid.

Besides, who knew what else was waiting for them in the desert. Trying to go around the mountains might be what got them killed.

They climbed over a group of boulders and into a rocky area where a small path emerged. It weaved between the rocks and around the black, craggy spikes jutting into the air.

When the path ended in a solid, rock wall, Orin stared at the steep surface towering hundreds of feet above his head. Rocks jutted from the wall, and grasping one, he lifted himself as he tested his weight on it.

"Shit," Sahira muttered.

Orin lowered himself as the others turned in a circle to survey the area. They either went up or turned back; one of those choices wasn't an option for him.

"I hope you're good at climbing," he said.

"We're going to have to be," Zeth said.

Orin secured his sword while the others strapped their spears to each other's backs. When their weapons were locked in place, Orin grasped the handhold again and pulled himself up.

Refusing to look back, he found more hand and footholds as he scaled the wall. Cool, black stone bit into his fingers and burrowed beneath them as he dug his nails in for better purchase.

The bite of stone against his hands and beneath his nails didn't deter him from climbing onward. He didn't look back at the others, but he heard their feet scraping against stone, and occasionally a rock would rattle against the wall as it fell free.

He ignored the hunger twisting in his belly as he focused on the task at hand. It had been over two weeks since he last fed on the energy created when he and Sahira had sex.

She didn't know that, no one here did, but if he didn't have sex soon, his malnutrition would weaken him further. He could already feel differences, not just in how his clothes fit but also in his decreasing energy level.

It was dangerous to be out here while feeling like this. He had to get Sahira to feed from him, and she was being stubborn about it.

She would cave if he could get her to drink his blood again. Getting her to do it was the tricky part.

She didn't want Elsa or Zeth to get hurt; he could use that to his advantage. Surprisingly, this was one game he wasn't eager to play, and he so loved his games. The moves, the back and forth, and the banter were great fun to him, but not this one.

His anger with her faded after her revelation about Zeth and his family. Yes, she'd misled and flipped the tables on him when she'd fed from the demon instead of him, but she hadn't betrayed him.

Betrayed me? Where had that thought come from?

They weren't in a relationship; there was *nothing* to betray. Yet, now that he was halfway up a four-hundred-foot wall, Orin realized that's exactly what he'd felt when he believed Sahira slept with the demon.

And he'd been jealous—that ridiculous emotion he'd never experienced before her—because of it. He'd hoped never to experience that emotion again, but when Zeth and Elsa offered her their blood, his entire body clenched as he prepared to murder someone.

There was no way he would let her drink from anyone but him, and he didn't care how much she fought him. He wouldn't stand by and let someone else take care of her when he could.

What kind of an idiot was he becoming? What kind of an idiot had *she* turned him into? And *how* had she done it?

Sure, she was a great fuck, but he'd had those before. Maybe nothing as intimate as what passed between them that night, but still fantastic. He'd have great fucks again too. He hadn't yet, but he would.

Maybe you should tell her there hasn't been anyone else.

Have you completely lost what's left of your mind?

He wasn't sure about the answer, but everything in him rebelled against admitting that to her. He should have moved on after her; he'd tried and failed.

The woman already had too much of an effect on him. However, he'd never give her that knowledge; he didn't know what she'd do with it, and there was *no* way he'd ever leave himself vulnerable to the unknown.

No, she could stay angry at him for the nymph, but eventually, she'd get over it. And she would never know the truth of it.

CHAPTER SIXTEEN

THEY WERE ONLY twenty or so feet away from the top of the cliff when a shadow fell over his face. It was barely more than a flicker but briefly blocked the sun.

Tilting his head back, he searched the top of the mountain; nothing moved up there, and no clouds floated across the pristine, blue sky. Orin's fingers tore into the stone as he froze.

He almost looked back at the others but stopped himself from making what might be a terrible mistake. Heights weren't exactly his favorite thing, and while being on this wall was better than being on the back of a dragon, he still didn't like it.

Ensuring his feet and hands were secure on their holds, he leaned back a little to try to see more of what was above. Still, nothing stirred, but he hadn't imagined that shadow, and since there were no birds in this realm—at least not yet—it hadn't been from one of them soaring overhead.

He wished there were birds here. He missed the crows the dark fae used for messages. Sometimes the beautiful, highly intelligent, black birds would sit on his shoulder for a while. He'd always kept dried fruit in his pocket as treats for them.

"What is it?" Zeth asked from below and to his left.

"I don't know, maybe nothing."

"But maybe something?" Elsa inquired.

"There's *always* maybe something in this realm."

He studied the top of the wall a minute more, but nothing emerged to cast a shadow over him again. Someone else might have convinced themselves the shadow was only their imagination, but he didn't have a good imagination, and he'd never made mountains out of molehills.

When he saw things, he *saw* them.

However, they couldn't stay here, clinging to the side of a mountain. Eventually, someone would fall.

Going back down wasn't an option either. They'd have to return to the desert, losing more days, time, and supplies along the way. They'd committed to this course and would have to see it through, even if something waited above for them.

Keeping more of his attention focused overhead, he started climbing again. He steadily closed the distance to twenty feet, then ten, and finally five.

His fingers ached from the rocks and his weight; he was tired and famished, but he would gladly kill anything that came at him. The only problem was he had to go over the wall without a weapon in his hand as he didn't have the room to maneuver his sword free.

He stopped to survey the top again as he prepared to scale the remaining distance before launching himself over the top of the wall. He'd have to move fast once he got up there and roll to avoid whatever might be waiting for them.

Shoving aside his exhaustion and hunger, he scaled the last few feet and planted his hands on top. He pulled himself up and over in one swift move that had him rolling away from the edge while reaching for his sword.

The blade made a snicking sound when it slid free of the leather sheath. He bounded to his feet as he prepared to slice through any attacker.

When he saw nothing, he spun in search of an enemy while he braced for something to crash into his side, emerge from the rocks, or descend from above. Nothing moved.

As the realization that he was alone sank in, so did the reality of what was before him. Despite knowing he hadn't imagined the shadow, Orin lowered his sword.

If a threat lurked here, he would kill it, but until then, he could only stand and gawk at the display before him.

"What the fuck?" Zeth blurted from behind him.

Those words perfectly described Orin's thoughts about something he would have considered impossible before scaling that mountain.

CHAPTER SEVENTEEN

IF SAHIRA COULD LIFT her hands, she would have pushed her jaw back up, but she couldn't do that when shock held her immobile. She glanced at Elsa to ensure she wasn't somehow imagining this, but she was also gawking at the display across from them.

So, not my imagination and not a display.

It was another town that looked eerily similar to what they'd left behind almost a week ago. Except no extra houses crowded the street. Only the seven original buildings from Belda's town stood here.

"Is that the *pub*?" Elsa asked.

It sure looked like it; this building even had balconies on the front. No one danced on them, and immortals didn't flow in and out of the structure, but from what she could see, it was a duplicate of the one they left behind.

Here, on top of a mountain, the town wasn't surrounded by sand. Instead, black rock created the roadway; the sun's reflection off those rocks cast the town in a grayer, drabber light, but there was no denying the similarities between this one and the last.

"What is this?" she breathed.

Orin lowered his sword to his side as he started forward. His head turned slowly back and forth as he searched the town. "I don't know, but we're going to find out."

Sahira removed her spear from where it had been attached to her back and started after him. She didn't see or hear anyone or anything here, but her heart still raced, and sweat beaded her forehead while she waited for something to leap out and attack them.

The hair on her nape rose as the sensation of eyes burning into her neck tugged at her. But that was impossible; they were at the top of a mountain. The only thing behind them was a cliff.

Still, she felt eyes boring into her. To some unknown enemy, this could all be some giant game more atrocious than Orin's.

As they crept down the rocky street toward the pub, she spotted the library, stable, jail, infirmary, mercantile, and granary. The further they moved into the town, the more she could see there was no eighth building here either.

The idea the figure eight symbol in the original buildings of Belda's town might represent a possible eighth building could be wrong, but it made sense to her. Nothing made sense anymore as a chilly wind blew through the town.

The temperature here wasn't unbearable, but the higher they climbed, the more they left the perfect temp of the desert behind. Sahira shivered as she huddled deeper into her cloak.

"What in the name of Hecate is going on?" she whispered.

"Maybe you should ask your goddess to get us out of here," Orin said.

Sahira shot him a look but refrained from saying anything. Pointing out that wasn't for the goddess to do, or how she worked, would be pointless to this Neanderthal, and she wouldn't argue with him about it in the middle of this place.

When they stopped in front of the pub, she examined the wooden facade. A sign with the word *Pub* carved into it hung above the door.

Nothing stirred as they moved down the road, and a heavy silence blanketed the air. From the outside, all the other buildings appeared the same too.

She couldn't be certain, but the structures all looked like they were also in the same locations as the ones in Belda's town. The distance between the buildings felt greater without homes and other businesses crowding the original ones.

"My dad used to say curiosity killed the cat," Elsa said. "Why do I feel like that cat right now?"

Sahira felt the same way as she stopped to study the library's windows. Nothing moved behind their panes, but she felt eyes following her every movement.

Turning, she searched the distant cliff, waiting for a horde of monsters to climb over the wall and charge them.

CHAPTER EIGHTEEN

SHE HELD her breath as she waited, but nothing stirred. In some ways, the absolute stillness was more unnerving. She knew how to fight a horde; she didn't know how to fight whatever this was... if it was anything.

Without speaking, they seemed to decide to search the buildings later as when they arrived at the end of the road, they all turned back. The sun was starting to set, and the pub was the only place that might offer a place for them to sleep.

Orin's booted feet thudded off the first step as he climbed them to the doorway. The heavy front door was closed, and she half expected it to be barred, but when he turned the handle, the door swung inward with a creak Belda never would have allowed in her pub.

When Orin went through the door, Sahira's heart leapt into her throat. She hadn't expected her sudden rush of concern or urge to lurch up the stairs after him.

She restrained herself as Zeth went through next, and she and Elsa followed. The wooden walls, three crystal chandeliers hanging from the ceiling, and elegant bar with mirror backing were all the same.

Some stools lined the bar but not as many as in Belda's pub. Just two tables sat in the middle of the room, while Belda's pub was full of places where immortals could sit, relax, and enjoy a few drinks. It was an inviting place where they could forget they were trapped and scarog beetles could arrive to kill any of them.

Belda's pub was spotless, despite its location in the center of the desert. This one was full of cobwebs, and dust rose to swirl in the air as Zeth, Orin, and Elsa moved through the building. The air was thick with a musty, stale aroma that hung thickly over everything.

Sahira remained in the doorway while she took it all in. She didn't know where those cobwebs had come from; she hadn't seen a spider in this realm since arriving, but those abandoned webs rippled in the air currents created by Orin's passing.

Edging into the building, Sahira ran her fingers across the top of the bar and lifted them to reveal the dust sticking to their tips. Her passing had created two perfect streaks on the surface.

"There's alcohol," Orin said from where he'd strolled behind the bar to examine the contents. "There might also be water stored somewhere."

That would be fantastic, and so would a bathroom and a shower. Her eyes drifted to the archway leading to the restrooms downstairs; there wasn't a shower down here, or at least there wasn't in Belda's pub, but the bathroom above had one.

She shifted her attention to the stairs as longing twisted in her chest. She'd give anything for a hot shower and a chance to scrub away the sand stubbornly stuck to her.

She had to see something before she could give in to her urge for a shower. Elsa flicked the switch beside the door, and after a couple of seconds of flickering lights, the chandeliers blazed to life.

The dust coating them dimmed their glow, but the magic flowing through them illuminated the room. A chair scraped the wooden floor as Zeth pulled it out to settle his massive frame on it.

He pulled off a boot, tipped it over, and dumped sand and rocks on the floor. Sahira winced at the mess, but it didn't make much difference in this place.

"I wasn't expecting that much," he muttered. "I hope there's a broom around here."

"With all this dust, I don't think your pile matters," Orin said.

"I don't want to leave a mess."

Sahira stepped into the archway as Orin set four glasses on the bar. Their clatter against the top was abnormally loud in this strangely hushed town.

Lifting her gaze, Sahira's eyes widened at the symbol carved into the wall above her. The figure eight, or infinity symbol, or whatever it was supposed to be, stood straight up and down as it did in Belda's pub and was almost identical, except for one difference.

The symbol in Belda's town had three arrows piercing diagonally through it. One went straight through the top and pointed downward with a set of feathers on the other end. The one in the middle had an arrowhead on each end instead of feathers. And the arrow at the bottom also pierced straight through the circle, except this one pointed upward.

There was a difference between the symbol here and the one in Belda's pub. The very top of the circle didn't have an arrow piercing through it. Instead, someone had etched an arrow into the wall beside it.

That arrow lay on its side next to the figure eight. And instead of the top of the symbol only being the wall behind it, scratch marks had turned the entire top circle darker.

She tried to puzzle the thing out but was beginning to think she could ponder this for a thousand years and never understand it. Rubbing her temples, she closed her eyes against her dull headache.

Orin's body warmed her shoulder as his cinnamon and clove scent filled her nostrils. She wasn't in the mood for him right now, but she couldn't deny that the strength of his presence helped calm her.

"What does that mean?" he muttered.

CHAPTER NINETEEN

SAHIRA HAD no idea what this change meant. None of this made any sense.

Zeth and Elsa entered the alcove. It was a little too crowded with them standing in the small space, but she didn't try to retreat. Instead, she stepped closer and, rising onto her toes, tried to touch the symbol. It was too far over her head, and her fingers fell short.

"What are you doing?" Elsa asked.

"I have no idea," Sahira admitted. "I touched all the other ones, and nothing happened, but I feel like I should."

"I'll get you a chair," Zeth offered.

He retreated from the alcove and returned a few seconds later. Sahira took the chair from him and positioned it beneath the symbol.

She climbed onto the chair and rested her hand against the symbol before tracing its contours. Like before, she felt absolutely nothing from it.

"There's no spark of magic or anything," she murmured.

"Should there be?" Zeth asked.

"Symbols are usually used for magic or to represent something... *anything*."

"It represents something," Orin said. "We just have no idea what it is."

When a shiver ran down her spine, Sahira pulled her hand away. He was right; someone put these symbols here for a reason. They just had no idea *why*.

They retreated from the alcove, and Sahira returned the chair as Orin poured them drinks. He carried them over to the table.

She'd much prefer a shower and bed, two things they might find above, but her fingers encircled the glass full of amber liquid and brought it to her mouth. She welcomed the burn as it traveled down her throat and into her stomach.

Warmth spread through her limbs, and she didn't turn away the second glass Orin poured.

~

"THERE'S metal shutters on the windows here too." Orin twisted his glass between his fingers and watched the amber liquid sway back and forth.

The others shifted their attention to the windows. Elsa tensed a little, but Sahira and Zeth were already rigid though they'd each drank three glasses of whiskey.

"The scarog beetles must come through here too," Zeth said.

Orin studied the shutters. "Or some completely different thing. We have no idea what happens here."

"That's the only thing we know for certain about this realm," Sahira muttered as she sipped her drink. "We know absolutely nothing."

"Well, I'm going to find out one thing for sure—if the shower works here or not." Elsa finished her drink and rose. "I'll let you know."

Dust kicked up behind her and floated through the air as she crossed the room to the stairs. The tiny particles danced in the glow of the chandeliers and dwindling sun filtering through the windows.

"Do you think these buildings are made of steel too?" Sahira asked.

"With those shutters, I'd assume so," Zeth replied.

"So at least they're safer."

"But if the scarogs arrive, they'll seek flesh from one of us."

Sahira shuddered. "Let's hope they don't come."

Orin knew she didn't have it in her, but he'd gladly sacrifice Zeth or Elsa if the beetles descended on this town. If push came to shove, he'd be the one they sacrificed; he had to make the first move.

Elsa released a happy little shout from above before racing out of the bathroom. She bounced on her feet while clapping her hands. "The water works! There's hot water!"

Before any of them could respond, she ran back into the bathroom. Sahira smiled before starting to laugh until her shoulders shook.

She hunched forward in her chair and wiped tears from her eyes before lifting her head to grin at them. "There's a shower!"

Without thinking, Orin rested his hand over hers as her joy made him smile. "There is."

Her hand relaxed beneath his for a second, and her laughter faded as they stared at each other. Then she stiffened and pulled her hand away.

She finished her drink before rising. "I'm going to see what the bedrooms are like."

Orin watched her glide across the floor and up the stairs. He felt the demon's eyes on him but didn't look at him as he leaned back in his chair and studied the open door.

"We should secure this place for tonight," he stated.

"We'll have to explore the rest of the town tomorrow."

"I have a feeling we're going to find exactly what we found

here… nothing. During your time in this realm, have you ever heard of anyone coming across something like this while in the Barren Lands?"

"No. If someone did, they didn't return to Belda's town to tell us about it. They either perished out here or broke free."

"No one's broken free of this realm. I'm certain of that."

When Zeth didn't argue with him, it only confirmed the demon felt the same way. Orin remained determined to leave this place, but sometimes it felt hopeless.

Rising, Orin strolled over to the front door and closed it as Sahira emerged from the bedroom that was hers in Belda's town. He wondered if the room here also had a secret trapdoor that led to a small room and a hidden door in the back of the pub.

"There are beds, too," she announced.

Orin bolted the door shut. "At least there's two good things about this place."

CHAPTER TWENTY

ORIN DIDN'T KNOW what time it was when he woke in a dark room. They'd closed all the shutters before retiring for the night, and unlike Belda's town, there wasn't a clock on the wall downstairs to answer the mystery.

Swinging his legs out of bed, he tried again to open a portal but failed like every other day since arriving in this forsaken realm. He glanced around the room similar to the one he'd resided in before leaving to explore the Barren Lands.

He'd redecorated that room, moved in a different bed, draped some red gauze across its poles, and turned it into his own. This room was boring and devoid of any character or furniture outside the bed.

Sitting on the edge of the bed, his hands squeezed on the mattress as a wave of hunger rocked him. He closed his eyes against the dizziness as his entire body cramped and stabbing knives twisted through his belly. His breath whistled in and out through his teeth as he worked through the pain gripping him.

Finally, his body relaxed a little as the cramps made their way out of his muscles, and his stomach stopped twisting. When he rose, his muscles protested the movement, but they had no choice as he shuffled forward before being able to walk normally again.

He had to feed soon, or things were going to get ugly. He might be able to sweet talk or romance Sahira into his bed, but he'd never been good at either of those things, and there wasn't anything romantic about this realm.

As he walked around the room, loosening his muscles and joints more, he enjoyed not having sand stuck in his ass and to his balls. He would take at least three more showers before they moved on from this place.

Stopping to stretch, he surveyed the shutters before removing the pole keeping the window bolted shut. He set it down and pulled open the shutters.

The sun had poked its head over a distant mountain peak. An array of colors spread across the sky, streaking out toward them as the sun rose higher.

He searched the rocky land for any hint of what caused the shadow he saw yesterday, but nothing stirred. So far, this town had been quiet, but he didn't trust it.

Something lurked here, and it would make its presence known. When it did, he'd be prepared for it.

He closed and barred the shutters again before turning away to get dressed. Before leaving the room, he secured his sword onto his back.

He went to the bathroom, brushed his teeth, and washed his face before emerging again. When he stopped at the balcony railing running along the second floor, he spotted Sahira sitting at one of the tables with a piece of bread and a glass of water beside her.

She didn't look up at him but stiffened when he descended the stairs. Their feet had left marks through the dust, but he kicked up more when he grabbed the chair across from her.

He turned the chair around and straddled the back of it as he settled onto the seat. On the table before her was a large piece of parchment.

He leaned closer to examine it but couldn't get a good view. "What's that?"

"The town's layout, or at least I assume it's this one."

"There's not much to lay out."

"No, there's not, but someone did."

She turned the parchment toward him, and he pulled it closer to inspect the seven buildings situated around the town. Each one was labeled; all those labels were the same as the seven original buildings in Belda's town—the pub, mercantile, library, stable, granary, jail, and infirmary.

"Why would someone bother?" he asked.

"I have no idea. But the better question is, *who* bothered, and where are they?"

Orin tapped his fingers on the parchment as he pondered this, but like in Belda's town, they uncovered more questions than answers here.

Sahira leaned across the table and pitched her voice low. "There's also a trap door in the room Elsa and I slept in last night. It goes down to a stone room and out to the back of the building, just like the one in my old room in Belda's pub."

Orin lifted an eyebrow at this revelation while his shaft stirred at the memory of what transpired between them there. Hunger clawed at his insides again, but it wasn't as crippling as before.

"We had a good time in that room," he murmured.

Sahira's lips flattened into a thin line as she sat back and crossed her arms over her chest. He should have kept his mouth shut. She'd been conversing with him, and now she was back to hating him; he'd have to do some prodding to get her to relax again.

"Did you show the trapdoor to Elsa?" he asked.

She hesitated long enough that he didn't think she'd reply,

but eventually, she did. "No. She was still in the shower when I checked it. I cast a protective spell over it, but it seems we're alone in this town."

Smart girl.

He knew she liked the witch, but if they returned to Belda's town, she'd return to her old room. The fewer immortals who knew that door existed, the better for her. Radagast had already used it to try to kill her; it had to remain a secret.

"I'm not sure we're alone. I know I saw that shadow when we were climbing the mountain. It passed over the top of me."

When she nibbled her bottom lip, his eyes fastened on it. He restrained himself from leaning across the table to run his finger along the delicate curve.

His fingers dug into the back of the chair as he resisted the impulse; he'd chase her away if he did, and the more they talked, the more she relaxed. It would be easier to get her back into his bed if she liked him, something he wasn't sure was possible, but he could try to make it happen.

"There are no birds here," she said.

"And there were no clouds in the sky. I think something leaned over the cliff to look down at us before disappearing."

"A big something?"

"The shadow wasn't big, but that doesn't mean whatever cast it isn't."

Sahira drummed her fingers on the table as she pondered his words. Above, the bedroom door to the left of the bathroom opened, and Zeth emerged. He yawned and stretched his arms over his head as he plodded down the hall to the bathroom. The door closed behind him.

"I haven't seen signs of anything else in this town," Sahira said.

"It's here; I know it."

She gulped, and her eyes darted to the parchment. "Do you

think there are other trapdoors in these buildings? We know there's only one in the pub, but what about the others?"

The possibility had occurred to him when they were still in Belda's town, but if they'd started searching for them, they would have drawn attention, and the others would have demanded answers. They couldn't give those answers without revealing, or at least indicating, they'd already found one hidden room.

"I'd say it's a very good possibility, but if we start looking for them, Zeth and Elsa will learn about the one above. Besides, given how well hidden that one is, we could search for years and might never find them. Or they don't exist, and there's only the one."

"Yeah," Sahira murmured.

"If there are other doors and rooms, then they're probably as useful as the one above. I wouldn't worry about them having some secret way out of here."

Though the possibility niggled at the back of his mind. Unfortunately, they didn't have the time to search for something that might not exist.

"What if something else in this town has found one and is hiding there?" she asked.

"Then we'll kill them when they emerge."

Sahira pondered this as her gaze fell back to the parchment. "I'm curious as to why the symbol is different."

"We all are, but I doubt we'll uncover the answers here unless we find something that can give them."

"Do we want that?"

That was a good question. Resting her fingers on the parchment, Sahira pulled it away from him.

Her attention shifted back to the drawing. There might be answers somewhere in this realm, but there weren't any answers on that parchment, and finding them may prove impossible.

CHAPTER TWENTY-ONE

THEY SAVED their exploration of the library for last, and when they arrived, Sahira wasn't sure what to expect. Would it be full of books like the library in Belda's town or empty?

The other buildings had all been identical to the ones in the last town, except they weren't as full of supplies and had no animals. They did find some grain in the granary, but it was mostly a pile of mold and dust.

Orin walked beside her as they crossed the street toward the library. Despite her dislike of him, she leaned slightly toward him while they moved.

She didn't realize she was doing it until their arms brushed and a little electrical thrill ran through her. Stepping to the side, she moved away from him, but it took a few seconds for that to happen.

Orin didn't look at her, but the corner of his mouth quirked toward a smile before slipping away again. Sahira kept her attention straight ahead as she tried not to look at him, but she could feel the pull of his body.

He was like the moon, and she was the waves, helpless to

resist his magnetic pull. It would be so easy to give in to the temptation of him again.

She could lose herself in his arms and forget all about this mess for a little bit. And he could make her forget, he'd done so before, but she couldn't come away from a second encounter without hating herself afterward.

She hadn't exactly been proud of herself after she screwed him the first time, but she could live with it. Everyone made mistakes.

After his parade of women following their night together and how badly it cut into her heart, even though she'd prepared herself for it, she couldn't give in to him again. If she did, she'd only be setting herself up for more hurt and humiliation.

Together, they ascended the steps to the library's front door, and Orin opened it. A cloud of dust rained down on them, and the hinges creaked as they swung open.

Sahira waved the dust particles away from her face and blinked away the stuff coating her lashes. Despite the extra layer of grime on the floors, walls, and ceiling, everything in the entryway looked the same as the building in Belda's town... except for the symbol above the archway to the library itself.

Like in the other buildings they'd explored, this symbol differed from those in Belda's town. It was the same as the one in the pub and the other structures.

That different symbol was starting to piss her off more than being unable to open a portal or use her vampire ability to transport. She still didn't understand how this realm kept them from doing those things, but it had to be something to do with physics or...

"Oh my, Hecate," she breathed.

CHAPTER TWENTY-TWO

"What is it?" Orin demanded.

She ignored him as she crept toward the symbol to study the shaded area on top, the arrows, the figure eight... or not a figure eight. They'd also speculated it could be an infinity symbol.

Time was infinite yet still measured by immortals and mortals alike. And one of the first ways of measuring time was with an hourglass.

"What if it's an hourglass?" she whispered.

"What?" Elsa asked.

"We can't open a portal out of this realm, and vampires can't teleport here. Both things are done by immortals who can bend or manipulate time. It's also a manipulation of physics, but I'm no expert in that. I do know we influence matter to open portals or teleport ourselves.

"When we do, we also manipulate time by moving from one place to another in a flash. While time remains consistent through all the realms, we create a hole through the fabric of time to get us from one place to another.

"What if this"—she waved a hand at the symbol—"is an hourglass? And here, in this town, is where the sand"—she pointed to the shaded area at the top of the figure eight—"has started running through it?"

"It's a pretty shitty-looking hourglass," Zeth said.

"Everything in this realm is shitty," Orin retorted.

They looked dubious, but Elsa's face started softening as her mouth parted. "But if it's an hourglass, what do the arrows mean?"

"Another way to tell time was with a sundial," Zeth said. "The symbol doesn't look like a sundial, but it could be something like that."

"If there was a clock around it, what numbers would the arrows be pointing toward?" Elsa asked.

Sahira imagined a clock surrounding the arrows in her head. "The one at the top is pointing toward the three, the one going through the middle would point toward the five and ten, and the arrow at the bottom is pointing toward the eight. I don't think any of them would line up perfectly, though."

"So, the arrows could represent all those different combinations of time," Orin said.

"Or *any* other combination," Zeth said. "We have no idea how time runs here. It could be upside down, reversed, or completely different."

"So, if it is an hourglass, the shaded area must represent the sand in it, but what does that mean?" Orin inquired.

"Maybe it means we're heading toward the end," Sahira suggested. But she had to add the other option, even if she didn't like it. "Or we're running out of time."

She didn't mean her words to sound so ominous, but they sure did.

"So does that mean there are other towns out there like this one?" Elsa asked. "With other hourglasses?"

"Maybe," Sahira murmured. "Or maybe it all means nothing, and it's not an hourglass. We've gotten as many answers here as in Belda's town."

Feeling disheartened and more irritated by this place, she broke away from the others. She strode across the dusty floor and beneath the archway to the main part of the library.

As she crossed the threshold, she stopped to take in the vast, three-story room so similar and different from where she'd worked in Belda's town. There, thousands of books lined the shelves.

Here, the shelves were bare of anything but the dust coating them. The lights were the same, but no tables or chairs sat out for someone to relax in while reading near the windows.

Her eyes scanned the room as she strolled toward the main desk. She stopped there and rested her fingers on the only book in the room.

She recognized the tome immediately; it was the book where everyone in Belda's town wrote their stories to prove they existed. It held the lives of the immortals trapped in the Cursed Realm.

Opening this book, she expected to see pages of different handwriting and assorted tales, but blank pages greeted her. She flipped through the entire empty book before closing it again.

"Anything?" Orin asked from behind her.

"No."

He glanced around the massive, empty room before shaking his head. "We'll leave here tomorrow."

They had to keep going, but Sahira wasn't ready to leave her newly found bed and shower. However, there was less here for them than in Belda's town. Sure, there was water in the pub, and they'd discovered a small river behind the buildings, but the food supply was less, and they hadn't come this far to stay here and rot.

"We should go back to the pub," she said. "At least we can wash our clothes before leaving."

Trying not to feel defeated, but unable to suppress her disappointment, Sahira followed the others outside. After exploring the pub last night, she hadn't expected answers from this town either, but she was incredibly sick of dead ends.

Lost in her melancholy, she trudged fifteen feet behind the others with her head bowed and her shoulders slumped. At least she'd have a bed again tonight, even if she had to share it with Elsa, who muttered in her sleep.

They were almost to the pub when a small, scratching sound traveled to her. The noise wasn't loud, but it was as if dozens of rats were running across the rock, and then it stopped.

Sahira stopped to search the town but didn't see anything. Orin's words about the shadow returned to her, and she lifted her gaze to the sky; it remained clear and blue. The roadway also remained empty.

What was that? She hadn't imagined it, she was certain of that, but what caused it, and where had it gone?

When he realized she'd stopped walking with them, Orin turned back to her, but Elsa and Zeth continued.

"What is it?" Orin asked.

"I heard something."

"What?"

"I don't know."

He started back toward her and had almost returned when a flurry of movement erupted from the ground. Sahira stepped back as small creatures released a vicious war cry while scampering toward them.

CHAPTER TWENTY-THREE

ORIN'S EYES widened at the movement racing toward him and Sahira. He pulled his sword free as the dozens of small bodies flowed over one another like water over rocks.

It took him a second to realize they weren't running over each other. There were so many that they became a rolling tidal wave coming toward them.

"What the fuck?" he muttered.

They didn't unnerve him; the damn things were so small he could stomp on them, but he had no idea why the small creatures were screaming at them while they charged. *What are they doing?*

With the speed of a passing second, they piled up in front of him, rising high until one of them stood directly across from him. Its whiskers twitched as it thrust a tiny spear forward; the weapon stopped inches from Orin's nose.

His eyes crossed, and his lip curved into a sneer as he looked from the weapon to the six-inch man holding it. He had a mouse-like face with a pointy nose that wiggled when he spoke.

"You're trespassing on our land."

The tiny voice, with its hint of a Scottish brogue, was

stronger than Orin anticipated. The man, and many of his friends, wore brown pants and a matching brown coat that revealed the bare skin of his chest.

His big front teeth became visible when he spoke, and scraggly brown hair poked out from beneath a lopsided, brown hat. A tail twitched behind him before standing up behind his back and going still.

Orin had never seen anything like it but heard Sahira whisper, "Brownies."

The one in front of Orin thrust his spear forward again. "You're not welcome here."

Orin rolled his eyes and looked past the tower of tiny immortals blocking his way to discover another one in front of Sahira. Her lips parted in awe, but he knew she was having trouble suppressing a smile when the corners of them twitched.

These brownies had to know they were a bit of a joke, but he suspected laughing at them might incite a tiny, spear-pointing frenzy from them. It wasn't like they could do much damage; all he had to do was kick out the bottom one, and they'd topple like dominoes, but these feisty critters didn't realize it.

"Get off our land," the one before him shouted.

Apparently, he was the leader. Orin ignored the spear to survey the rest of the creatures. Over a dozen stood before him with their feet on the shoulders of the one below.

With a glance back, he confirmed that more towers of brownies had assembled behind him. One stood before Elsa, another stood between her and Zeth, and a third was behind Zeth.

They each held a weapon while maintaining perfect balance on the ones below them. This must be their way to fight anything, and since they'd survived this long, it must be at least somewhat effective, but he doubted they'd ever taken on someone the size of him or the *demon*.

They were either as dumb as a box of rocks or had balls the

size of cantaloupes, even the women, as he spotted some of them in the tower too. Since he didn't see anything the size of a cantaloupe hanging between their legs, he was leaning toward them being stupid.

These things must have been the source of the shadow he saw. They'd emerged from a hole in the ground to attack and probably had dozens of them dug throughout the town and the cliffs.

One or more of them must have either leaned over the cliff to look down or poked their head out a hole in the wall that he hadn't noticed.

"We're only here for a couple of days," Sahira said, "and we're not here to cause trouble; we're just looking for answers."

The one in front of her waved his spear in Sahira's face. Orin didn't care about the weapons pointed at him, but his hands fisted as the imbecilic creature threatened *her*.

"There are no answers here," the brownie told her with a hint of the Scottish brogue the one before Orin had displayed.

"Get that thing out of her face!" Orin snapped.

"We'll do what we want, dark fae," the tiny creature spat at him.

"Should I cut off his dick, Puth?" one asked.

Something poked him in his crotch, and Orin glanced down to discover another prodding him with a small sword. He would prefer not to smoosh the annoying creatures; he wasn't a bully who enjoyed picking on things smaller than him, but if that asshole didn't stop, he would learn how to fly.

"He's a dark fae; it's probably rotted off by now," Puth retorted, and Sahira snorted a laugh.

Orin glowered at the brownie in front of him. He was sure this creature was aware immortals didn't get diseases like that, something the rat confirmed with a smirk.

He smiled in return before ripping the spear from the brownie's hands. "Now, get that weapon out of her face!"

The force of him tearing the weapon away caused the brownies to sway before they regained their balance and went ramrod straight again. Puth cursed Orin and pulled a sword from the sheath on his back.

When he pointed it at Orin, he almost ripped it away, but Sahira's words soothed the growing fire inside him. "It's okay, Orin. I don't think they mean us any harm."

Orin rolled his eyes; even if they did mean them harm, there was little these tiny imbeciles could do. He ignored the paper cut he received when he shoved Puth's sword away and stalked past them to Sahira.

CHAPTER TWENTY-FOUR

CLASPING HER ELBOW, Orin drew her closer to his side as the tower that had guarded him turned and rushed over with surprising speed. She stiffened against his side.

"What are you doing?" she hissed.

"*No one* is going to wave a weapon in your face."

"They're harmless."

"We are not!" the one in front of her squealed. "We'll kill you for that."

"Easy," Sahira said. "I didn't mean anything by it."

"The hell you didn't!"

She bit her bottom lip to keep from laughing, but whereas these annoying gnats amused her, Orin had had enough of them.

"I'm sorry I insulted you," Sahira apologized. "I didn't mean to."

The top brownie scowled at her while Puth returned to pointing his sword at Orin. He had to give them credit; they were still trying though they had to know they couldn't win a battle like this.

Orin started to tell Sahira not to apologize to these things, but as much as he'd like to flick Puth in the head and walk away, these creatures might have some useful insight into this realm. It was doubtful, but if they did, he wouldn't get it by deciding to turn them into darts.

He could play nice... sometimes.

When the brownie in front of Sahira waved his spear in her face again, Orin forgot all about playing nice as he pulled it away from the man and snapped the six-inch-long weapon between his fingers.

"We're not attacking you," he growled. "You'll offer us the same courtesy, or I'll kill you all."

"Orin," Sahira gasped.

"They're *not* going to point a weapon at you, and that's final."

"No one tells us what to do!" Puth declared.

A second later, a sharp sting ran up from his shin. He glanced down to discover one of the creatures had stabbed him with its spear.

Before he could restrain himself, instinct took over, and he kicked the thing. "Motherfucker."

He managed to pull his foot back enough not to kick the rat with all his strength, but the brownie soared through the air and spun around before crashing onto the ground. All its friends watched in horror until it bounced up, spitting like a rodent on a rampage, and charged back toward them.

In a flash, the ones before him disassembled their tower and pulled their spears free to charge at his legs.

"I can stomp some rats," Orin told them.

"Enough!" Sahira shouted. "All of you, that is enough! And you"—she pointed a finger at him—"stop instigating them."

"He *stabbed* me."

"Yes, he was wrong, but you're not helping this situation, so let's all *settle down*." She shifted her attention to the brownies. "We don't want to fight you. We're here in search of a way out of this realm."

"He kicked one of us!" a brownie shouted and pointed at Orin.

Orin lifted his leg to point at the hole and spot of blood on his pants. "He stabbed me first."

"That's because you're a dick."

"They have you there," Sahira muttered.

Orin shot her a look. He was defending her, and she was siding with the little rat monsters. Typical, but he still wasn't leaving her side.

"We're searching for a way out of this realm," Sahira said. "We came from a town *many* miles away, but it's similar to this one. All the buildings here are also in that town, except the immortals there have grown and expanded by building more residences and businesses. They also have the symbols, but those are different there."

As her words sank in, the angry chatter of the rodents ceased around them. "Do you think she's telling the truth?" one whispered.

They all had similar features and wore brown clothes, but some women wore skirts while the men wore pants. A few of the women also wore pants.

"You didn't travel here from Belda's town?" Sahira asked.

"Who's Belda?" Puth inquired.

"She's the alpha lycan who runs the town we came from."

"Did she chase you out?"

"No, she'd welcome us back if we returned, but we're trying to find a way out of this realm."

"There is no way out," one of them murmured.

"Why do you say that?" Orin demanded.

The brownie lowered her spear. "We've never been able to escape."

"Have you ever left this town?"

"It's a little too big for us out there," Puth said.

"So, you don't know for sure there's no way out."

"No, not for sure."

"She could be lying," another one whispered.

"I'm telling the truth," Sahira said. "The journey is dangerous, but Belda's town is out there."

"They didn't arrive here like we did," another brownie whispered. "We saw them climbing the mountain. They came here a different way."

"We entered this Cursed Realm via portals of our own making; they led us to Belda's town. I'm assuming you opened a portal into *this* town," Zeth said.

"Yes," Puth answered. "We were looking for a place to hide from the ghouls invading our realm. This is what we discovered."

CHAPTER TWENTY-FIVE

ORIN DIDN'T BLAME them for hiding from the ghouls. He'd never encountered the flesh-eating monsters before and was happy to keep it that way.

"We have no idea what became of our families," another one said.

Sahira's sound of sympathy caused Orin to roll his eyes. These little, violent cheese eaters didn't deserve any compassion.

"There is a brownie realm," Sahira said. "I've never been there, but I've heard of it. I don't know when it was established; it could be the realm you all left—"

"Doubtful," Puth interrupted. "They had destroyed most of what remained of it. Many others fled before us; we were some of the last to flee their wrath."

"Then your families still exist... somewhere."

"How long have you been here?" Elsa asked as she and Zeth walked over to join them.

Their towers had dispersed and now trailed them.

"Some of us have been here for almost three hundred years," the brownie before Sahira said. "The rest were born here."

"Shit," Zeth breathed while rubbing his bald head.

As he spoke, more brownies emerged from the ground. Some of them came forward while others hung back, watching.

Most of those who hung back were around two or three inches tall and clearly children as they clung to their parent's legs. One woman held something so tiny in her arms, Orin could only tell it was there because she rocked back and forth with it.

Regret over kicking the one tugged at him, but he buried it. He hadn't kicked a kid, and the one he booted did *stab* him, so it deserved to take flight. Play stupid games, win stupid prizes.

"And you've been in this town the whole time?" Elsa asked.

"We can't leave here," Puth said. "The mountains are difficult enough to traverse, but the desert beyond...." His voice trailed off as he placed his hand against his forehead to shade his eyes. "Some have tried to cross it, but they didn't get far."

"Did they make it back?" Sahira asked.

"Two did, but two others went out, and we never saw them again."

Orin pointed in the direction they hadn't explored yet. "Have you tried going that way?"

"We have. We've tried going all the ways, but it's all mountains except for the desert. We didn't make it far into those mountains."

"So, there could be something else out there," Orin pressed.

Puth shrugged, and the other brownies all looked at each other. "Yes, but we've never found it."

They hadn't found Belda's town either, so that didn't mean anything.

"It's hell out there," a woman said. "I went into the desert, but it's no place for a brownie."

"Have you seen any other immortals here? We've had some leave our town who have never returned," Zeth said.

"No. You're the first we've ever seen. We thought we were the only ones in this realm," Puth answered.

"Did any brownies make it to your town?" one of them asked hopefully.

"They weren't there when we were," Elsa said.

"I've never heard of a brownie being there," Zeth told them.

All their shoulders hunched forward in disappointment.

"It's no place for a brownie out there," the woman said again.

"Do the scarog beetles come here once a year?" Sahira asked.

"We've never seen those monsters here," Puth gruffly replied.

"Does something else come here to kill you once a year?"

They all exchanged looks before shaking their heads.

"Not once a year." Then Puth pointed at them. "Unless it's going to be you."

Sahira held up her hands while Orin said, "No one is here to hurt you. And it's not like we couldn't easily kill you."

"I don't like you, dark fae."

"Few do," Sahira said.

He shot her a look, and she smiled as she batted her eyelashes at him. With her wiseass comments, she was starting to remind him a little too much of *him*.

He didn't like it.

"Does that happen where you come from? The scarogs come in and try to kill you?" another brownie asked.

"Yes," Zeth said. "Once a year, the beetles arrive, hunt everyone they can for twenty-four hours, and after that, if they haven't killed someone, they hunt until they succeed."

"That sounds horrible," a brownie murmured.

"You should tell us more about your town over drinks," the leader said. "It's been a while since we've been in the pub, and now's as good a time as any."

With that, he turned on his heel and marched toward the pub.

CHAPTER TWENTY-SIX

OVER DRINKS, Sahira and the others learned the leader of the brownies, Puth, was married to Eisel. They had eight children.

Sahira couldn't remember the names of their children or most of the other brownies, though they'd all introduced themselves. Puth and Eisel did most of the talking afterward.

"What do you eat here?" Orin asked.

"We hunt small rodents and insects. Initially, the grain was good, but it eventually turned bad, and we had nowhere to grow any more."

"You are small rodents," Orin muttered under his breath.

She kicked him under the table. Yes, they'd stabbed him and threatened all of them, but he shouldn't be such an ass to them.

He grunted and rubbed his shin while scowling at her. Ignoring him, she turned her attention back to Puth and Eisel; they sat on the bar's edge with their legs kicking back and forth while they sipped whiskey from tiny thimbles they'd said came from the mercantile.

Many of the other brownies also sat on top of the bar. Some also drank from thimbles, others shared glasses, and some chased the children around while they laughed uncontrollably.

Most of the kids had jumped off the bar to run around the dusty floor while their parents and older siblings watched in amusement. The sound of their laughter made her smile. It had been far too long since she'd heard such joy from anyone, and she hadn't realized how much she missed it.

It reminded her of when Lexi was a little girl and they would chase each other around the manor, playing hide-and-seek. Lexi was the worst hider.

She'd sit there and giggle behind doors, or if Sahira called out, "Where are you?" she'd yell back, "I'm in the living room."

Sahira had to stifle her laughter while trying to act like she still couldn't find her young niece and her increasingly high-pitched giggles.

With the joy of that memory came sadness. She was stuck here, away from the family she loved so much, and they were no closer to escaping than they were before.

But they *had* to be making progress. They'd gotten further than anyone else who'd left Belda's town, the symbols were different here, and everything would eventually make sense… it had to.

"How did the grain get here?" Orin asked.

"We have no idea, just like we have no idea about the furniture, the alcohol, or anything else in this realm. It was all here when we arrived."

"Shit," Zeth muttered as he downed his drink.

"And *no* other immortals have come here since you arrived?" she asked.

They'd already said no, but she had to confirm it.

Eisel bounced a two-inch tall toddler on her knee as she spoke. "Not in the nearly three hundred years since we've been here. With the grain being here, the buildings, and things in the mercantile, there were signs of someone having been here before us, but the place felt so empty, and there was enough dust to make it feel like no one had been here for years before we arrived."

"Some of those who left Belda's town behind still could have gone and found answers," Zeth said. "Just because they didn't find this town doesn't mean they didn't find *something*."

"They never found anything to help them escape," Orin stated.

She glanced at him as he leaned back in his seat and drummed his fingers on the table. His attention was on Puth and Eisel, but when his gaze shifted to hers, their eyes locked.

For some unknown reason, she had to restrain herself from walking over to hug him. She needed comfort or something to let her know she wasn't as alone as she felt, but seeking it from him would be a big mistake. Still, her traitorous heart ached for it.

Breaking his stare, she shifted her attention back to Puth and Eisel. "And you live underground?"

"Yes," Eisel said. "Originally, we stayed up here, but we prefer being underground, and we've made a home for ourselves down there."

"Will you continue through the mountains?" Puth asked. "Or stay here?"

"We'll continue," Sahira said and looked to Orin, Zeth, and Elsa, who nodded their agreement. "With the difference in the symbols between this town and ours, we've found something here. I'm not sure what it is, but it's more than anyone else has ever found, and we have to continue."

"There's no other choice," Orin agreed.

"When will you leave?" another brownie inquired.

"I think we've spent enough time here; tomorrow morning is as good a time as any."

Sahira wanted to argue with him. They had a shower here, a roof over their heads, and warm beds; they didn't have to rush out tomorrow. If they did some hunting, they might find more food, but she kept her mouth shut.

If they spent much more time here, she might decide against leaving. Orin was right; it was better if they left tomorrow before they got too comfortable here.

CHAPTER TWENTY-SEVEN

ELSA WAS MUTTERING about chocolate chip cookies when Sahira crawled out of the bed they'd shared for the past two nights. She padded across the cool wooden floor to gather the clothes she'd set out to dry after washing them last night.

She didn't look at the trapdoor as she crossed it but was acutely aware of its presence. It was another mystery and oddity about this realm.

Who had constructed these buildings and towns so similar to each other, yet each with tiny differences? And why?

She was beginning to fear she'd never uncover the answers. A growing concern they would continue endlessly through this realm, finding more towns and more questions but never anything to help them solve the mysteries, was building inside her.

If she let it, her thoughts would give way to a panic she couldn't control. It would become a runaway monster that steamrolled through everything, including her.

She had to keep it controlled and locked away, but that was easier said than done. This realm had a way of stripping away everything; she could feel it chiseling away at her, trying to steal pieces of the sanity she was desperate to cleave to.

Twisting the knob, she opened the door and slipped into the hall. She tiptoed to the bathroom, stripped out of the clothes she'd slept in, showered, dressed, and brushed her teeth before reluctantly leaving the bathroom behind. She was going to miss that shower and hot water.

Descending the steps, she made it to the bottom before realizing Orin sat on a stool at the bar. He'd rested his elbow on the bar to face her.

He must have opened the shutters as the early morning sun spilled through the windows and across the floor. It did little to illuminate him as he seemed made of shadows, but his crow-black eyes latched onto her.

The predatory gleam in those eyes caused her to gulp as a thrill pulsed through her. She shouldn't be here; she should turn around and go back upstairs. She didn't care if it made her look cowardly or let him know how much he affected her.

The second the idea crossed her mind, she cursed herself. She wouldn't let him intimidate her, no matter how much he rattled her.

Throwing her shoulders back, she walked proudly across the floor and settled onto the stool beside him. She tried to ignore the heat of his eyes as his gaze ran over her, but she felt it as acutely as if his hands were caressing her.

How could one look turn her legs to rubber and cause her heart to lodge in her throat? She didn't know, but Orin had a way of battering down her defenses.

He'd lost weight, and his coloring wasn't as healthy as normal, but he still looked good enough to lick. And she yearned to taste him *everywhere*.

"Good morning, little witchy witch," he murmured.

Sahira swallowed to wet her suddenly parched throat before

responding. She'd probably jump out of her skin or into his lap if he touched her now. She wasn't sure which would be worse.

"Good morning. You're up early."

His knee brushed her leg when he turned on his stool a little more. Sahira clamped her teeth against the visceral *need* gripping her.

With one simple touch, he could make her feel more desire than anyone she'd ever known before. It wasn't fair.

But then, nothing was in life, especially in this realm, but *why* did it have to be him who could make her feel this alive and aware of another living being? Why couldn't it have been one of the other billions of men in all the realms? She would have preferred a human to Orin.

He was one of those crazy, unfair things many faced and her cross to bear. She wasn't sure how long she could carry that load before she broke.

CHAPTER TWENTY-EIGHT

"I CAME DOWN HERE TO THINK," he said.

"Don't hurt yourself."

The corners of his oh-too-alluring mouth twitched toward a smile. "Why, Sahira, I believe you've been hanging out with me too much. You're adopting my sarcasm."

"I believe I have too. Maybe it's time we stop."

He chuckled. "Now, what fun would that be? This realm is boring enough without the entertainment we provide for each other."

Sahira didn't agree about this being entertaining. It was more a slow form of torture that would eventually drive her out of her mind... or to the murder of one *very* annoying dark fae.

Spinning to face the bar, Orin clasped his hands before him while studying the wall of drinks. There was nowhere near as much alcohol here as Belda's pub, but enough for at least another week of solid drinking.

"Already thinking about a drink?" she asked.

"I wouldn't mind being drunk right now, but no. I'm thinking about what traveling through more of the mountains will be like."

"I'd like to say it can't be any worse than what we've already faced, but I'd probably jinx us."

"At least I don't have sand in my ass and stuck to my balls anymore."

"That's a lovely picture."

Instead of some wiseass retort, his gaze remained fixed ahead as his mouth flattened into a thin line. "We have to go."

"I know."

He turned on his stool to face her again and tilted his head in that, what she hated to admit, endearing way he had of studying her. He'd shaved the stubble from his cheeks at some point to reveal the perfection of his face.

"Aren't you concerned we won't find anything?" he asked.

"We've already found something, and according to the brownies, it's something more than anyone else from Belda's town ever found."

"True."

"It just wasn't a way out."

"Not yet."

Unable to stand the intensity of his gaze, Sahira shifted her attention to the bottles behind the bar. "Do *you* still think we'll make it out of this?"

"I know we will, don't you?"

Sahira pondered this for a minute. "Yes."

Maybe she wasn't as convinced as when she first arrived in this realm, but finding this town had given her hope again. There was more to this realm than met the eye. There had to be a way to get out.

She had no idea how everyone was trapped here, but she believed she might be right about this realm having something to do with time. The symbols *had* to be hourglasses; maybe they weren't the standard hourglasses they were all used to seeing, but what else could they be?

"What happens when the sand reaches the bottom of the hourglass?" she pondered.

"We get out of here," Orin said.

Sahira hoped he was right and that something more ominous wasn't coming for them. But it didn't matter because they would continue onward no matter what.

"Are you ready to go back out there, witchy witch?" he asked.

"No," she admitted. "Are you?"

The arrogant grin he flashed normally irritated her, but now it caused a little flutter in her dumbass heart.

"I'm always ready for anything," he said.

Sahira rolled her eyes. She should have known better than to expect a serious answer from him.

When he leaned closer, his scent filled her nostrils and fueled the thirst clawing at her with increasing frequency for days. She'd once again gone too long without feeding because of him and was on the verge of losing control.

If he hadn't threatened Elsa and Zeth, she would have fed from them by now, and she should find her friends, but she couldn't drink from them. She could smell their blood without contemplating jumping on them and drinking from them, but his scent was like waving a piece of raw meat before a wolf.

Her mouth watered, and her fangs tingled as her gaze involuntarily fell to his neck. Memories erupted in her head, and she recalled what it was like to sink her fangs into his flesh to drink.

His potent blood was a rush of power the likes of which she'd never experienced before. It had sated her in a way no other's ever had, and she craved *more*.

She was tired of starving and denying herself what she wanted... *him*. She easily recalled how her body came alive beneath his hands. It was impossible to forget what he'd felt like inside her as his arms enveloped her.

For that moment in time, in a place where everything she'd

ever known and loved was ripped away, she felt safe and happy. The passion he'd so easily evoked in her had consumed her, and she'd give anything to be devoured by it again.

The man was sin itself, the devil waving the apple to Eve, and she was more than ready to burn in the hellfires of hedonism he promised. She was treading a treacherous path but didn't care as her gaze fastened on his neck and the vein pulsing beneath his skin.

CHAPTER TWENTY-NINE

ORIN STIFFENED when red flashed through Sahira's eyes. Her fangs had lengthened to the point where their outline was visible against her compressed lips.

He had no idea if she knew she was losing control, but he felt it slipping away as something more primeval emanated from her. Something inside him stirred in response before rising to the surface.

He'd done his best to keep his dark fae appetites suppressed and not to reveal how much time had passed since he last fed on sex. It was impossible to control it when her gaze focused on his neck and the scent of her arousal permeated the air.

He was a dark fae, a man and creature attuned to the needs of women, and for some reason, he was more aware of *hers*. She also evoked a more visceral reaction from him than any woman before. He *had* to satisfy her; the impossible-to-ignore instinct clamored across all his nerve endings and throughout his cells.

Was it because she was so stubborn and difficult that he found the challenge of her so irresistible and fun? Or was he actually developing feelings for this little witch who was more of an enchantress that had turned his life upside down?

Before meeting her, he would have believed it impossible to *consider* caring for another in such a way, but he couldn't deny his fascination with her. He also hadn't been with another woman since she arrived in this realm.

That was also something he would have believed impossible for him to experience before her, but she'd changed everything. He just didn't think it was for the better.

He had no idea why he'd pushed himself to the brink of exhaustion and starvation for her. None of it made any sense.

Maybe that would change once they were out of this realm and he had more women to choose from. He'd always been so certain it would, but some of his certainty was starting to fade.

The only problem was, Sahira was determined to defy him. That might be why he desired her so much. He'd always enjoyed a good challenge; she was the biggest, most fun, and exasperating one he'd ever faced.

And he was more than willing to meet that challenge again. He knew how to get the vampire within her to cave to him even if the woman was still determined to deny them both.

When he leaned closer, he turned his head to expose more of his vein. Her gaze fastened on his neck, and she licked her lips.

Suppressing his rising feeling of victory, he focused on what it was like to have her lips against his. She not only smelled of honey but tasted of it too, and he would never forget that.

Unable to resist, he leaned closer to run his thumb across her delectable bottom lip. When he pulled it down a little to reveal the tips of her fangs, blood rushed to his cock.

Having her feeding from him, and that mixture of pleasure and pain, was an erotic combination he craved. He'd been with plenty of vampires over the years and experienced their bite countless times before, but her bite made it impossible to recall theirs, something that had never happened before.

Leaning closer, he moved his thumb away as his lips hovered centimeters from hers. He could already taste her lips and feel the tightness of her sheath as he sank his shaft inside her, but he hesitated to kiss her.

If she pushed him away, he'd tear this place apart. Another rejection from her, when they were this close, would tip him over the edge and into a fit of rage the likes of which he'd never unleashed before.

While he waited, no words left her enticing lips as her red-streaked, amber eyes held his. When he didn't close the distance between them, she did.

CHAPTER THIRTY

WHEN HER MOUTH TOUCHED HIS, a firestorm of passion erupted inside him. Gripping her arms, Orin dragged her off the stool to pull her flush against him. Her lush breasts flattened against his chest, and he released one of her arms to wrap his around her waist.

Had anyone ever tasted or felt as good as her? If they had, Orin couldn't recall, and he was sure he would, because no matter how many more women he screwed, he'd never forget her.

Rising from his stool, he kept his arm around her, carrying her further into the pub while their tongues entwined. Her legs encircled his waist, and she rubbed enticingly against his erection, demanding release.

If he let her breathe or think, she might stop this, so he wouldn't give her a second to do either. Clasping the back of her head, he held her close as he kissed her senseless.

Bloodlust didn't compel her to do this. She could try to convince herself of that when this was over, but he knew the truth... she wanted him as badly as he did her.

She could have fed from Elsa or Zeth. He'd told her not to,

but she'd never listened to him before; she wasn't about to start now.

Of course, she could try to blame it on him, and most likely would, but she could restrain herself from letting bloodlust take over. She'd done it with Zeth and told him she'd done it with countless others before him.

He carried her toward the storage room of the pub. If he had his way, he'd fuck her on the bar, but he wasn't going to let anyone get in his way or interrupt him, and Elsa and Zeth would be waking soon.

If Sahira heard them, she'd pull away and end this. He wouldn't let that happen.

Having worked in the pub for Belda, he knew where everything was inside it. Since there was less furniture in this place, it was easier to maneuver around, and he didn't bump into anything before reaching the storage room.

Releasing her with one hand, he found the knob and twisted it. He pushed the door open and carried her inside. He wanted to kick it shut but couldn't wake anyone else or draw their attention.

Once they were inside, with the door shut, all pretense of calm vanished. Resting her back against the wall, he found the edge of her shirt as his heart raced and his dick ached from the blood filling it.

Their tongues continued their dance as he pushed her shirt up to expose her flat belly and round hips. His fingers glided over her silken skin, tracing the curves he'd memorized the last time they were together.

Those curves sent his blood pressure through the roof as whatever primordial force this woman unleashed in him roared to the forefront. His fingers found the button on her pants and undid it.

When his hand slipped inside, he discovered how wet she

was for him. Sahira could deny it until the day she died, but she couldn't hide that she wanted him as badly as he did her.

She released her grip on his waist and lowered her legs as he pushed her pants further down her hips. He managed to maneuver her pants the rest of the way down while keeping her in his arms.

Her fingers entwined in his hair, tugging at it as she kicked her boots then pants off. Her fangs grazed his lips, drawing blood.

Any resistance she'd managed to maintain fell away as she released his hair and started yanking at the bottom of his shirt. He was no longer afraid she'd bolt if he broke the kiss and did so as she tugged it upward. She was as far gone to him as he was to her.

When he lifted his arms, she pulled the shirt over his head and threw it aside. In the dim light spilling through the window in the back, her eyes were completely red as they met and held his while he slid her shirt up.

His fingers skimmed her curves as he lifted the shirt to reveal the swell of her beautiful breasts behind her simple, black bra. He dropped her shirt on the ground, and his mouth watered as he grazed his knuckles down the valley between her breasts.

Her breath caught, and she swayed toward him as her heartbeat thudded in his ears. He trailed his hand along her skin up toward her hair.

Grasping the stick she'd used to secure her bun, he pulled it free. Her mahogany hair smelled of lavender as it tumbled around her shoulders and down her back in waves.

He ran his fingers through the silky strands, letting them fall around her shoulders and exquisite face again. She was magnificent.

She held his gaze as she undid the button on his pants. He stepped out of his boots before pulling off his pants and kneeling before her.

When his knees hit the ground, the hardwood floor bit into them. *How do we keep doing this without a bed?*

But as his knees protested his weight and the wood digging into them, he knew there was no way he'd stop this now... not when his prize was so close.

He'd experienced far more agony in life and had no doubt he would again, but from now on, he would make sure they did this somewhere more comfortable.

Who are you kidding? he thought as he drew her thighs over his shoulders. *You'd screw her on a bed of nails if necessary.*

And he would gladly do so as her scent engulfed him and he lowered his mouth to her core.

CHAPTER THIRTY-ONE

SAHIRA THREADED her fingers into Orin's hair as his mouth settled between her thighs. Her head and back fell against the wall, and her legs hung over his shoulders as he licked, teased, and stoked the fires of passion into an inferno.

The man was pure magic with his tongue, and when a part of her screamed to stop this before it was too late, she shoved it into the deepest recesses of her mind. It would come back to torment her later, and she would hate herself for this, but for now, she was too lost in the moment to care.

That was the way she liked it.

Right now, she couldn't hate herself for this weakness when it felt so good. He tongued her clit while his hands caressed her ass, drawing her closer until she was on the verge of screaming as the high she rode crested and broke apart.

The sting of her fangs piercing her lower lip was nothing compared to the ecstasy he unleashed. She was still coming down from the high he'd created when he removed her legs from his shoulders and rose over her.

She grasped his hand, dragging him down before he could

pull her into his arms. She *needed* control over this. Maybe then she could fuck whatever this was between them from her system.

When he was kneeling before her, she planted her hands on his chest and pushed him back so he lay on the ground. She climbed on top and straddled him.

When his eyes met hers, she saw confusion and yearning in them. She wasn't the only one who didn't understand what this was between them.

And she wasn't the only one who didn't like this but couldn't stop wanting it. He was as baffled as her, but that wouldn't stop either of them.

He seized her hips as she settled over him; she was desperate to feel his cock within her again. Shifting her hips, she moved to take his rigid shaft into her.

She groaned at the familiar sensation of him filling her as he spread her further and sank deeper. Every part of her became hyperaware of him as a feeling of belonging and rightness stole through her.

But how can this feel so right when everything about it is so wrong?

She didn't have time to ponder that question as he rose a little, wrapped his hand around the back of her head, and pulled her down for a kiss. Pressed flush against him, with his fingers in her hair and their bodies entwined, the rest of the world faded until it was only them and the amazing way he made her feel.

As they moved, she felt him pulling on the sexual energy they created to feast on it and sate himself. She hated this man almost as much as she desired him, and the conflicting emotions would destroy her, but she loved being the one who could do this for him, as he could do it for her.

Bending her head, she rested her mouth against his throat. Her lips skimmed back before her fangs punctured his vein.

The sweet, coppery tang of his blood filled her mouth. It

infused her with strength as the tension building inside her unraveled, and she came again with a loud cry that his skin muffled.

His fingers biting into her, Orin thrust his hips up, and his back bowed. Deep within her, his shaft pulsed as he came.

CHAPTER THIRTY-TWO

ORIN STARED at the ceiling as he drifted down from the high being with Sahira created. The witch could screw, and once again, she'd sated his hunger like no other.

Her power and energy had seeped into every part of him and infused him with strength. The desert had taken a lot out of him, as had climbing the mountain, and they had further to go.

Now he wouldn't have to worry about going hungry in the Barren Lands. He had a little witch to keep him happy.

And speaking of the little witch... he looked over to find her staring at the ceiling too. Instead of looking perfectly sated and happy like him, despair etched her face.

He'd never seen that expression before on a woman he'd been with, and he didn't understand it. She'd come; she could never deny that.

He'd felt the muscles of her sheath contracting around him and experienced the quake of her body as she let go. His chest bore the marks of her fingers, and blood still trickled from the punctures she'd left on his throat.

Without a word, she rolled away and rose in one fluid

motion. She fumbled for her clothes, tossing aside his as she searched for what she sought.

Propping himself up on an elbow, he frowned at her hectic motions in the dim room. "What's the rush?"

"This shouldn't have happened. It was a giant mistake."

"And why is that? We're both happy, fed, and sated, though I wouldn't mind going for another round."

"Because you make me miserable. You make me *hate* myself. I don't understand how I can dislike someone so much and still have sex with them."

"You don't have to like someone to fuck them."

"I do!"

He pondered her words as she lifted a pair of pants. She started tugging them on before realizing they were his and throwing them at him.

They hit his face, and he almost laughed as he pulled them away, but the look on her face killed his amusement. He dropped his pants on the ground.

"That sounds like a *you* problem and one you should get over," he said. "There's nothing wrong with doing something that makes you feel good, even if it's with someone you don't like. And come on, admit it, you like me a little."

She stalked toward him and stopped when her feet connected with his leg. "Don't you understand? This *doesn't* make me feel good."

"You came."

"So what? I got off. I can do the same thing with my hand."

Feeling as if she'd slapped him, he recoiled from the insult. Had she really compared sex with him to masturbating? He was a *far* better option, and countless women would agree.

"I'm far better than any hand," he retorted.

"Sure, your moves are better, you have a tongue, and your blood is a bonus, but how you make me feel afterward…."

"And *how* do I make you feel?" he demanded when her words trailed off.

"Dirty, used, *weak*."

When her voice broke on the word weak, he lifted an eyebrow. Orin considered her one of the strongest women he'd ever met; he admired and respected her, which wasn't something he could say about many, and he'd met a lot of immortals in his lifetime.

Out of all those immortals, he could count on one hand the amount he respected... who weren't part of his family. Sahira and Lexi were two of them.

How did he upset her more than the witches and warlocks who despised her because of her vampire blood? All he'd ever done was make her feel good, irritate her, and play some mind games... but that was all in good fun.

"You're not weak, Sahira."

"No, I'm a fool. I'm just a hole for you to pass the time and someone to feed from until we're out of here. This won't happen again."

Her words irritated him for some reason, and he scowled, though she probably couldn't see it through the shadows while she jerked on her pants. He didn't like how she talked about herself or that he'd somehow made her feel that way.

"You're more than a *hole* for me to pass the time with," he told her.

"Why do you keep coming after *me*? Why can't you leave me alone? But I might not have to ask that for much longer; once you find another willing body, you'll move on to them."

He hadn't been able to do that so far, but there was *no way* he would let her know. And she was right; even if he hadn't screwed the nymph or the other women he'd flaunted in front of her, he planned on finding many more beds to warm once they were out of here.

That was who he was. It was what he did, and he wasn't going to change.

Then why did a part of him protest that, and why did he feel... *sadness*? Was that actual sadness over moving on to other women? How was *that* possible?

It wasn't. Dark fae didn't get sad over fucking; it was what they did and who they were. It was who *he* was, but he'd grown to like her.

CHAPTER THIRTY-THREE

"I'LL STILL CONSIDER US FRIENDS," he said.

"Friends," she scoffed, moving forward so he could see her better. "You'll consider us *friends*?"

"Wouldn't you?"

"No. My friends don't manipulate and play games with me. What happened today was my choice, but let's face it, that's all you want from me. I'm a plaything to you, someone to torture and pass the time with while we're stuck here.

"As soon as we're out of this realm, you'll be in someone else's bed, and I doubt you'll ever talk to me again unless it has something to do with Lexi and Cole. Friends have dinner and drinks together, socialize, and keep in touch, but you'll be gone the second we're out of here. We're not friends. *You* don't *have* friends."

He couldn't argue with that; he found friends to be a nuisance. He had his family, and that was what mattered, but when Lexi and Cole married, Sahira would become family too.

Plus, he didn't find the idea of drinks with Sahira as annoying as he would with anyone else. He'd enjoy sitting down, catching up, and maybe getting her back into his bed. She might not be on board for that last part, but he was sure he could get her to change her mind.

She'd also become more than a plaything to him, but he could never tell her. The woman had no idea how much of an effect she had on him; if she had the slightest notion, it could get ugly for him.

"I hope you're at least still on birth control. I didn't bother to bring any with me; I *never* thought this would happen again."

He was glad she'd been wrong about that. "I'm always prepared for that." There weren't going to be *any* babies in his future.

"Of course you are; it's always any port in a storm for you."

"I do like it when things are wet and rocking."

"You're disgusting."

"And you should let go and enjoy things for a change. Your life would be much happier if you stopped overanalyzing *everything*."

Red burned in her eyes. Leaning back on his elbows, he smiled. This wasn't how he'd expected this to end, but he enjoyed irritating the little witch.

"Fuck you," she spat.

"We've got plenty of time to do that again."

Wrath radiated from her, and he braced himself for an attack. It would start violent but end with him inside her; he was certain of that and would welcome it.

Instead, she spun away and stalked toward the door with her clothes and boots in hand. Leaping to his feet, he raced across the room and planted his hand against the door before she could open it.

Her honeyed scent, now mixed with his, teased his nostrils and tantalized him more. When he leaned closer, she planted her hands against his chest and pushed away.

They'd stepped more into the shadows, the things that were a part of him and all dark fae. They were his refuge from the world, the places he could slip into and hide, and now they hid more of her from him.

"Get away from me!" she snapped.

"We both enjoy this; I don't understand why you fight it so much."

"Because I won't be a whore of convenience for you!"

"You can't be a whore; I'm not paying you."

He blamed the darkness for keeping her fist hidden from him; it wasn't because a part of him actually believed he deserved the blow and *that* was why he didn't see it coming. No, it wasn't that at all, but when her punch connected and pain erupted through his jaw before spreading into his cheek, he welcomed it.

He rubbed his jaw. She had a nasty right hook.

"Get. Out. Of. My. Way," she bit out.

Orin didn't move. "You and your niece love to hit."

"I helped Del teach her to fight. Now *move*."

Orin stood his ground. "Why are you denying yourself something so good? I give you pleasure; you can't deny that."

"Why don't you go find a nymph to fuck, Orin?"

He blinked at her statement as he tried to understand what she was talking about. Then he remembered the nymph he had sitting on his lap when she returned to the pub after the first time they fucked.

Is she jealous?

The possibility excited him. It meant he wasn't the only one jealous of possible other bed partners.

He'd hated the jealousy eating at his belly and tearing him apart when he believed she'd screwed Zeth. He couldn't understand it then and still didn't, but the idea of her with the demon made him want to tear those horns off Zeth's head and shove them up his ass.

But she was jealous too, and he could end that and maybe screw her again before they left this room. He could tell her the nymph was another game he'd played with her, but not real.

He'd been waiting for Sahira to return to him and taunting her with other women. He never screwed them but couldn't let her know that.

Even as the truth rose in his throat, it strangled there. If he told her, she would know she was different and had some control over him.

That was a vulnerability he refused to expose or possess. He'd rather have her storm out of here, hating him, than tell her the truth and have her use it against him.

And she would, of course she would. He'd most certainly use it against someone, and after everything he'd done to her, he'd probably deserve it, though he'd never admit that.

Lowering his hand, he flashed his teeth at her. "Go on. I'll be here when you're ready for more."

He saw her hands coming this time but didn't stop her as she planted them against his chest and shoved him back. He'd deserved that one and possibly more.

Sahira pulled open the door and tugged on her clothes as she stormed across the pub. She undid the barricade on the front door and left.

He stood there, resting his hand against the doorframe after Sahira vanished. It wasn't until he felt eyes on him that he lifted his gaze to discover Elsa on the stairs.

The witch's scathing gaze raked his body before she descended the rest of the way and followed Sahira out the door.

CHAPTER THIRTY-FOUR

SAHIRA HAD no idea where she was going, only that she needed to get away. How had she been so stupid and weak *again*?

Why did she keep giving in to him, and *why* did she still crave more even while she berated herself? What was it about him that she couldn't resist? It certainly wasn't his sparkling personality.

She should have climbed off her stool and walked out of the bar an hour ago. Or, better yet, never sat next to him at all.

Instead, she'd done all the *wrong* things and succumbed to that hideous man's temptation again.

But what a marvelous temptation it was.

She couldn't suppress the shiver racing up her spine as she recalled the feel of him moving against her. His hands were so warm on her skin, and his tongue on her clit had undone her completely.

Unlike any of the other men she'd been with, he possessed and owned her in a way no other had. He made her forget everything but him as the pleasure he gave became the focus of her world.

She hated him for it.

She was almost at the end of the street and near the library when she heard someone calling her name. Turning back, she spotted Elsa striding toward her.

Sahira's heart sank. She didn't want anyone else to know how weak she'd been *again*, but if Elsa was here, she'd seen or heard something.

Desperate to be somewhere less exposed for this conversation, Sahira hurried up the steps of the library. She opened the door and entered the dusty building.

She wanted to run until she couldn't anymore, but she'd cornered herself here, and it was time to own up to her weakness. Her feet thudded against the wooden floor as she strode into the main part of the library with its three stories of empty shelving.

She'd never been much of a reader, but these barren shelves were as depressing as her inability to resist a dickhead dark fae with a god complex. Sahira stood in the middle of the room as she closed her eyes and restrained the scream reverberating in her head.

Elsa's nimble steps barely made a sound against the floor as she approached. Sahira opened her eyes to take in the dust particles dancing through the air around her. The sunlight spilling through the open windows did nothing to warm the coldness seeping through Sahira.

"Are you okay?" Elsa asked.

"No."

"Did he hurt you?"

Only my heart, but Sahira kept those words and their awful truth to herself. She was already ashamed of herself; she couldn't admit she had some very complicated feelings for the dark fae douche.

"No, he would never do that," she said instead.

"Good."

Sahira kept her attention on the specks of dust as Elsa came to stand beside her. "If it makes a difference, I think he cares for you too."

"I don't care for him," Sahira said far too quickly. "He drives me insane. He's an asshole, and I hate him."

"Sure, you do."

Elsa's voice dripped with sarcasm as she drew out the word *sure*.

Sahira wanted to be annoyed with her, she hadn't asked Elsa to come here and be insightful, but all her irritation remained focused on herself and Orin.

She sighed as she tried to catch a speck of dust and failed. "I really do hate him."

"I'm sure part of you does; he makes it quite easy to hate him, but there's more to it than hate. That would be too simple."

"Yeah, it would. It's all so complicated, but none of it matters because he's a dark fae, and we all know what *that* means."

"We all know what it usually means, but like I said, I think he cares for you too. That doesn't mean it's healthy or something good for you, but I believe it."

Sahira started to deny it, but curiosity got the best of her. "Why do you say that?"

"If that thing in the desert had captured *me*, he would have let it eat me."

"That's not true."

But as she said it, she pondered if it was true. Orin wasn't exactly selfless; he was more likely to save himself than lend a hand.

"Yes, it is," Elsa said. "He probably would have used the thing eating me as a distraction to slip away."

Sahira laughed humorlessly because it was true. "He'd do the same to me."

"But he didn't do the same to you. I was there. You couldn't see him because that thing was trying to eat you, but I did. He didn't hesitate before chasing after you; Zeth did.

"I like Zeth, but he has a family to get home to, and I saw that on his face before he went to help. He still went but thought of them first, as he should. Orin only thought of *you*."

Sahira felt Elsa's eyes on her, but she couldn't look at her friend. She had no idea what to say.

"He went to find you when the scarog beetles attacked, too," Elsa continued. "And he was *pissed* when the brownies pointed their weapons at you."

He had found her when the scarog beetles attacked. After the beetles invaded the library and she was separated from the others, she'd been desperate to flee those monsters. And then Orin had been there, pulling her against him while he enveloped them in shadows.

She hadn't expected him to risk himself in such a way, but there he was, and she'd survived because of it. Some of her coldness melted, which was a dangerous thing for her. Orin would destroy her heart and soul if she let her guard down around him. She had no doubt.

"The brownies wouldn't have done anything," she said.

"That's not the point. It upset him, and he made it clear to *everyone*. He does care for you in some way."

"How much can a dark fae really care for anyone?"

Elsa shrugged. "They've fallen in love and gotten married before. I have a feeling that creatures who are always so cold, distant, and self-centered might fall *harder* when their heart finally becomes involved."

"Hmm," Sahira murmured. "Well, it doesn't matter because I prefer to hate him."

"There's a reason they say there's a fine line between love and hate." When Sahira shot her a look, Elsa lifted her hands in a calming gesture. "I'm just saying."

"It's not like that."

"Isn't it?"

Sahira bit her bottom lip and pondered this. No, it wasn't

love, it couldn't be, but the damn man had managed to work his way under her skin and become a festering thing she couldn't get rid of.

However, no one described love as a festering *thing,* and that's what Orin was to her… most of the time.

"You could always try women; we're a lot easier to deal with," Elsa suggested.

Sahira laughed, and the sudden release of tension felt good after everything they'd endured since entering this realm. She grinned at Elsa as she nudged her friend's shoulder with hers.

"There are billions of men who would disagree with that statement," she said.

Elsa chuckled. "True, but I don't want to have sex with them."

Neither do I. There was only one man who interested her anymore, and out of the countless realms with innumerable men in them, he was the worst one for her.

"I'm not hitting on you," Elsa said. "I much prefer blondes."

Sahira laughed again. "I didn't think you were, but I could turn you on to brunettes."

Elsa chuckled as she hooked her arm through Sahira's and clasped her hands together. Gently, she turned away from the empty library and led her back across the floor. "I have no doubt, my friend. Come on, let's get out of here. This place is depressing."

Sahira couldn't agree more. Gripping Elsa's arm, she squeezed it. "Thank you."

"I'm here if you need to talk, but I know this is between you two, and you'll eventually figure it out or destroy each other. I'd much prefer it if you didn't destroy each other."

"Me too."

CHAPTER THIRTY-FIVE

ORIN FOLDED his arms over his chest and scowled at the women strolling down the street arm in arm. Their heads were bent close together as they smiled and talked.

Sahira looked a *lot* happier than the last time he saw her, when she'd told him he made her miserable. That had been the last thing he expected after she'd so enthusiastically given herself to him. No one should be unhappy after orgasming *twice.*

He didn't understand how she could be. It was one of the many annoying mysteries of her, and he was not happy about it.

They should be preparing to leave, and these two were doing who knew what. They also looked far too cozy for his liking.

He didn't think Elsa had any interest in Sahira sexually; he would understand if she did, *his* witch was irresistible, but he didn't get that sense from Elsa. Sahira and Elsa were good friends, and neither wanted anything more. He still didn't like it.

Sahira didn't consider him a friend, and he certainly wasn't going to talk about her feelings or anything like that with her, but he found himself wishing it was *him*. He craved a bond like this with her.

His scowl deepened over this realization. He'd never sought a bond with anyone other than his family... but he did with her.

He hated this shit.

Zeth settled onto the porch and draped an arm over his knee as the brownies emerged from their holes and gathered closer. They had dug far more of them into the ground than Orin had realized, and they came from everywhere.

When they were only a few feet away, Sahira and Elsa stopped walking. "Where have you been?" Orin demanded more harshly than he'd intended.

Sahira frowned at him while Elsa grinned.

"That's none of your business," Sahira replied.

She *really* loved pissing him off, but he probably said the same thing about him.

"We should have left by now, but we've been waiting for the two of you."

"You're free to go off on your own."

They glared at each other as Elsa laughed and disentangled her arm from Sahira's. Zeth's eyebrows rose as his gaze shifted from him to Sahira and back again.

"Let me get my stuff." Elsa jogged up the steps. She stopped beside him and leaned closer to whisper, "Maybe you should try not being an asshole for a change. It might get you a lot further."

His eyes narrowed on the pretty witch who grinned at them. "Didn't you say you had to get your shit?"

"Easy there, tiger, I'm getting there. I just thought you should know that plenty of men and women would gladly scoop her up."

"Does that include you?"

"Maybe."

She winked at him before continuing into the pub. His jaw clenched as his teeth ground together until he was sure they'd crack.

The witch was messing with him and trying to prove a point, but he wasn't in the mood for mind games. *He* was the only one who could play those.

He had enough problems with one witch; he didn't need more with another one. If Elsa tried to take Sahira from him, he'd gladly kill her.

Sahira climbed the stairs next. Her gaze held his before she turned her nose into the air and stalked past. Orin rolled his eyes and almost started after her, but he refused to chase her.

Let her throw her little fit, she'd return. She could say she wouldn't, but she'd proven that wasn't true this morning. He doubted she'd have any more restraint next time.

Orin felt the demon's eyes on him and turned to meet Zeth's steady, yellow eyes. "You're looking a lot better."

Orin didn't respond. His relationship with Sahira wasn't any of the demon's business, and if he tried to push it, Orin would make sure he regretted the decision.

"She deserves better," Zeth said.

"Maybe so," Orin agreed, "but *I'm* what she'll have."

Zeth's eyes narrowed before he shifted his attention to the road again. Orin thumbed the handle of his dagger as he contemplated slitting the demon's throat.

They might require the demon's help to get through this realm, but Orin wasn't sure it was worth keeping him alive. However, it would infuriate Sahira if he killed her friend.

No, it would hurt *her if you killed him.*

And it would hurt her; she had a heart and cared for her friends. She'd be pissed and devastated if he killed this sanctimonious bastard, but it would be fun.

She'd truly hate him if he did, and not just claim to. She'd never forgive him for killing Zeth.

The certainty of that stayed his hand, and finally, it fell away from his dagger. He couldn't believe he was letting a woman have any influence over this decision, but if she wasn't involved, he probably wouldn't feel so much animosity toward the demon.

She kept fucking with his world, and while he thoroughly enjoyed sex with her, it was starting to annoy him. They had to get out of this realm so he could get away from her and get his head on straight again.

CHAPTER THIRTY-SIX

THE BROWNIES GATHERED CLOSER but didn't say anything as Puth and Eisel moved to the front. Behind the leaders stood four more brownies, each with a tiny bundle tied to their backs.

Orin eyed the tiny bags and spears in their hands. *That can't be good.*

But before he could learn more, Sahira and Elsa returned. The door creaked as it swung shut behind them.

"We have four who would like to go with you," Puth said.

"No," Orin said while Elsa and Sahira said, "Sure."

Orin turned to face them. "They can't climb those mountains, and they'll only slow us down."

Not to mention these two witches would risk themselves to save these rodents, especially Sahira. He wasn't about to let her endanger herself for some rats.

"They don't have to climb the mountains," Sahira replied. "They can ride in our packs, on our shoulders, or in our pockets. They probably each weigh five pounds at most; that won't slow us down. They'll be fine."

"They'll be a distraction."

"We want out of here too," Puth said. "These four would like to help make that happen. More of us would go, but we have children to care for; we can't leave or take them with us."

"Of course you can't," Sahira said sympathetically.

Orin rolled his eyes; it was already starting.

"We also thought that sending more than four would result in a bigger protest," Puth said.

Puth gave Orin a pointed look; Orin smiled in return. The man was right, but none of these little hairballs were going with them.

"If you manage to get free," Puth continued, "they won't forget us and will find a way to help us break free too."

Orin admired their determination, but they couldn't have these four little vermin tagging along with them. "We'll make sure to let your people know you're alive and where you are when we get free."

"Not good enough," Puth replied.

Everybody wanted to piss him off and argue with him today. What was so difficult about just doing what he said? He'd survived *far* more battles than anyone else here; he was trying to keep them all alive and safe.

"You're fighting over something that shouldn't be an argument," Sahira said.

"They'll be a distraction," Orin told her.

"No, we won't," the single female brownie with a pack retorted.

"I don't see how they could be," Sahira said. "They're asking, and we're saying yes. They know how dangerous this journey is and that there's a chance they won't survive."

"We do," the woman brownie said. "We're very aware we're less likely than you to survive, but we've been here for centuries and want to see our families again. Our children deserve to grow up free to roam and to know our families and friends... if they still live. Our loved ones also deserve answers about what happened to us."

"All four of us have been here since the beginning; it's time for us to go," the brownie to her right stated.

He felt all their gazes on him as he tried to control his temper. This was a *bad* idea, but none of them wanted to hear it. Because of that, they could suffer the consequences of their bad decisions, but not him.

"Fine," he relented. "But none of you are riding with me, and I won't do anything to save your asses if you get in trouble."

"Always the gentleman," Sahira muttered.

"Are you going to risk your life for them?"

He didn't know why he bothered to ask; he already knew the answer. And if he was smart, he'd let her do it and not do anything to intervene. She would deserve whatever she got.

Sahira lifted her chin as she stared haughtily back at him. "Yes."

"You're a bigger fool than I thought."

He considered shaking some sense into her. She should be concerned with her life and her life alone, but though she was smart and strong, her big heart made her weak.

He didn't like it.

"Let's go," he said.

Elsa and Sahira bent to help a brownie climb onto their shoulder; Orin bit back a sound of disgust when the demon lifted two onto his shoulders and they settled into the crux of his horns. A bunch of bighearted morons surrounded him.

And it would get one of them killed.

CHAPTER THIRTY-SEVEN

OVER THE NEXT FIVE DAYS, they climbed higher into the mountains and scaled cliffs thousands of feet over her head. By the end of every day, Sahira's fingers were often bloodied and raw from digging into rocks with a death grip that kept her from falling thousands of feet to her death.

Thankfully, they healed overnight, but by nightfall, she was dejected, sore, and desperately clinging to the hope they would make it out of this. That hope faded a little more every day.

Often the tops of the mountains they climbed were impossible to see while hanging onto the sides of them. It was difficult to tell how much further they had to go until they either found the top or a shelf big enough for them all to rest.

Her muscles ached, and her legs wobbled, but she pushed onward. They all did.

As they traveled, they got to know the brownies better. Pipper, or Pip as she preferred, was quick-witted and loved to sing ballads as she sat, cradled on one of Zeth's horns.

Fath was quiet and watchful. He observed the world around them far more than he commented on it, but he would offer a short opinion when asked a question. Most of the time, he was content to sit on Sahira's shoulder while his friends talked.

Gior had brought a small flute he often played to accompany Pip's singing. Settled onto Zeth's other horn, Gior often swayed to the music as it flowed through the air.

Loth thoroughly enjoyed their exploration of the realm, probably because he didn't have to climb these awful mountains. He often gasped, pointed, and commented on each new thing they saw.

Because they were usually in the middle of climbing, they didn't get to enjoy the mountains or the view as much as the brownie, but that didn't stop him from rejoicing in the wonders around them. Elsa often had to tell him to stop bouncing as he rode on her shoulder.

As they climbed, the conditions became increasingly worse. The air grew colder, thinner, and more difficult to breathe. Since Belda's town had been a place of nearly perfect temperature, and the brownie town had been a little cooler but still comfortable, they weren't prepared for this cold.

They'd brought extra clothes, but too many layers slowed them down and made climbing more difficult. Sahira had wrapped some socks around the middle of her hands to keep them warmer, but her exposed fingers were as numb as they were bloody. She couldn't use them to cover her fingers, though; they hindered her ability to grip the rocks too much when she did.

By the end of their fourth day, they'd climbed so high, clouds floated past them, and ice coated the rocks. Scaling the mountains became increasingly difficult as her hand slipped off rocks or her feet suddenly skidded out from under her.

More than a few times, she was jerked to a stop by her fingers catching on something as her feet fell away. Once, she slid down a few feet as rocks tore and battered her belly before she regained purchase and jerked to a stop.

Her shoulders and back screamed a protest against the abuse

and her weight pulling on them, but she somehow managed to regain her footing. Pulling herself closer to the wall, she stood trembling and unable to move for a few minutes before regaining the strength and confidence to do so again.

"Careful," Fath had murmured.

Gritting her teeth, Sahira resisted the impulse to flick him from her shoulder. Like she needed to be told that or was enjoying nearly falling thousands of feet to a sudden, splattered stop.

However, the brownie's voice had wavered with fear on that one word. She didn't like his backseat driving but understood it. She pushed on without hurting a tiny creature who didn't deserve to have her terror taken out on him.

At the end of the fifth day, she was frozen, her limbs shook, and blood dripped from her fingers, making the already slippery climb more difficult, when the summit of another mountain came into view only a few feet over her head. Exhausted, she wasn't sure she had the strength to pull herself over the top, but as she stretched her hand up, Orin grasped her wrist and helped pull her over.

Even battered, bruised, frozen, and about to collapse, a tingle ran through her as his hand warmed her more than the fire they would build once they settled in for the night. When she tugged on her wrist, he released it.

"Thank you," she murmured.

He nodded briskly before turning away. They hadn't talked much since leaving the brownie town behind.

It wasn't because of their argument over the brownies; they annoyed him, but he wouldn't withdraw and stop pestering her over them. Instead, she saw something watchful and uncertain in his eyes when they met hers.

She didn't understand what brought about the change; maybe their fight in the storage room after they had sex, or perhaps he was done with her. He could try to go for Elsa, but Sahira knew her friend had no interest in him, and Orin probably realized the same.

Maybe he'd decided he could hold out until they escaped this realm and he found someone else to occupy his time. He looked a lot better than he did before they had sex.

She'd noticed his weight loss and increasingly pallid skin tone, but since it was gradual, she hadn't realized how bad it was until his skin regained its glowing vitality and his cheeks filled out some. He'd still lost weight, they all had, but he looked like he'd put five pounds back on.

He might be able to hold out for another woman until they left this realm behind… if they found a way to do so soon. If not, she fully expected him to start annoying her again, but she would hold out this time.

As she thought it, she felt that niggling weakness deep inside her. Why couldn't things be simple with him?

But that would be like asking why the Earth couldn't stop spinning. Some things were simply impossible.

Now, as his wary eyes held hers, she had no idea what was going through his mind. Before, she'd always known what Orin was thinking. He tended to have only one thing on his mind... other than breaking out of this place.

She had no idea what was going on with him, and as much as she welcomed this distance from him and a reprieve from the madness of their strange relationship, she almost asked him what was wrong. Thankfully, she managed to restrain herself when he turned away; some things were better left alone.

CHAPTER THIRTY-EIGHT

SHE BENT to help Elsa over the mountain's edge while Zeth hoisted himself over and fell to his knees. When Elsa collapsed beside him, Loth scrambled from her shoulder, stopped to pat her head, and whispered, "Thank you. Rest now, dear."

The brownie scampered away while Fath climbed down Sahira's back and walked over to join his friends. Gior pulled out his flute and played while Pip sang a haunting melody of unrequited love that set Sahira's nerves on edge.

Determined to ignore the singing, Sahira knelt at Elsa's side and rested her fingers against her friend's arm. "Are you okay?"

"I can't feel my arms and legs, but I think they're still there."

Sahira pretended to look her friend over. "They're still there."

Elsa lifted her hand to give her a thumbs-up before dropping it again. Sahira patted her shoulder. "Do you want me to stay with you?"

"No, I'm going to sleep or die here, whichever comes first."

Sahira chuckled as she squeezed her arm. "I'm going to see if I can find some wood. A fire will make us all feel better."

So far, they'd been lucky enough to find wood at their other stops. Scraggly trees speckled the mountains, and their broken limbs and branches littered the ground.

She didn't know how long that luck would hold out, but she hoped to find more of it here too. Sahira shifted her attention to the mountain they'd climbed and the beautiful view of the craggy, snow-topped peaks rolling out around her.

Clouds drifted in and out of those peaks as they kissed their tops and parted around them. During the climb, she'd touched some of those clouds—or tried to as her fingers fell through the misty creations floating around her.

Despite her lingering unhappiness and the wind howling around her, it was beautiful. Pulling her cloak tighter, she huddled under the hood as she turned to survey the land.

They might have finally scaled to the summit of the mountains as the land before her was flatter than before. If it wasn't the summit, at least they'd have a break from climbing for a little bit tomorrow.

She welcomed that reprieve and compelled herself to move before she turned into a block of ice. As Zeth rose, Sahira reluctantly left Elsa to help the others scavenge for wood.

It took at least an hour for her to gather a couple of armloads of wood and bring them back to a rocky outcropping that helped protect them from the worst of the wind. She'd chop off a finger for a cave or some shelter, but she hadn't seen anything like that here, and it was too windy to set up a tent.

The wind howling across the land made it feel like a knife was cutting across her face with each icy burst. She'd lost the feeling in her arms and legs but still had some in her cheeks and the tip of her nose.

She stared at their small pile of wood. They hadn't found as much here, and the fire was smaller than on previous nights, but at least it offered some warmth as smoke wafted into the air and flames danced around the sticks.

Elsa had risen to start the fire and now had it going as much as possible. If they kept it small, they might keep it burning through the night.

She was so tired of being cold; she craved warmth as birds sang and the sun beat down on her. But there was no evading the relentless, icy air.

Not even with the bigger fires on the other nights had she completely warmed. Some part of her always remained frozen, and she feared she might never get warm again.

When they left this realm, she would never sit on another beach or go anywhere below sixty degrees again. She'd find somewhere tropical, consume a lot of fruity drinks, and sit in a field of grass while downing them all.

It was such a lovely image that she smiled a little before another gust of wind swirled over the top of the rocks. It found crevices in her cloak and blanket and caused the fire to jump around.

Pip had stopped singing, but the notes of Gior's flute filled the air as the sun sank behind the mountains. What had been a chilly day turned into a frigid night.

Sheltered as much as possible behind the rocks, Sahira hugged her knees to her chest as she huddled in her cloak and blanket. She stared at the small, crackling flames barely warming her cheeks while listening to the haunting strains of the flute.

Elsa was curled into the fetal position on the other side of the fire. She'd passed out without her blanket on; Zeth removed it from her bag and draped it over her.

The other three brownies had hunted for insects and returned with scarce findings they offered to share; they all turned them down. Soon, they might have no choice but to eat the insects as their food supply dwindled.

Orin wasn't the only one who had lost weight. She could feel that in how her clothes fit and how the ground dug into her bones while she tried to sleep.

They were all exerting too much energy without a steady

food supply, but they couldn't do anything about that. When they left on this journey, they'd assumed they could hunt and eat the monsters in the desert.

They didn't have much luck with that, but if they were back in those arid lands, they would find and kill something, even if it was one of those tongue things. They hadn't planned for this mountainous terrain or the lack of life amongst it.

The reprieve from things trying to kill them made her both upset and grateful, but as her stomach rumbled, she wished for a monster to eat. Trying not to think about what would happen when the food ran out, her stomach turned when Gior bit off the head of an insect.

When bile rushed up her throat, she swallowed it and rested her head against the rock behind her. Maybe if they cooked the insects first, they'd be more appealing.

Sahira doubted it, but she also doubted she'd turn them down when she was starving. She'd do whatever it took to survive this land, no matter how much it disgusted her.

Feeling eyes on her, she lifted her head and met Orin's gaze across the fire. Unable to suppress her visceral reaction to him, a thrill ran through her as her heart rate increased and her skin came alive... and this time not from goose bumps.

How this man could affect her so much with only one look was something she'd never understand or get used to. Despite her unending exhaustion, her frozen body came alive beneath his gaze.

He sat ten feet away from her and across the flames, but he didn't feel as distant now as he had when he stood beside her earlier. Barely able to breathe and unable to break his stare, she held it until a large boom quaked the earth.

Rocks broke free of the mountains surrounding them. They bounced and rattled as they tumbled from the walls.

In the distance, a plume of smoke rose into the night sky. It turned the middle of the full moon a shade of gray.

CHAPTER THIRTY-NINE

ORIN LEAPT to his feet as he broke eye contact with Sahira. He turned as the plume of smoke rose higher before dispersing into the ever-present wind.

Now what?

He didn't know the answer to that as the smoke had been at least a mile away, and he couldn't see what caused the explosion. They should rest, but this was the first new development in days.

It was the first sign of something other than themselves in this wild, unforgiving land. Though he'd far prefer to sleep and check it out tomorrow, that couldn't happen. He had to make sure they weren't in danger.

"What's going on?" Elsa inquired in a groggy voice.

"Something just exploded or... or... I have no idea," Sahira replied.

Elsa shoved herself up and rose as Orin bent to start shoving things back into his sack.

"What are you doing?" Zeth inquired.

"I'm going to check it out," Orin answered.

"We can do that in the morning. We need to rest."

"Can you sleep after seeing that?"

Zeth hesitated before his shoulders slumped. "No."

"Then I suggest you start packing too. If there's nothing there, we can come back."

With obvious reluctance, the others rose and returned their things to their packs. The brownies grumbled about it, but considering they just rode around on everyone else, he didn't understand why they were so exhausted.

It only took a few minutes for them to be ready to leave, and by then, the plume of smoke had completely dissipated. Orin's body thrummed with excitement as he stared at the luminous moon hovering over the land; *finally*, something different was happening.

Climbing the mountains had been an exhausting endeavor, but the endless sameness of it all was disheartening. The possibility they could spend the rest of their lives climbing through this rocky terrain and never find answers kept trying to take root.

The worst thing that could happen in this place was losing hope. Once they did, they'd die; he was certain of it. And he was certain he wouldn't let it happen to him.

But now, something had changed, and he had to know what it was.

When Sahira lifted her brownie onto her shoulder, he turned away. So far, the tiny immortals hadn't hindered them as much as he'd assumed.

They were more annoying than he'd anticipated. Too many times, he'd contemplated breaking that flute in half.

No one should be playing such cheerful music while sitting on the shoulders of a demon who was doing all the work by carrying it higher into the sky. He'd restrained himself from doing so only because Orin had to admit the female brownie could sing.

Her voice was a reprieve from the drudgery of their days. He had no idea what their names were and no intention of learning them, but he liked her voice.

Thankfully, the rodents were silent as he led the way through a rocky path between the mountains. Sahira followed on his heels.

Towering cliffs no longer blocked their way, but large **stones** did. He rested his hand on the frigid boulders to boost himself onto and over them.

He turned back once to offer Sahira his hand, but she wasn't paying attention or was purposely ignoring him. Trying to disregard the sting of possible rejection, he lowered his hand and continued down the other side of the **boulder**.

He climbed over another set of rocks and followed the path cutting through the terrain.

The blast and smoke had been farther away than it looked as they continued to go down. He had to turn sideways in some areas to keep rocks from scraping his skin and tugging at his clothes.

With his bigger, bulkier frame, the demon fared worse and barely squeezed through some of the passageways. After what felt like hours, but was probably only one or less, they made it out of the constricting confines reeking of minerals and ice.

Orin frowned as he emerged from the mountainous spaces and onto the edge of an enormous, rocky field thousands of feet wide and long. It was so vast, he couldn't see the end though the moon hung in the sky behind it.

Raised mounds, no more than a few inches high in some places and as tall as a foot in others, peppered the field. He couldn't detect the initial coil of smoke, but something smoldered to his left.

He couldn't quite make out what had tendrils of smoke rising from it as glowing embers lit the night around what was little more than a charred blob. He studied those mounds and then the thing to his left again.

He had no idea what had created those masses on the field or if they were an entrance to lairs beneath the earth, but he suspected they were deadly. Approaching them might prove fatal, but staying here wasn't an option.

Staying away from the start of the field, he approached the smoldering thing. It wasn't until he was nearly upon the blob that he realized it was the charred remains of an immortal.

What remained of its charcoaled skin glowed like hot coals as it burned off its face and fell to the ground. No flesh remained on its hands or torso, and he had no idea where its legs had gone, but they were no longer attached to its frame.

"Shit," Sahira whispered from behind him.

He'd been so focused on getting to the thing and discovering what it was, he hadn't heard her following him. Glancing over his shoulder, he checked to ensure nothing nefarious approached her before focusing on the field again.

Where did the fire come from that torched this guy?

He searched the night as he recalled the tower of smoke. It must have come from somewhere out there, but where?

"What is it?" Sahira whispered.

"I think it was an immortal."

"Can you tell what kind?"

"No. There aren't enough remains left."

Bending, he found a loose rock on the ground, lifted it, and tossed it in his palm as he studied the field. Like he was skipping stones across the water, he pulled back his arm and threw it sideways across the area.

It made it ten feet before gliding over one of the mounds. The second it skimmed across the top of the pile, a blast of fire erupted; it launched the rock fifty feet into the air.

He never saw where the stone landed or heard it rattle against other rocks. It was most likely vaporized by the blast... like this poor bastard's legs.

CHAPTER FORTY

"Oh," Sahira breathed.

"Go back to the others."

Orin was too close to the field to maneuver around her, but they needed to return. She briefly met his gaze before plastering her back against the rocky wall and sliding along it toward where the others waited.

The brownies had all descended from their customary perches to gather at the edge of the field. Their tails twitched as they studied the land.

"This realm keeps getting better," Zeth muttered.

"What was that thing over there?" the female brownie asked.

"The remains of an immortal," Orin answered. "They're burnt beyond recognition."

"Delightful," Elsa muttered.

"How do we get around a field of fiery geysers?" Sahira asked.

"A field of fiery 'blast off your legs and barbecue off your testicles' geysers," Orin said.

The three male brownies grabbed their crotches while Zeth

shifted uncomfortably. Orin studied the field as he tried to figure out their next step.

"If someone was coming this way, then there has to be something over there," Sahira said.

Their attention shifted to the still-smoldering immortal who had become a mystery.

"Not anything good if that unfortunate immortal was trying to escape it," the female brownie said.

"Our town wasn't so bad, and we sought to escape it," Zeth said. "You're here, but you were surviving in your town. We all have families we'd like to get back to."

"I have six children I left behind," the flute-playing brownie said. "Ghouls killed my wife before we all fled. Our children were older and could take care of themselves, but I *miss* them. I could have grandchildren that I don't know. I need answers about what happened to them and where they are."

Zeth rubbed his chin as he spoke. "So do I."

"My ma and pa must miss me terribly... if they're still alive," the female brownie said.

The other two male brownies nodded.

"I also had a girl I planned to marry," the quiet one of them said. "She was beautiful."

Orin doubted that. From what he'd seen, the brownies all looked alike, which meant they resembled overgrown mice, but to each their own.

"She's probably moved on by now and found someone else," he murmured.

"I miss my siblings," the other one said. "There were fifteen of us. You'd think we wouldn't really know each other, with our age differences and the fact there were so many of us, but they were my best friends."

Orin could understand that. He'd fought endlessly with his eight brothers but also loved every one of them. And when he lost five of them, it changed him. It changed all of those who remained.

He wouldn't lose any more of them, but for all he knew, he already had. According to Sahira, Brokk still hadn't returned from Doomed Valley when she arrived here.

Cole and Varo could also be dead. He doubted much could kill the Shadow Reaver, but he had no way of knowing what had become of his brothers, and he *hated* it. It had also been far too long since he'd seen his mother and sister; while they were most likely safe, he wanted to confirm that for himself.

His hands fisted as he studied the vast, endless field. He had to get back to his family; if Brokk still hadn't returned, he would find his brother.

"I want to be free," the female brownie whispered.

"We all do," Orin said. "We wouldn't be here otherwise."

"If someone was coming from the other way, then there's something on the other side," Sahira said again.

"What if they were coming from this way?" Elsa inquired. "What if it was someone from Belda's town who's been wandering out here and just started across the field?"

Zeth rubbed his chin as he answered. "Before us, it had been a while since anyone left our town."

"But it would be easy enough to get lost out here," Sahira said. "They could have been out here for years, surviving on what little they found to eat and drink."

"We haven't found any water outside the brownie town," Orin said.

The female brownie looked at him. "You're the first to come through our town in centuries."

"I'm sure there's a way to get here without going through their town first," Sahira said. "It's so easy to get turned around out here."

"True," Orin agreed.

Elsa huddled deeper into her cloak as she shifted from foot to foot and rubbed her hands together. "I don't think they came from Belda's town. It would be too difficult to survive out here for this long."

"I think she's right," Zeth said, "but it is a possibility. I think it's more likely there's something on the other side of this field."

"Which means we have to cross it," Sahira said.

"We've come this far," Elsa stated. "I'm not turning back."

"Neither am I," Orin said.

"That settles it then." Zeth turned away from the field to survey the rocky land behind them. "We should probably wait until morning to leave. The field will be easier to navigate in the daytime."

One of the brownies jerked his thumb toward the still-smoldering remains. "Why didn't they wait until daytime to cross?"

"Maybe they just came across this field and decided to keep going," Elsa suggested.

"Or maybe they did start in the daytime, and the field is so big night descended by the time they got this far," Sahira said.

Orin hoped that wasn't true. "Whenever they started, they almost reached the end, which means we will too."

"Or they were coming from our way and didn't get far at all."

Sahira's ominous words hung heavy in the air. No one responded to them; there wasn't anything to say. They had no choice but to continue.

CHAPTER FORTY-ONE

THEY DIDN'T BOTHER FINDING wood to start another fire or to return to the one they left behind. It would take too much time to return, and by the time they finished gathering enough sticks for another fire, the day would be upon them.

Instead, they settled near the edge of the fiery geyser field. They gathered all their blankets and huddled together for warmth.

The brownies burrowed in to nuzzle securely against them. When the wind picked up, it found crevices that let it blow down the blankets; the small immortals shivered in response.

Sahira spent most of the night trying to ignore that she was wedged between Orin and Elsa. Every time she nodded off, her head inevitably fell onto his shoulder; the second it did, she'd pop back up.

Whenever it happened, he'd smirk at her in that annoying way he had. He had no idea how close that smirk brought him to having his throat ripped out.

She glowered at him and contemplated moving, but she'd have to get up and walk to the other side of Zeth, which meant she wouldn't be between him and Elsa and would have one side exposed to the cold.

As much as Orin infuriated her, she couldn't tolerate the idea of being more exposed to the frigid elements. She'd had enough of the cold as her teeth chattered and her toes were caught somewhere between being completely numb and an awful pins-and-needles sensation that never ceased in this *horrible* place.

Eventually, exhaustion won, and she passed out. She woke to discover her head on his shoulder and his arm draped protectively around her. His body was like a small furnace she'd burrowed close to.

She tried to deny it but stayed there far longer than she should have while savoring his warmth and scent. He was more addictive than any drug.

While she would never become one of the dark fae's mindless, sex-craved shadow kissed, she understood how those immortals and humans could fall so completely under the spell of the dark fae. They were a deadly, nearly irresistible temptation.

But she would resist.

As the first rays of the sun touched the horizon, she stirred from his arms and sat up. Yawning, she instantly missed his warmth but pretended not to as she rubbed her eyes before studying the vast field.

Not being able to see where it ended was a little unnerving, especially considering they were only a hundred feet away from a dead immortal who had failed to traverse it.

Sahira rubbed her hands together before breathing on her cold hands. She wasn't looking forward to this.

She'd prefer to climb another mountain today... maybe. Her fingers ached as she recalled gripping those icy stones while pulling herself higher. She'd prayed to Hecate to keep her from making one small mistake that could send her spiraling toward a bloody, broken oblivion.

On second thought, she'd prefer not to scale anything again today.

As the sun crept higher, Elsa stirred, and Zeth rose to stretch his back. The sun's rays revealed more of the field, stretching endlessly before them.

She certainly couldn't see the end of it, and the more she saw, the further her heart sank. It had to be at least two or three miles across the thing, if not more because she still couldn't see the end.

And then something strange started happening. At first, she couldn't tell what was going on; it was too far away to process it, but as more of the sun's light touched the field, it drew closer to them.

Then her jaw dropped as understanding dawned. What was coming toward them was small puffs of smoke as the geysers closed and sucked into the earth with tiny pops that left only tendrils of smoke behind.

The geysers disappeared completely into the earth, leaving only a vast, barren landscape of flat rock. Only fifteen feet away from them, the last one vanished so completely she couldn't tell the difference between the rock and the place where the geyser once stood.

"What the fuck?" Zeth breathed.

The brownies had crept out from beneath the blankets and stood shivering at the edge of the field. While Elsa and Orin rose to examine the now blank canvas, Sahira remained where she was, her head resting against the rock, as a sense of understanding and doom descended over her.

When Orin lifted a rock from the ground, she didn't have to see what would happen when he threw it sidearm across the field; she already knew the answer. Orin's stone made small clicking noises as it skipped over the flat rock like it was passing over water.

As she'd known it would, the rock only made it ten feet

before a geyser sprouted from the field. It propelled the rock upward in a fiery blaze that most likely incinerated it. The geyser vanished again with a pop, but smoke lingered above it.

"Now we know why that immortal didn't wait until the sun rose to cross." Sahira pointed to the remains that had finally stopped smoking. "It's safer to cross at night."

"Son of a *bitch*!" Orin exploded.

Sahira winced as his words echoed throughout the passageways behind them and across the land. When the words finally died away, an ominous hush descended.

"Now what?" Elsa whispered.

"Now we wait until nightfall," Sahira said. "Until then, we might as well gather firewood."

"We can load up on rocks and use them to help guide us across the field," Orin said. "We'll throw them out to discover where the geysers are."

"And if we run out?" Zeth asked.

"Then we'll stop and wait for nightfall."

"There's no way we can guarantee that rocks will uncover all the geysers as we go. One or more of us will end up getting cooked."

Sahira knew that was a chance Orin was willing to take. He was cocky enough to believe it wouldn't happen to him and would willingly sacrifice some of them to get across.

When he glanced back at her, the set of his jaw changed.

"We can take some rocks, but the amount it would take to get us across would slow us too much," Zeth continued.

"I hate this," Orin growled, but as he stepped away from the field, it was clear he wouldn't push it.

With reluctance, Sahira shed the warmth of her blanket and rose. She didn't look at the others as she slipped back into the winding crevice that brought them here.

They'd come this far and wouldn't turn back, but things had gone from pretty terrible to worse.

CHAPTER FORTY-TWO

SAHIRA DIDN'T KNOW how much time had passed since she last saw Orin and Zeth. She'd returned several times to the edge of the field to deposit her armloads of wood onto the growing pile.

Maybe it wasn't the best idea to have separated from Orin and Zeth, but she required some time to herself. She'd barely had a minute to herself since starting this journey and wanted to be alone.

Elsa remained there, tending the fire while the brownies huddled around it. "How's it going?" Elsa asked.

Sahira set down her newest find and stepped closer to the fire. She rubbed her hands together while she warmed them over the flames.

"I found a spot with a bunch of dead trees and branches. If I return to it a couple more times, it should give us enough until nightfall."

"Okay."

Elsa placed another stick on the fire. Zeth and Orin had returned since her last time here, as the pile was almost twice the size as the last time she saw it.

"We might have enough once they return with their next find," Elsa said.

She was probably right, but Sahira wanted more time to herself. Thinking wasn't the best for her right now as her mind bounced between Orin, the field, and how much she missed her family, but at least she was moving.

If she stayed here, her thoughts would do the same, but she might have to talk to someone too. She wasn't in the mood for that.

"I'd like to make sure of it," she said.

"Be careful," Elsa said, and the brownies all gave her a small wave.

Sahira turned and made her way back onto the path cutting through the mountains. As she walked, she scaled more boulders and took a right onto another, smaller path she hadn't noticed while they were walking toward the field last night.

She paused for a second and tried to open a portal. She'd attempted it a few times since wandering off alone, but the idea of crossing that field made her keep trying... and failing.

When she once again didn't succeed, she trudged forward again. Winding in and out of the tiny passage, she made her way to the rocky shelf she'd discovered on her second trip out here.

Several dead trees growing out of the rocks had gotten enough nourishment to make them a few feet tall before dying. They remained standing on the shelf.

She stopped before the mountain wall and tipped her head back to study the shelf a couple of feet above her. She couldn't see much from her angle, but she already knew what was up there.

Lifting her arms, she planted her hands on the edge of the ledge and braced her toes against the mountain. She pulled herself up and climbed onto the ridge, where she knelt to examine the space.

It went at least twenty-five feet back. A cave was etched into the side of the mountain; she had no idea how far it went, but she'd traversed at least fifty feet before the darkness made it impossible to continue.

She had no idea what might lurk within those shadows, but given everything else they'd encountered in this realm, she wouldn't take the chance of going further into it. If something didn't attack or eat her, she could get lost and wind up stuck in that cave forever.

Pulling her cloak tighter, she shuddered at the possibility as the wind howled across the land. Nothing moved inside the cave, but she sensed eyes watching from the shadows.

A few scraggly trees grew out of the rocks over the entrance; their dead branches drooped, and pieces had broken off to litter the ground. Taking her time, she cleaned up the limbs and piled them close to the edge for her to take later.

She bent to gather more branches, but a change in the shadows caught her attention. Sahira's hand went to the dagger at her side; the spear was still strapped to her back, but she didn't have time to pull it free before it attacked.

Then the shadows shifted like a flower opening to the sun; Orin materialized as the shadows pulled away from him. She didn't know whether to feel relieved or to start yelling at him.

He'd been in that cave, watching her, and most likely tried to scare her because games were what he liked to play. And he looked far too amused about it for her liking.

"You've found a treasure trove of firewood," he said.

"What are you doing here?" she demanded.

There was that damn sly smile again. "Waiting for you."

"And purposely trying to scare me?"

"Not at all. I decided to explore the cave a little and figured it would be safer if I cloaked myself in shadows first. That way, if there was anything in there, it wouldn't eat me."

"I couldn't get that lucky."

"You'd miss me."

She scowled but didn't argue his words. The truth was, she *would* miss him.

It was something she'd concluded during her hunt for wood. She wanted him out of her life, but when they left this realm and he did walk away, she'd miss him.

He'd somehow wormed his way into her heart, or the vicinity of it. He drove her nuts, he was nothing more than a womanizing dark fae who loved messing with her mind and feelings, but despite all his *many* faults, she'd started to care for the annoying bastard.

He did have some good qualities, not many, but they were there. He was loyal, protective, loved his family, and had saved her from the scarog beetles and that awful monster with too many tongues.

Elsa's words from the other day in the brownie town returned to her. *"He didn't hesitate before chasing after you."* And in the end... *"Orin only thought of you."*

She didn't understand why that was and would never get her hopes up that it meant he had feelings for her too. Sahira had no idea how she got to this point, but here she was, with too many feelings for a dark fae who only cared about himself.

And he could *never* know.

CHAPTER FORTY-THREE

"WELL, you've found me; what do you want?" she asked.

Her voice came out far testier than she'd intended. She hated letting him know when he'd gotten under her skin; he'd use it against her later.

"Is that any way to talk to someone trying to be nice to you?" he asked.

"You're never nice for no reason, Orin. So, what do you want?"

When he moved away from the cave opening and glided toward her, his fluid agility mesmerized her. The man was literally sex walking, and even as she debated leaping off the edge and fleeing back toward the fire, her body tingled with awareness for him.

Orin stopped a foot away from her. He wasn't so close he crowded her, but his body emanated heat against her as his scent filled her nostrils.

Her heart rate increased as her skin prickled with awareness. She recalled waking, nestled against his side, and the safe feeling of having his arm around her.

Safe and Orin were two words she'd never thought would go

together, but somehow they had this morning. It was a scary sensation that should have made her run as fast as she could from him, but her feet remained planted.

Oh, Hecate, he was gorgeous with his crow-black eyes and hair the color of a raven's wings. He also had a face that could stop traffic in the human realm, and the son of a bitch knew it.

She no longer knew if she hated that about him or admired it.

When she was younger and learned how much the witches despised her because she was half vampire, it rattled her confidence. Over the years, she'd regained it and learned not to care what they, or her mother, thought of her.

But she'd *never* possessed the sort of overwhelming, in-your-face confidence Orin exuded. Maybe it was because he was born a dark fae prince with wealth, power, and everything he'd ever wanted at his fingertips. Or perhaps it was just who he was.

His brothers were also arrogant, but not to his level of it. They also weren't pure dark fae, and she'd never met a dark fae who didn't think their shit didn't stink.

"It's been almost a week since you fed," he said. "You must be hungry."

Of course. She should've seen it coming but hadn't. Her stomach rumbled as she recalled the taste and scent of his blood.

Has it really been that long?

She struggled to recall how much time had passed since she last drank from him, but the arduous climbing had blended one day into another. She thought it was six, but it could be five, seven, or ten.

What do I know anymore?

"That's okay; I'm good," she told him. "And like I said, you're never nice for no reason."

His eyes glittered with amusement. "Always so quick to think the worst of me."

"You're always so quick to prove me right."

His smile grew as he held out his arm with his wrist turned toward her. "I expect nothing in return."

She eyed his wrist as the blood pulsing through the vein called to her with every beat. It took everything she had not to lick her lips.

"I'm telling you the truth," he said. "I expect nothing in return."

"That's because you think the bloodlust will overtake me and I'll have sex with you again."

"I wouldn't say no if it did, but it won't. It didn't last time."

When her eyes met his, they held a challenge, but she didn't argue his words. He was right; she didn't have sex with him the last time because bloodlust took her over; she did it because she chose to.

Just like she had their first time together.

"We're about to cross that field, and we have no idea how long it will take or how bad it will be. You should be at full strength for it."

"And not you?" she countered.

"I feel great."

"It's okay; I'm not hungry."

But as she said it, her traitorous stomach growled.

"Go ahead, Sahira. I promise you, I don't expect anything in return."

She shouldn't trust him, and while she didn't believe him, his expression was so earnest it made her pause. Sahira glanced at his wrist before meeting his eyes again.

She could say no; she wasn't starving and had gone longer without blood, but it was so enticing. Everything about him was.

Then she recalled the vast field with all those geysers waiting to destroy them. They had no idea how far they would have to walk before they were free of that deadly place.

Her resistance started to crumble, and she enclosed her

fingers around his wrist. Tiny electrical pulses moved from his skin to her fingertips, making her come alive.

She restrained herself from closing her eyes and savoring the tantalizing sensation of the flesh she knew so well. Beneath her fingers, his ciphers twisted out before coiling up beneath his sleeve and vanishing.

She couldn't let herself get caught up in him; this was a simple blood exchange, nothing more. But as her fangs extended and she bent her mouth to his wrist, she knew she was lying to herself again.

CHAPTER FORTY-FOUR

WHEN SAHIRA'S fangs pierced his flesh and his blood filled her mouth, she bit back a groan as the ambrosia of it hit her tongue. She'd never get used to how amazing he tasted.

But even though every part of her body became hyperaware of him, she kept her bloodlust leashed. It took everything she had, but she managed to control it.

When her eyes lifted to his, the ravenous gleam in his gaze curled her toes. It simmered in his eyes like a pot about to boil, but, true to his word, he didn't touch her or come any closer.

Instead, he gave her the distance she often craved from him... but not this time.

She itched to move closer as those eyes, burning into hers, set fire to her body. Never in a million years could she have imagined a look could turn her on so much, but what a searing, ravenous, all-encompassing, sinful look it was.

It was impossible to break eye contact; she could no more do so than she could will her bones to break. When his eyes roamed over her, she felt them like his hands skimming over her.

When his gaze returned to hers, it was hungrier than before, something she wouldn't have believed possible only seconds ago. Her knees shook, her fingers trembled, and wetness spread between her legs even though he didn't touch her.

Reluctantly, she retracted her fangs, licked the blood from his wrist, and released it. A bereft, empty feeling filled her at the loss of contact.

"Did you get enough?" he asked.

Still so rattled by his presence and the searing intensity of his gaze, it took her a few seconds to answer. "Yes."

"Good."

With that, he turned and walked over to the pile of wood she'd gathered. His gait was more awkward than before; she assumed it was because he was as turned on as her and his erection made it difficult to move.

The possibility made her mouth water, but she didn't move. She was as rattled by the fact he'd turned and walked away, like he'd promised, as she was by what transpired between them.

She could only stand there shivering as she tried to process what happened while emotions and lust battered her. While feeding, she'd shut down the bloodlust, but not the truth... she wanted him.

When he rose with an armload of firewood and turned toward her, she closed the distance between them, clasped his stubble-roughened cheeks, and kissed him. He went rigid against her, but when her tongue stroked his lips, they softened.

For the first time, she didn't have to bury her doubts about this as they kissed. The wood he held clattered to the ground a second before his arms enveloped her.

Breaking the kiss, he leaned back to look at her. Even with the rigid evidence of his arousal prodding her belly, he said, "This isn't what I was after."

She believed him. Instead of responding, she kissed him again.

CHAPTER FORTY-FIVE

ORIN REALLY HADN'T BEEN angling for sex when he offered Sahira his blood. He'd prefer she didn't go onto that field of fire and death hungry and exhausted.

She should be at full strength to face whatever lay ahead of them; he intended to ensure she was. Altruism worked better than he could have imagined to excite women, but he'd never tried it before.

He wasn't exactly one for self-sacrifice... until her.

Her fingers found the rope he'd started using to keep his pants up. Even after he fed from her the last time, they were still much looser than they were before he left Belda's town.

With nimble fingers, she undid the rope, and his pants slid down his thighs. Breaking the kiss, her eyes held his before she knelt before him.

He'd vowed the next time they did this, it would be in a bed, or at least somewhere far more comfortable than their previous encounters, but he wasn't about to stop her. Though the rock had to be biting into her flesh, she didn't show any signs of discomfort as, while holding his gaze, she clasped his cock and ran her tongue around the head of it.

His breath sucked in, and his head almost tipped back from the glorious sensation of her mouth working over him, but he couldn't take his eyes off her as she drew him deeper. They'd done many things together, but she'd yet to suck his dick; it was far better than he'd imagined.

As she worked him with her lips and hands, he clasped the back of her head and guided her. The fangs she couldn't fully retract grazed his shaft.

He wanted her to bite again. "Feed from me."

When she started to pull away, he kept her head in place. "Do it."

The witch's eyes narrowed a little before her lips slid back toward the base of his erection. Her fangs extended against his flesh, and when she bit deep, pleasure and pain coursed down his spine.

He released the groan he'd suppressed as her tongue swirled over his flesh. The urge to thrust into her mouth and fuck it until he came gripped him, but he couldn't with her fangs inside him, so he remained still while the anticipation of what was to come built higher and higher.

When her fangs retracted and she started moving over him again, he'd had enough of the waiting. Bending, he placed his hands under her arms and lifted her.

She licked his blood from her lips as he undid the string holding her pants in place and watched them pool around her feet. Beneath the first pair was a second, and he untied them as she kicked off her boots.

As their clothes fell away, she stepped into him, but he grasped her waist and turned her around. Bringing her down, he positioned himself behind her as her hands and knees settled on the ground.

He ran his hand over the exquisite curve of her back, tracing her spine and relishing the feel of her silken skin. She was magnificent, and while he would love to spend the rest of the day savoring her, the wind howling down the mountains and causing her flesh to pebble wouldn't allow such wonder.

When he entered her, Sahira gasped, and her back arched as he settled deep inside her. Unable to resist, he removed the stick from her bun to let her hair spill free.

He wrapped her glorious mane around his wrist and fisted it as he drew her head back while leisurely moving in and out of her. His other hand slid around to find her breasts and tease her nipples.

When she pushed back onto him, he tugged a little on her hair and leaned over to kiss the delicate curve of her cheek before their mouths met again. His hand grazed the hollow of her belly before slipping between her thighs.

He teased her clit as the sexual energy she exuded grew thicker on the air, gathering around him and demanding he feast, so he did. And what an exquisite banquet she was as she infused him with strength while leaving him weak for her.

He couldn't get enough of her, his fierce, proud witch with a steel spine and uncanny ability to piss him off while exciting him more than anyone else he'd known. Whatever this was between them was as unnerving as it was exciting, and he wanted more.

When she cried out and her sheath clenched around his shaft, he smiled as her orgasm nearly pulled his own from him, but he wasn't ready to find his release. He was so obsessed with her and how she made him feel that he didn't feel the cold anymore.

Releasing her hair, he adjusted her so he took the brunt of the rock as he lay on the ground. He moved her on top of him, with her back facing him, and planted his hand on her back to guide her while she rode him.

He ran his hand down her spine to the curve of her ass as her hips moved and delicious sounds of ecstasy issued from her. She was a masterpiece, and she was *his*. After this, she would know who owned her.

Guiding her faster, he planted his feet on the ground and

arched his hips up as they fucked until they were both sated and neither could move.

CHAPTER FORTY-SIX

As the sun set, the geysers resurfaced across the field. With small pops, they rose from the ground to create a deadly trap that could destroy them before they ever made it across.

Orin looked to where Sahira stood beside him with her mouth pursed and determination in her amber eyes. They'd all managed to take turns napping around the fire this afternoon, but none of them were as rested for this as they should be.

They had no idea how long it would take or what they would encounter out there, but it wouldn't be easy. Right now, he was more concerned with her than the field.

After their time together, something had changed in her. He wasn't sure what it was, but when they finally finished with each other, she hadn't jumped up like last time and run away because she was disgusted with herself.

Instead, she'd lain nestled against his side while he tried to cover them the best he could with their clothes. The cold drove them apart and back into those clothes far sooner than he liked, but he'd had those few minutes to lie there and enjoy her.

And what a glorious few minutes they were.

They might have been better than the sex, something he

never would have believed possible, and it wasn't something he'd ever admit to anyone. But for those few minutes, he'd experienced a sense of contentment he never had before.

Orin had been many things in life, but content was never one of them. He'd always sought more... more fun, more sex, more adventures, just *more*. He didn't crave power and more carisle—the immortal's currency—he already had those, but he'd never been satisfied.

Until then.

And lying on those rocks, with her in his arms, he'd experienced a stillness to his life that had never existed before. She was *peace*, and while he'd never known it was missing from his life until her, it was an amazing feeling that he never wanted to end.

However, all good things must end, and the cold forced them apart. Some of that feeling waned once she was out of his arms, but if he searched for it, he could find it again, especially if he looked at her.

He didn't know what to make of this change inside him and didn't analyze it too much, as standing here on the verge of death, it didn't matter.

Then she met his eyes, and he realized it *did* matter. He didn't understand any of this or what she'd done to him, but it mattered.

He jiggled the rocks in his pants. He hadn't loaded up with them, but he was bringing some just in case; he'd seen the others gather some too.

"Are you ready for this?" he asked her.

"I have no choice but to be ready."

"Yes, you do."

"Is turning back really an option?"

"To some."

"Not to me."

He smiled as she said what he'd known she would. "Me either."

When the sun finally set completely and the last geysers emerged, he looked to Sahira. "Be careful."

When she met his gaze again, he could tell she wanted to make some wiseass response but instead said, "You too."

Without another word, they all started onto the field. The brownies had chosen to navigate the geysers on their own rather than riding with someone.

With their much smaller size, it was a wise choice. They were much more likely to avoid the geysers than the rest of them, especially the demon.

Thankfully, the flame-throwing death traps were spaced far enough apart that they could navigate them though it was tight in many areas. However, there was a reason the other immortal failed to complete the crossing; Orin suspected it wasn't because they stumbled or rushed at the end.

The going was slow, with only the radiance of the moon, stars, and two candles to guide them. They had more candles but were running low and had decided against using them for this.

As of now, the candles Elsa and Sahira carried cast enough illumination to help all of them navigate the field. If clouds rolled in, they'd need more candles, but right now, they had a clear night to help guide them.

CHAPTER FORTY-SEVEN

THE BROWNIES WEAVED in and out of the geysers with far more ease than the four of them, but they all made steady progress.

After a couple of hours of walking in silence, the girl brownie started singing in her haunting, clear voice that carried across the land. The one with the flute didn't join in, probably because it would be almost impossible to play while ensuring he didn't step on a geyser.

Orin was grateful for this. He could handle the singing, but that flute made him want to gouge out his eardrums.

"What are their names again?" he asked Sahira, nodding toward the brownies.

Even in the dim light, he saw her eyebrows shoot up, and she gave him an incredulous look.

"What?" he inquired with a laugh. "I'm a curious immortal."

"You've only referred to them as rats or rodents since we left their town behind."

"Well, that's what they look like."

"Fuck off, dark fae," the flute-playing brownie retorted.

"That's Gior," Sahira told him.

The brownie didn't turn around to give Orin the finger while he skirted the edge of two geysers. Wedged so close together, Orin had to move closer to Elsa to avoid stepping on a geyser.

"Pipper, or Pip, as she prefers to be called, is singing," Sahira continued. "Fath is closest to me, and Loth is closest to Elsa. Are you actually going to remember their names this time?"

"I'm not making any promises."

Sahira shook her head, and they stopped speaking again while Pip continued singing. Her voice and the wind howling across the vast land were the only sounds.

Exhaustion crept in as they traversed further across the field, but Orin shoved it aside. It was a good thing he fed off Sahira earlier, or the call of sleep would be a lot worse.

After a while, he looked back to see how far they'd come. The mountains had vanished from view; all that surrounded them was a vast landscape, peppered with mounds waiting to kill them.

Though he had no intention of turning back, he didn't know if it would take more time to return to the mountains or finish crossing the field. He had a feeling he wasn't going to like the answer.

After hours of traveling, his feet ached, and he would gladly kill something if it meant he could sit and rest, but there wasn't enough room between the geysers for that. They had no choice but to keep going as they dragged themselves forward.

He had no idea how far they'd traveled as they carefully navigated the field, but he was blinking far more often to keep his eyes open. He stopped to rub his eyes and blinked again before squinting at the horizon.

Is it getting lighter over there?

The sky was definitely starting to look grayer at the edge, but it couldn't be sunrise already, could it?

When his eyes met Sahira's, he saw the fear in their bloodshot depths and knew he wasn't imagining it; the sun was starting to rise. *Shit!*

The others had all stopped walking to gaze at the sky with horror and resignation. He should have seen this coming.

He should have known when this started, they wouldn't make it across in one night. That they would be stuck out here, with nowhere to sit, but he'd been too determined to make it across to think it all through.

They'd still be here even if he had known because he wouldn't have turned back. He doubted any of the others would have either.

"Find a place where you can safely stop," he said.

The brownies looked around before settling onto the ground and drawing their knees to their chests. Unfortunately, the space between the geysers didn't offer anyone bigger than the rodents anywhere to sit.

As the light spread across the earth, the geysers vanished with a small sucking sound. Standing there, surrounded by flat earth, Orin rattled the stones in his pockets and surveyed the land around them.

He didn't take them out and toss them across the earth; they wouldn't get him far enough for it to matter. All he could do was stand there and wait until sunset.

CHAPTER FORTY-EIGHT

SAHIRA'S HEAD snapped up when her chin hit her chest. She blinked at the barren earth surrounding them before rubbing her eyes.

Exhaustion was an understatement as her legs ached, her feet throbbed, and her eyes burned like someone had thrown acid in them. She'd give anything to sit down, but that was impossible when she no longer knew where the geysers were.

Besides, when she *did* know where they were, it hadn't been safe for her to sit, so she could only stand, barely moving in this spot. The most she could do was shift her weight from side to side, but it didn't give her any relief.

So, Sahira stood in misery, trying not to pass out on her feet. She didn't dare move too much, not only because she was afraid of getting a stream of fire up her ass but also because if she turned around, with this sea of sameness surrounding her, she'd never know for sure which way she'd faced before.

Granted, the others still faced the same direction, but she was scared they might also move and get turned around. If that happened, they could roam these barren fields until exhaustion caused them to step on a geyser.

As it was, she didn't know if they were heading out of this field or deeper into it. That dead immortal had come from somewhere, so there had to be a way out, but they might be walking away from it.

Or the immortal could have started from their side, which meant there was nothing out there and they'd wandered out to meet their deaths. Shaking her head, she tried to clear it of the exhaustion clouding it while not giving in to the panic clawing at her insides.

They were going the right way. They had to be.

She rubbed her eyes again before looking at Orin, who remained steadfastly staring ahead, glaring at the horizon like it was the enemy. They would keep going straight, as that's the way they'd gone the whole time, and to change course could prove disastrous.

For all she knew, they were supposed to go to the left or right, and straight could continue forever into this horrible land. And if they stayed straight, they could turn around and head back.

Returning to the mountains would be admitting defeat, but they'd be alive. It wouldn't be much of a life, but at least it was one.

She wasn't ready to cave, but the idea of continuing was terrifying. The further they went, the tougher it would be to return. Orin seemed to be thinking the same thing as he glared at the land.

Sensing her gaze, his head swiveled toward her. When his eyes met hers, they burned with a steely determination. He was still convinced he could bend the world, and everyone around him, to his will.

The Cursed Realm should have taken some of that confidence from him, but it hadn't, or at least he didn't act like it had. Outwardly, he remained determined to show this realm they would conquer it, and she truly hoped he would.

She had no idea how he felt about it inwardly and preferred not to know. They all needed his confidence to help them through this because hers was dwindling beneath her exhaustion.

As the day crept onward, the icy bite of the wind whipping across the plain didn't stop sweat from beading on her brow and slipping down her nape. The strain of standing in one place for so long was taking its toll, but she wasn't about to give in to her body's demand for sleep.

"I guess we know how that immortal made it so far before they were burnt to a crisp," Zeth said as the sun reached its pinnacle in the sky.

"By the time he got to the end, he was so exhausted, he messed up and stepped on a geyser," Elsa said.

"He also could have traveled out here for weeks before then."

Sahira gulped as she tried not to think about the horror of that possibility. After more time passed, she maneuvered her pack from beneath her spear and carefully held it above the field while removing some dried meat and water.

Supplies were running low, but that was the least of her problems right now. She sipped some water while chewing the meat. It helped revitalize her, but not enough that her eyelids didn't droop before opening again.

The brownies, far more secure in their locations, drifted in and out of sleep. At one time, Gior's tail waved in the air like he was dreaming about something good; she wondered if it was his children and possible grandchildren.

"I don't know if it's possible to destroy a realm, but if we get out of here, I'm going to find out," Orin said.

The Lord had destroyed so many realms when he controlled the dragons, but any dragon sent here would be stuck. Besides, Lexi wouldn't unleash the wrath of the dragons on this place.

"There are still so many trapped here," Sahira said. "It can't be destroyed."

"Their lives aren't much better than death anyway."

Sometimes, she could forget how brutal he was. Then he'd slap her in the face with it, and she'd question how she could forget.

His brutality no longer unnerved her; she was starting to believe it wasn't as soul deep as he portrayed. There was a softness to him when they were lying together earlier.

His arms had been secure around her, his body warm as he tried to cover them with their clothes. The cold made it impossible for her to lie there and enjoy it as much as she would have liked, but there was a tenderness to him that wasn't a game.

Orin didn't do gentle as a game. Hell, he didn't do gentle *at all*, and he'd already had sex with her again. He didn't have to stay, but he did.

He portrayed himself as an uncaring oaf, but there was more to this man than met the eye. She wasn't sure what that meant for her or them.

"That's not for you to decide," she told him. "Even if they're stuck here, I'm sure most of the immortals in Belda's town and the brownies would prefer to live than die."

When Orin scowled at her, she realized he was in a pissy mood and looking to vent his frustration. She chose to ignore him.

Sahira yawned as she rubbed her burning eyes before closing them. She didn't realize she'd dozed off again until her chin hit her chest and her head popped up again. She had to stop doing *that* before she became a steaming pile of meat.

Shaking her head again, she focused on the others to distract herself from her exhaustion. They all had bloodshot eyes, and Elsa's were swollen from rubbing them every few seconds.

Sahira liked the brownies, but when Loth started snoring, she had to restrain herself from kicking him across the field. It was great they could sleep, but did they have to flaunt it so much?

Orin wasn't the only one in a bad mood, she realized as her

festering resentment battled with her sleep deprivation for control. If she could, she might burn this realm down, too, as the day stretched endlessly onward.

Finally, after what seemed like weeks of this torture, the sun set, geysers emerged, and without a word, they started across the land once more.

CHAPTER FORTY-NINE

With every passing minute, Orin became increasingly incensed with their current situation. He wanted to stalk across the land, hunt down whoever did this to them, and make them pay.

If he could get his hands on whoever, or whatever, made this realm so miserable, he'd tear them apart joint by joint until all their pieces littered the ground around him and their blood dripped from him. Once he finished, he'd curl up in the middle of his carnage and *go to sleep*.

The idea was so appealing he rubbed his hands together while he walked. Oh yes, he would enjoy making whoever did this pay. He just didn't know if he'd ever have the answer to who it was.

He had no idea how long they'd been walking as the waning moon shone down on them and the geysers blurred before snapping into focus again. The wind continued to howl, but his need for sleep outweighed his dislike of the cold.

He stepped around a geyser as the flute-playing rat—*Gior*, he reminded himself—scampered around the side of a mound. As he did so, his hand skimmed the top of the geyser.

Elsa yelped, and Sahira jumped when flames erupted into the night. Zeth leaned back as if about to step away from the fire a foot to his right, but he caught himself in time and stopped.

None of them saw what happened, but Orin had been watching the brownie before he disappeared into the torrent of fire. Unlike the immortal, Orin doubted any of Gior's remains still existed as the geyser abruptly shut off.

He hadn't expected one of the rodents to slip up and set off a geyser, but unlike the others, the explosion didn't shock him. And as they were again plunged into darkness, what happened fully sank in to the others.

"No!" Pip screamed.

She lunged for the place where her friend once stood, but nothing of him remained. So caught up in her concern and sorrow for her friend, she didn't realize she was heading straight for another geyser.

Other than instinct, Orin wasn't quite sure what propelled him. He didn't care about these things, or at least that's what he told himself, even as his feet remained planted while his hand swung out.

Flames erupted into the night as a roaring inferno shot fifty feet into the air. He yanked the rat away from the fire, but not before the flames raced up her back and burnt his fingers.

Orin pulled the idiotic creature away from the fire that would have destroyed her while cursing his stupidity. From the knuckles up on his right hand, his fingers were red, black, and blistered. Some of those blisters popped and oozed while new ones formed and his skin peeled away.

Pip whimpered as he gently placed her on the ground, but he didn't know if that was from the agony of her burns or the loss of her friend. Loth and Fath scampered to her side as Orin studied his burnt hand.

It would heal, but because of their conditions, it would take longer than he would have liked. At least the throbbing pain radiating through his body with each beat of his heart would help keep him awake.

If they had ointment or access to a decent meal, it would heal faster, but it would still heal. Fortunately, in this endless geyser wasteland, there weren't any monsters seeking to kill them, and he didn't require the use of his hand too much.

He shifted his attention to the burnt brownie as she lay unmoving on the ground. Her clothes had melted to her back, her flesh was blistered, and half her tail had burned away. The tip of it was a still-smoldering, glowing nub.

With his burnt fingers, he bent and squeezed the tip of her tail to put out the remnants of the fire. He didn't feel the ember extinguishing beneath him, and she didn't move.

"Pip! Pip? Pip! Pip? Pip?" the other two eagerly chattered as they hovered beside her.

The brownie with the beautiful singing voice moaned in response but didn't say anything. He didn't know if she would make it. Under normal conditions, sure, but this was all far from normal.

Elsa swung her bag from her shoulder and set it on the ground. "I have some ointment. It will help her heal."

Elsa dug through her pack before handing it over to him. When she spotted his burnt fingers, her eyes widened on them. "You should use some of it too."

"Are you okay?" Sahira asked from his other side.

"I'm fine." He knelt beside the brownies and unscrewed the small jar of ointment. He held it out to the rats. "Here."

Loth dipped his fingers in to remove a scoop of the white ointment. Pip moaned and twitched when her friend dabbed it on her blistered back.

It took some time, but Loth and Fath finally finished and knelt beside her. They rested their hands on her shoulders while whispering words of encouragement.

Orin ignored the tug of sympathy pulling at his heart. Why

had she been so stupid to try and help her friend? She had to have known it was already too late.

He should be angry over her ridiculous decision but didn't have it in him. He was too angry at this realm for that.

Removing some ointment from the jar, he smeared it over his fingers. The witch's concoction immediately dulled the pain while coating his flesh.

"She can't walk," Loth said mournfully.

Orin recapped the ointment and returned it to Elsa, who tucked it away. Without a word, he gently plucked Pip from the ground and settled her on her belly in the hollow of his shoulder.

She was so close to his cheek, he could feel the warmth of her tiny nose as her whiskers tickled his neck. He should have tossed her to Elsa or Sahira, but he'd saved her life and would see her the rest of the way through this.

"He'll never see his children again," she whispered mournfully.

"No, he won't, and if you're not careful, you'll never see your ma and pa again either," Orin told her. "Or *his* to tell them what happened."

She sniffled before relaxing into the crook of his shoulder. When he glanced at Sahira, curiosity and disbelief shimmered in her tear-filled amber eyes. She looked at the geyser that killed Gior before wiping the tears from her eyes.

"Are you sure you're okay?" she asked him.

He sensed she wanted to say or ask more but restrained herself. He was grateful for that, as he didn't know what to make of this either; he never should have saved the brownie. At any other time, he would have let any other immortal suffer the consequences of their stupid decisions, but not this time.

Why not?

He had no answer, as he had no idea what had compelled him to save her. Sure, he liked her voice, and admired the courage of the brownies, the crazy bastards had formed a tower to try to take him on after all, but that wasn't a reason to burn himself for her.

"I'm great," he muttered.

"You remembered that she wanted to see her parents again," Sahira said.

"And?"

"You didn't bother to learn her name for days, but you remembered that."

When he scowled at her, she smiled as warmth filled her eyes. He'd seen that warmth in her gaze before but never directed at him.

He didn't know what to make of it or the strange flutter it created in his heart. Whatever this was, he didn't like it... or did he?

CHAPTER FIFTY

THEY WERE STILL in the middle of the field when the sun rose again. Sahira resisted the urge to cry while blinking away the tears burning her eyes.

She didn't shed any tears but inwardly sobbed against the unending torment of this place as exhaustion made it almost impossible to remain standing. If she sat, she'd die, but it was all she yearned to do.

She was so tired she'd fallen asleep while walking earlier. It was a deadly mistake, thankfully, caught by Orin, who grasped her arm and jerked her awake.

After that, they all held hands. Every few seconds or so, someone would squeeze to make sure the others were awake, and it would run through the chain of them.

Her fingers entwined with Orin's, and she held on tighter than she should have, but thankfully it had mostly healed and he didn't complain. On his other side, he held hands with Elsa, and Sahira had taken Zeth's.

Their joined hands were slick with sweat, but no one released anyone. They were probably as afraid as her that, if they let go, they'd lose someone.

Sahira pried her eyes open as the sun beat down on them. Grainy and dry, they felt like they had a pound of sand caked onto them as blinking became a monumental effort.

Her stomach rumbled, but the idea of moving to take off her pack and find food only made her more tired. Not eating might also be a deadly mistake; she was willing to make it, as it took every ounce of energy she had to stay awake.

Once the sun set again, they would continue. They didn't have a choice, but she had no idea how she'd dredge up the strength to do so.

Closing one eye, she kept the other open as she glanced at Orin. Pip remained sleeping on his shoulder with her hands propped beneath her head.

Am I hallucinating?

Considering the severe lack of sleep she'd experienced these past couple of days, it was a good possibility. This was Orin, the biggest asshole out here, with a *brownie* on his shoulder.

Because he saved her!

The memory of Orin pulling Pip from the fire blasted across her foggy mind. He'd saved Pip from the flames while also burning himself.

If someone had ever asked her if she thought such a thing was possible, she would have laughed. Until last night, Orin would have been more likely to kick one of the brownies into the fire than pull one from it, but he had; she'd seen it herself.

Or did I? Is he really here? Am I here?

The questions churned in her mind as she tried to process everything, but she couldn't think straight. Everything was so difficult right now, and trying to process anything was nearly impossible.

She'd give anything to fall asleep. To lay down, put her head on the ground, and let it all go. Sleep would be so....

A jerk from Orin alerted her that she'd passed out again. This time, her chin didn't hit her chest; she'd stood there, eyes closed, and her face pointed straight ahead.

"Is this real?" Her voice sounded as grainy as her eyes felt.

Orin's thumb stroked her skin. The tender gesture was nearly her undoing as more tears surged into her eyes.

She was overtired, that's why she was so emotional, but she was on the verge of losing it. Breaking down here could spell doom, because once she started crying, she wouldn't stop, and standing might prove impossible as sobs wracked her body.

"It's real," Orin said.

"Are you sure?"

His hesitation before he replied told her he wasn't entirely sure, but he said, "Yes."

She had no idea how they made it through the day again. Probably through their squeezes to stay awake and the steady reassurance the others were here.

And they were all counting on each other to stay alive. If one failed, they could all fail.

When the sun set again, they continued across the field. Travel was becoming increasingly slow and difficult as her vision often blurred, and the geysers became two or three in some places.

She sometimes had to stop for a few seconds, if not more, to make sure what she saw was real. She wasn't the only one, as the others also called a halt to ensure they were stepping in the right place.

Since they hadn't eaten or drunk much since entering the field, their bathroom breaks were far less frequent, which was the only silver lining in this mess. Trying to relieve herself hadn't been fun with the others around, even with their eyes closed. No one dared to turn away for fear they would lose their direction and end up going the wrong way or start meandering in circles.

Fath and Loth, uninjured and more rested, guided them when

they asked questions about what they saw. The brownies were also exhausted, as their tails drooped, and they often wiped tears from their eyes. They hadn't endured as much physical exhaustion as the rest of them, but the loss of Gior had taken an emotional toll on them.

As the night wore on, Sahira couldn't tell if she was sweltering or freezing. Sweat beaded on her nape, but she couldn't stop shivering as the wind invaded any opening in her cloak.

Too tired to pick them up, her feet skimmed the ground with every step. It was the best she could do, considering every step took away what little remained of her energy. When she made it to a mound, she shuffled around it, carefully avoiding its deadly wrath while not pulling Zeth or Orin toward the geyser.

The moon was high in the sky and already beginning its descent. She tried not to think about being trapped out here for another day, but inwardly, she started sobbing again at the possibility.

Much to her dismay, this time, one of her tears slid free. She blinked the others away as she resolved not to cry again. No matter how battered and tired she was, this was not the time or place to lose it.

There was a way across this field. That other immortal had nearly made it to their side of the field, so it must end somewhere.

She couldn't consider the possibility they were going the wrong way; her brain wasn't functioning enough for that. All it could handle was one foot in front of another, one more step, and another and another.

Her entire existence had boiled down to steps and hand squeezes. They were all she had to give.

They only had about an hour of nighttime left when Loth suddenly exclaimed, "I think I see something!"

CHAPTER FIFTY-ONE

AT FIRST, it took a few seconds for his words to sink in as she remained focused on her feet and avoiding the geysers. When what he'd said finally penetrated, her brow furrowed as she tried to process it. The others must have had the same problem as they all ceased walking.

"What is it?"

Orin's words grated out from between his teeth. She had a feeling it would take too much effort for him to open his mouth and speak; she understood completely.

"I'm not sure. I'll be right back," Loth said.

With that, the brownie took off to dart in and out of the geysers as he crossed the field with far more speed than he exhibited while helping them. When he made it a couple hundred feet, Sahira lost sight of him amid the mounds.

"Do you see anything?" Zeth asked, sounding as exhausted as she felt.

Pip propped herself up on Orin's shoulders. She remained on her belly while resting on her elbows. "I see something, but I'm not sure what."

Sahira strained to see something, but only blurry, endless

geysers stretched before her. Some of them multiplied two or three times before becoming blurry once again.

"We should... we have to keep walking," she whispered. "It doesn't matter what's there; the sun is rising soon, and we have to keep going, or we won't."

When no one argued with her statement, she took a deep breath and focused on her frozen feet. It took every ounce of her willpower, but eventually, she got one of her feet to shuffle forward again.

One more step. One more step. One more step.

The words became such an unrelenting mantra that she forgot about Loth leaving to explore something else until the brownie returned. She blinked at him, uncertain where he'd come from as she struggled to function.

Loth jumped up and down while clapping his hands. "This is the end! It's the *end*!"

"The end of what?" Elsa inquired.

Sahira pondered the same thing as she tapped her temple with her palm to try getting the synapses in her brain going again. It didn't help.

"The end of the field! There's another town! Just like ours... or at least it's similar to ours. I didn't take the time to look around. I just came back here to get the rest of you."

"The end," Pip whispered.

Loth planted his tail on the ground and used it to lift himself while shouting. "The end! It's not much farther, and there are *no* geysers there!"

Sahira's heart crashed against her ribs as his news finally sank in. *The end!*

They could *finally* break free of this endless, torturous, lethal monotony. Then her eyes shifted to the sky.

Is it starting to brighten over there? Can we get to that town before we're trapped out here again?

She didn't think she could survive another day out here, even if they stopped only twenty feet away from salvation. Knowing they could get to safety but unable to do so, might make it worse.

"We have to move," Zeth said.

As they started forward again, Sahira's attention shifted from the field to the sky and back again. A new adrenaline rush staved off some of her exhaustion as she picked up her feet with more enthusiasm.

Her vision still wasn't the greatest, but it had cleared some, and she had more confidence in where she put her feet. Maybe a little too much confidence, but they had to escape here before sunrise.

This is why the other immortal died. He saw the end. This is why!

But she couldn't slow down as the warning screamed across her mind. She had to get there. Freedom from this field loomed on the horizon, and she would do anything to attain it.

Her heart raced, and everything inside her screamed to be free of this place. She wanted to run; she suddenly had enough energy to sprint miles, if necessary, but running would get her killed.

She had the energy to move faster, but the geysers blurred and shifted before her. If she started sprinting, she had no doubt she'd step on one of those death traps within twenty feet.

"That's it, come on, you're doing great. Keep going. We're almost there," Loth encouraged, while Fath, who was always much quieter, guided the way with his hands as he pointed in one direction then another.

After what seemed like an eternity, Sahira finally thought she saw it too. *The end!*

The outline of buildings wavered against the increasingly gray sky as more light spread across it. They still had at least fifty feet to go when the sun's rays broke on the horizon.

They didn't have much time before the sun touched the field, the geysers vanished, and they were trapped here again. She released Orin and Zeth's hands as they pushed faster while freedom beckoned.

As the sun's rays hit the earth and the pop of the geysers vanishing filled the air, they stepped free of the field. Relief, exhaustion, and fear battered her as she stared at the town with seven buildings.

CHAPTER FIFTY-TWO

UNLIKE THE LAST pub in the brownies' town, this building had no beds. Sahira barely noticed this while stumbling around to help the others close the shutters.

All she wanted was sleep, but they had no idea what else could be in this town. They had to secure the building against whatever monsters might lurk nearby.

They somehow managed to dredge up enough energy to lock everything down, simply because none of them would be any good for a while. If they didn't do it now, and something sinister lived here, they'd die in their sleep and never know it.

Her vision was blurring again, her head pounded, and she stumbled around as she locked the door to what she considered her room in these buildings. She closed the shutters before falling to her knees and blindly feeling for the trapdoor in the floor.

Her fingers finally located it, and she pulled it free. She slid down the stairs on her ass and checked the secret door that opened into the space behind the back of the pub.

Barely able to see anything beyond the door, she closed it again and half crawled back upstairs. She slid the trapdoor back into place and dredged up what remained of her energy to cast a protective spell over it.

The spell was far from her best work, but a scream would sound throughout the pub if someone broke it. She could only hope that would be enough to wake them once they passed out.

She unlocked the door, staggered into the hall, and bounced off the stair railing as she went downstairs again. Sahira could barely keep her legs and feet beneath her as she stumbled toward the center of the room, shrugged off her pack and weapons, and curled into a ball on the floor.

Her legs and feet, which hadn't gotten any rest for days, trembled now that her weight was finally off them. She almost wept over finally being set free from the field, discomfort, and misery of the past few days, but as soon as her eyes closed, she didn't know anything more.

When she woke again, the room was dark. She had no idea what time it was, as the shutters closed out most of the light, but some crept beneath the bottom of the front door.

Her hip and shoulder ached from lying on the cold, hard floor, but something softer cradled her head. When she inhaled the scent of whatever was beneath her, Orin's cinnamon and clove scent wafted to her.

Blinking away the sandy grit still clinging to her eyes, she rubbed them and yawned before nestling closer to his warmth. Her head was propped on his shoulder, and his body surrounded her.

She didn't recall pulling a blanket from her sack and was fairly certain she hadn't, but one covered her now. She should probably be annoyed he'd taken advantage of her exhaustion to sleep beside her, but she was too ensconced in the happiness and security he gave her.

She couldn't be mad when she craved this. He smelled so good, and the muscles of his lean body emphasized his strength as he held her close.

No one could hurt her while she was in his arms. He was the only one.

That cold reality put a damper on her mood. He'd break her heart, but she still didn't move as she idly traced the ciphers his shirt had pulled back to reveal on his arm.

She loved the sharp black edges of the marks that flowed like water across him. The man was magnificent and powerful, and despite all his *many* faults, she'd come to care for him.

There was so much she didn't like about him: his callous attitude, lack of empathy, and nonstop manipulation were just a few things. But despite all those faults, a good heart lay beneath his cold exterior.

He'd saved Pip, cared for her, and protected her after she was injured. She truly believed he'd come to her to offer his blood because he sought to make her stronger and not for sex. It had worked out that way for him, and for once, she didn't regret sleeping with him.

He'd kill anyone who got in his way, but she was beginning to see he had a kinder soul than even he realized. And he'd also kill anyone who tried to harm her.

She had no idea when that changed; it certainly hadn't been that way before the Cursed Realm, but she didn't doubt he'd protect her. He'd drive her crazy, play games with her, and they'd probably fight by the end of the day, but he'd also do everything he could to keep her safe, and she would do the same for him.

Before coming to this realm, she would have hesitated to throw him to the wolves only because he was Cole's brother. He might have hesitated to do the same to her because Lexi was her niece.

Now, she would also protect him. In this realm, they'd come to rely on each other, but they'd also seen different sides of each other.

She didn't doubt he'd run straight into the arms of another woman once they were free. He was a dark fae, after all.

The idea of losing him caused sadness to tug at her heart. She stopped tracing his ciphers and buried her sorrow as she shifted her attention to the empty room.

As much as she wanted to do so, she couldn't spend all day in his arms. She had no idea how much time had passed since they arrived in this town, and they needed to learn more about it.

They could have already been here for hours or days. Her full bladder demanded her attention as her stomach reminded her it had been a while since anything filled it.

CHAPTER FIFTY-THREE

As CAREFULLY AS SHE COULD, she inched away from Orin before rising. Stretching her cramped back, her feet, muscles, and joints protested movement as they screamed about the abuse they'd taken since leaving Belda's town.

She'd give anything for a hot bath, a steaming cup of eucalyptus tea, and a bed with thick blankets and an inviting mattress. They were all the things she'd always taken for granted and never would again.

When she finished stretching, her gaze fell on Orin, who remained on the floor. In sleep, his face was softer, his mouth parted, and though he lay on his back, his arm remained outstretched to where she'd been.

Her heart warmed so much that it took a few seconds to look away from him. Zeth and Elsa lay on their sides with their backs to each other as they slept beneath their blankets. Loth and Fath were snoring at the foot of those blankets.

Sahira searched for Pip before discovering her burrowed into one of Orin's shirts near his head. She lay on her stomach with her hands tucked beneath her head. Her whiskers twitched like she was dreaming of something; with a small sigh, she settled again.

Unable to ignore her bladder anymore, Sahira trudged upstairs to the bathroom. She could use one of the downstairs rooms, and she really should see the symbol, but it would still be there when she finished, and the possibility of a shower was far more alluring than those aggravating symbols.

In the upstairs bathroom, she was happy to discover the water worked, and after using the toilet, she took a hot shower. Resting her hands against the wall, she let it stream down on her back as she drank the liquid spilling between her lips.

The heat and beat of the shower helped ease some of the tension in her muscles but didn't get rid of it all. Still, she stayed in it for longer than normal.

When she finished, she stepped from the shower and searched for a towel, but there weren't any. Sahira leaned over the shower drain and twisted her hair to squeeze the water from it the best she could.

As she worked, she became increasingly chilled while dripping dry, and goose bumps covered her arms. Finally, she used her shirt to dry herself before reluctantly tugging her dirty clothes back on.

Later, when everyone was awake, she'd wash her clothes and take another shower, but for now, this was the best she could do. With her clothes cleaving uncomfortably to her still-damp skin, Sahira left the bathroom and walked over to the banister to look down at the pub.

The others remained sleeping below. Orin hadn't moved and was only ten feet away from Zeth and Elsa. No furniture of any kind filled the room. Behind the bar, the shelves lining the mirror were empty; not a single bottle sat on them.

Dust covered everything, and footprints swirled through the layer coating the floor. Most were from them, but one set tracked toward the alcove where the other bathrooms and the symbol were.

She didn't recall anyone going back there when they arrived, but she'd been so out of it that it could have happened without her knowing or while she was closing the windows up here. Anyone could have also gotten up to use the bathroom while she slept.

Sahira turned away and entered the room that was hers in Belda's pub. It was barren, something she vaguely recalled from her last time here.

She remembered closing the shutters but was surprised to see them bolted into place. She'd been so out of it that she wasn't sure if she recalled doing it or hallucinated the whole thing.

Running her fingers across the floor, she undid her protective spell before finding the hidden panel and lifting it away to reveal the stone stairs below. She was pretty sure she'd gone down there last night but not certain.

Sahira descended into the darkness; she'd become familiar enough with the hidden passage to have her instincts guide her. Reaching the bottom of the steps, she strode over to the wall.

Her fingers skimmed the cool rocks until she found the button to open the door. She pressed down until it clicked, and the door swung open to reveal bleak, black rock for as far as she could see.

The depressing view caused her to close the door. Once it shut, she tried opening a portal and failed again. She retreated upstairs, settled the panel back into place, and weaved a more intricate protective spell over it.

Feeling defeated, she stared at the panel as she tried to understand what they were doing as they traveled through hellish places only to discover one increasingly lacking town after another. Was this what they would experience for an eternity?

No, they wouldn't, but simply because they couldn't go for that long, especially without an adequate food supply, which they didn't have. They could keep moving and probably find another one of these towns with even less to offer them.

We should have stayed in Belda's town.

She couldn't deny it might have been better for them to have done so, but as disheartened as she was by all this, they'd done the right thing. She'd rather be here, without answers but *doing* something, than there.

If they'd remained in Belda's town, she would have spent every day questioning if they were making a mistake by staying. She'd also still be surrounded by witches and warlocks who hated her.

At least, out here, no one despised her simply because she existed. She'd take endless hunger over those jackasses any day.

And so far, she had discovered one answer, which was more than she had at Belda's. They'd traveled out from there and had uncovered nothing to help them break free of the Cursed Realm.

Sahira left the room and descended to the floor below. Everyone remained asleep, and Loth's snores sounded like a miniature owl calling to its owlets.

She crept past them and on toward the alcove. Her skin crawled, and for some reason, she didn't want to see the symbol but had to know if it was different too.

CHAPTER FIFTY-FOUR

SHE FROZE when she saw the symbol etched into the wall between the two bathrooms. Like the last symbol, the top arrow lay next to the figure eight, but now, the middle arrow had been etched across it to form an X beside the hourglass.

The dark coloring that marked the top of the etching in the brownies' town now shaded the middle half of the figure eight. The top quarter of the symbol was once again only a wall with no shading.

It's sand moving through an hourglass, and the sand shifts lower as each arrow is removed.

It couldn't be anything else. *That* was the only thing that made sense, but nothing in this realm ever made sense, so she could be completely freaking wrong.

Lowering her head, Sahira rubbed her temples as she battled a scream of frustration. She *loathed* this place.

Taking a deep breath, she focused on the symbol again as she pondered its existence and changes. If the shaded area was sand creeping through an hourglass, what happened when time ran out? And *where* did it run out? In the next town? Another realm? *Where*?

Orin's scent alerted her that he'd arrived before he spoke. "So, what do *you* think happens when the sand gets to the bottom?"

She recalled him saying they'd get out of here before, but it didn't sound like he still felt the same way. "I don't know. You think it's an hourglass too?"

"What else could it be?"

"I have no idea."

"Why put the arrows in, only to take them out?"

"Maybe to show the different stages before the sand reaches the bottom."

"Which should mean we only have one more town to find before... who knows what. And X usually marks the spot."

"I don't think it means we've reached the end."

"Neither do I. There's still another arrow to go."

And then what? She had no idea, but they had to continue.

She glanced at Orin over her shoulder and almost laughed at his disheveled hair standing on end. Before entering the Barren Lands, he was always immaculately groomed, but now thick stubble lined his slightly pointed chin and high cheekbones.

Pip sat on his shoulder, her burnt tail in the air behind her and her brown hair sticking out around her face like a lion's mane. Her black nose twitched as her brown eyes examined the symbol.

"If it is an hourglass, then all of this, this realm, *everything*, has something to do with time," Sahira said.

"What immortals can fuck with time that way?" Orin asked.

"The Dagadon."

But there was one problem with that...

"The Dagadon aren't real," Pip said.

"And humans didn't think immortals were real either until the Lord burst into their realm and tore it apart," Sahira said. "I know of no other immortal, real or otherwise, who could manipulate time enough to keep immortals from opening portals and vampires from transporting. There's a reason why myths exist, and the Dagadon are an immortal myth."

"Or maybe they're not." Zeth stepped into the doorway and yawned while he stretched his arms over his head. "I can't think of any better explanation for all of this than them. They were rumored to manipulate time and loved to play games."

"They were also known as cruel beings who enjoyed tormenting their prey," Sahira said.

"And *we're* that prey?" Pip squeaked.

"Seems that way," Zeth replied. "*If* they exist."

"We should explore the town," Orin said. "I doubt there's any answers here, but we have to know."

"I'm going to shower first," Zeth said.

CHAPTER FIFTY-FIVE

"IT LOOKS LIKE OUR BARBECUED, immortal friend was here," Orin said as he ran a hand through his still damp hair. He'd been the last one to get a shower, but it had been worth the wait as he finally got to shave that awful hair growing on his face.

The footsteps of someone else crossing the dusty floor of the library were as clear as day, and none of them had entered this building until now. Orin studied the booted tracks as they made their way over to the desk and back out again.

They'd also found evidence of someone having recently been inside the mercantile and granary. None of them could remember if footprints were in the pub before they entered, but he suspected there were.

Now that they had a better idea of what these boot prints looked like, he could recognize them in the pub once they returned. They hadn't searched the other buildings yet, but he'd bet they'd find evidence of Mr. Crispy in them too.

There was no evidence of the immortal living here or staying for an extended period, which meant they had to have come from somewhere else.

"It could have been someone else here," the demon suggested.

"Do you really think that?" Orin asked.

"No, but we have to analyze every possibility. Someone else could be moving through these outer towns or whatever they are. Plus, plenty of immortals left Belda's town, never returned, and could still be out here. There could be any number of towns out here that also have other immortals living in them… like the brownies' town."

"They are getting increasingly barren and less hospitable," Sahira said.

"Some immortals and creatures thrive in those conditions."

"I hate this," Elsa muttered.

Orin agreed. For every answer they found, they had a hundred more questions.

"Okay, so if it was the immortal from the geysers, and they weren't living here, then they must have been passing through," Sahira said.

"From where?" Elsa inquired.

"If that symbol is an hourglass, then the next arrow should be the final town," the demon said, "and must be where the immortal came from."

"If that immortal was leaving the next town, then there's no escape from there either."

Orin chose to ignore the panic tinging Elsa's voice. If the witch decided to fall apart now, he'd leave her ass here.

"We can't know that," Sahira said.

Since standing around and debating it wouldn't get them anywhere, Orin walked away from the others. Dust swirled around him and covered some of the booted footprints as he walked into the library's main room.

There was less here than in the town with the brownies. Shelves only lined the walls on the first floor; the second and third floors were bare.

What is going on in this realm?

He'd asked himself this question a thousand times since becoming trapped here and was no closer to the answer. If he could tear this whole realm apart piece by piece, board by board, and one mountain or dune after another, he would. He'd rip it to shreds and piss all over its remains.

Turning, he stalked out of the building, down the stairs, and to the black rock that was the base of this town. Nothing moved on the street; no birds soared through the air. There was nothing but an empty shell where life should thrive.

At least there aren't any threats... so far.

He didn't know how long that would last. If something came through here, he'd happily destroy it.

When the others joined him, they moved on to explore the other buildings. In each of them, they discovered the same things... proof another immortal had been here and the same symbol as in the pub.

They never uncovered any evidence that whoever came through before them resided here for any length of time. All the buildings were more barren than the ones in the brownies' town and emptier than the ones in Belda's.

They started on this journey with the intention of finding food or hunting to supplement their needs, but there was nothing here to hunt. The brownies hadn't found any insects to eat.

They explored every inch of the town and uncovered nothing of use. When the sun started setting, they returned to the pub, where Orin confirmed his suspicions about the burnt immortal on the geyser field... their boot prints also marked the floor here.

"Does anyone know how long we slept?" Sahira sat on the floor and crossed her legs as she asked this question. "Was it hours? Was it days?"

The demon pawed through his pack for food as he settled on the floor across from her. "No idea."

Loth and Fath sat in the middle of the loose circle they'd

created. Each munched on an insect leg they'd pulled from their tiny packs.

On Orin's shoulder, Pip finished her small meal and licked her fingers. He didn't mind the female rat riding around on him, even though she'd healed enough to walk; he kind of liked her company but would deny it until the day he died.

Elsa sat between the demon and Sahira and clasped her hands before her as she swayed a little. Her face was far paler than normal, and she squeezed her hands until they turned red.

While eyeing Elsa, he flexed the fingers that had completely healed since being burnt. Resting his elbow on the bar, he leaned against it as the witch continued to rock.

She wasn't handling this as well as she was before. He'd have no problem leaving her behind, but the demon and Sahira would put up a fight.

However, if the witch couldn't keep her shit together, she could take them down, and he wouldn't allow that. He glanced at Sahira as she carefully laid out what remained of her food and water.

She cared for Elsa, but he wasn't about to let the witch jeopardize Sahira's life. He wouldn't let anyone hurt her; if the witch melted down now, she risked doing that.

Elsa was still rocking when Orin stepped away from the bar, gathered his pack, and went to sit beside her. He settled on the ground and dropped his bag before him.

As he sorted through the remains of his food supply, he leaned closer to Elsa and told her, "If you fall apart, I'll kill you before I let you slow us down or put her in danger."

CHAPTER FIFTY-SIX

ELSA'S EYES shot to him as he looked pointedly toward Sahira, who stiffened at his words. On his shoulder, Pip stirred uneasily but didn't speak or climb down.

The demon's eyebrows rose as he looked from him to Sahira and back again. "You don't have a chance of that happening," Zeth stated.

Orin remained focused on Elsa, but he felt Sahira's shock. When he looked at her again, her eyes were circles on him.

Then her attention shifted to Pip, and her mouth closed as her lips compressed into a thin line. When her attention went to Elsa, a furrow appeared between her brows.

She was trying to understand him but failing to do so, when it was simple. He'd do anything to get them out of this realm, including killing the witch, even if it meant Sahira hated him afterward.

At least she'd be alive to hate him.

"I'm not going to fall apart!" Elsa snapped.

Orin grinned at her as he bit into a dried piece of meat. "Probably not now."

Elsa gave him the finger. "You couldn't kill me, dark fae."

Orin didn't doubt that he could, but she could have her delusions; everyone else here knew the truth. Sahira glowered at him before shifting her attention back to their dwindling supplies.

They would last the longest without food since they had an alternate supply... each other. But without regular meals, they'd weaken and eventually collapse too. With his massive size, the demon required the most sustenance, and his pile was the smallest.

Sahira pushed some of her dried meat toward him, but the demon waved it away. "Keep it."

Orin's eyes narrowed on the food between them. If the demon hadn't packed enough, that was his problem. She shouldn't be sacrificing anything for any of them.

"You need it more than me," Sahira protested. "And we're all going to get out of this together."

Orin suspected that last part was more for him, but he ignored it. He didn't care what Sahira thought; if she wouldn't do what was best for her because of her too-big heart, then he would.

How could someone with so much pride, smarts, and strength be so blind to things that might have to happen? He admired her determination and ability to care for others, but he wouldn't let them bring her down.

"She's right," Elsa said and glared at Orin. "We're all leaving here *together*."

He wiggled his fingers at her as he took another bite of meat.

"Fucking dark fae," the witch muttered; Orin chuckled.

"Keep your food... for now," the demon told Sahira. "If I run out before we find another source, we'll talk then."

"Your blood will help keep me going; take some of my supplies," Sahira insisted.

A growl rumbled up Orin's throat before he suppressed it. All his amusement vanished as he gritted his teeth.

He'd made it clear she wasn't to feed from anyone but *him*.

He thought she'd accepted this since she'd been coming to him, but he was wrong.

There was no way he would let her feed from anyone else, and he would make sure she realized it.

"You haven't required my blood in a while," the demon told her.

"I will in the future," Sahira insisted.

"Keep it, Sahira," Zeth said more firmly. "We can talk about an exchange if it becomes necessary, but I still have enough food to keep me going for a bit."

With a sigh, Sahira pulled the food back toward her and packed it away, except for a piece of dried meat. She chewed it while she sat back; her eyes traveling around the pub didn't return to him.

She could try to ignore him, but that would be impossible—something she should already know by now.

Pip rose and stretched before descending his arm to join the other brownies. She settled between them and lay back to stare at the ceiling with her hands propped behind her head; if she didn't fall asleep, she'd most likely turn his clothing into a bed again. He didn't mind, considering the creatures didn't bother him as much now.

When Sahira finished eating, she rose and wiped her hands on her brown fae pants. She didn't say anything before walking toward the alcove with the bathrooms.

Orin waited until he heard one of the doors shut before rising and striding to the alcove. He leaned against the wall to wait for the door to open.

When it did, she stepped outside and froze as she spotted him. Before she could react, he strode toward her, rested his hands on her hips, and guided her back into the bathroom. He kicked the door closed behind him.

CHAPTER FIFTY-SEVEN

"WHAT ARE YOU DOING?" Sahira hissed as he turned on the light.

"Do you really think you're going to drink the demon's blood?" Orin inquired while stroking her hip with his thumb.

She slapped his hand away and folded her arms over her chest. "If I require blood, then yes."

"If you require blood, you'll come to me. We've already established that."

Sahira rolled her eyes. "If we were somewhere else and with any other woman besides Elsa, who doesn't want you—"

"I'm not her type."

"I know. But if we were anywhere else, you'd gladly go traipsing off with another woman, so no, we haven't established anything. And if it takes me drinking his blood to get Zeth to agree to eat some of my food in exchange, I'll do it."

Despite the anger coiling in his belly, he released her hip to lean against the door while crossing his legs before him. "No, you won't."

She threw up her hands in exasperation. "For someone who was happily fucking a nymph the day after you screwed me, you're far too confident you have any say over my life and my actions. You. Do. Not."

There she went throwing the nymph in his face again. If she knew the truth....

What? What would that accomplish except revealing your weakness for her to *her? That could never happen.*

He smiled at her while speaking through his teeth. "For the rest of the time we're here, you're mine and mine alone, so you'd better get that through your thick head."

Red flashed through her eyes as her fangs elongated before retracting again. This brief loss of control caused a little thrill of excitement to run through him.

Normally he hated any sign of too many emotions, but she was amazing when she was out of control.

Sahira stalked across the room, shoved her finger into his chest, and poked him while she spoke. "And you better get it through *your* head that you *don't* control me."

He gripped her finger and held it while smiling at her. "No, but I own you."

Her eyes turned completely red as her face flushed, and she ripped her finger away from him. "*No one* owns me. Least of all *you!*"

"Don't I?"

When he prowled toward her, she backed across the room until her heel hit the wall, and she stopped. Her chin lifted as she glowered at him. "*Back off!*"

He stopped before her and rested his hands on her hips. She slapped at them, but he didn't stop as his hands slid up her sides to trace her curves.

She was so lush and supple. He'd never encountered anyone who smelled as good as her. His cock stirred at the memory of her and all the future possibilities as she decked him.

He'd been so focused on the wonder of her body that he didn't see her fist until it smashed into his nose and shot his head back. His hands flew to his face as he staggered away from her.

Throwing her shoulders back and keeping her chin high, she brushed past him as she headed for the door. Orin blinked away the tears that involuntarily sprang into his eyes when she'd battered his nose.

He should be pissed enough to make her pay, but he admired her feistiness and desired her too badly. There were other, far more pleasurable ways to make someone regret their choices. She'd be pleading for release and spewing apologies by the time he finished with her.

He caught her wrist before she reached the door and pulled her back. She spun and swung at him again, but he grabbed her hand and held it between them. He'd allow many things from her, but not that, not again.

"I *own* you, Sahira, and you're going to have to accept it. Your body is mine. You're reacting to me even now; you may hate it, but you can't deny it."

"That doesn't mean you *own* me, you conceited jackass!"

"Doesn't it?"

Before she could reply, he kissed her. He would show her that he owned her, make her pay for her defiance, and prove she couldn't resist him. She *would* learn where she belonged.

Instead of doing as he'd planned, she refused to ease into him as she planted her hands on his chest and bit his lower lip. It wasn't a playful bite either; it made it clear she wasn't happy.

Jerking her head to the side, she broke the kiss as she pushed against him. "A kiss isn't going to make this better, and I'm not having sex with you in a *bathroom* that probably hasn't been cleaned in centuries."

He laughed but didn't release her. "We've had worse conditions."

"You're gross."

"Sahira—"

"Let me go!"

The distress on her face caused him to release her. She was his, but he wouldn't force her into something she didn't want.

Sahira walked toward the doorway as she spoke over her shoulder. "If the hourglass theory is correct, then the next town should be the last one. After that, you'll be free to own whoever you want to... again. Since you have a thing for nymphs, you could always start with them."

Orin didn't realize he'd considered moving until he was beside her as she started to open the door. When he smashed his palm into it, the door slammed closed.

CHAPTER FIFTY-EIGHT

HER HEAD SHOT toward him as he leaned so close their noses nearly touched. It was on his tongue to tell her the truth, but again, the words lodged in his throat.

That admission would only make him more vulnerable to her. And standing there, staring at her, he realized he was already too weak when it came to her.

She made him feel and experience things he never had before, things he'd *never* wanted to experience. He tried to shut down the emotions battering him, but they refused to be caged as his heart hammered.

When her eyes met his, questions and something more shimmered in them. He had no idea what to say to make her stay... other than the truth.

Instead of revealing that hideous, festering secret to her, he said, "What does it matter *who* I fuck? We're not together, and I never made you any promises. Why do you care if I moved on after you? What is the big *fucking* deal?"

Her eyes slipped past him as her jaw locked, and she stared at the door. She didn't speak while he held his breath and waited for her to say something... *anything*.

Let her be the one to reveal things; it didn't have to be him. What would he do if she told him she didn't want him sleeping with other women and she wanted to be his only one?

Any other woman, he would have laughed the words off and gotten away from her as fast as possible. He didn't have time for that nonsense, and there were far too many beautiful women in the realms to be saddled to only one.

That was how he lived his life, and he'd been quite content to keep it that way... until her. And now, his stubborn little enchantress remained focused on the door when she should be answering his question.

He yearned to hear her say those words, and then he'd....

You'll what? Finally tell her the truth? Commit yourself to only one woman?

A few months ago, that idea would have curdled his insides. Just one woman? For eternity? Hell would have been a better alternative to that mundane existence.

Now, it didn't sound so awful. They might eventually kill each other, but they'd have a lot of fun before then.

Orin scowled as Sahira remained staring at the door. He wanted a response from her. "Are you going to answer me?"

Finally, her eyes flicked to him; they'd returned to their beautiful amber color. Strands of her mahogany hair had fallen free to frame her beautiful face as her bun had shifted down to her nape.

The stick she'd used to bind it up fell out a little, and his fingers twitched with the impulse to pull it free. He enjoyed running his fingers through the silken strands and the way the different hues of it glistened in the light.

"There is no big *fucking* deal," she said. "Have sex with anyone you want; I don't care."

He managed to keep himself from flinching as the words cut deeper than he'd expected or would have believed possible. Why did this woman affect him so much?

"Then why do you keep throwing the nymph in my face?" he growled. "If it doesn't matter, then let it go."

A muscle twitched in her cheek, and distress flickered through her eyes before she suppressed it and looked away again. It would be so much easier if she would let the nymph go; then he'd never have to tell her the truth.

But nothing with his stubborn witch was *ever* easy.

"Would it have made a difference if I didn't sleep with her?" he asked.

"A difference in what?"

"You know what," he snarled.

She flinched a little before closing her eyes and swallowing again. When she focused on the door again, a small tremor ran through her. As much as he'd like to choke her, he also longed to draw her into his arms so he could comfort her and forget this mess.

A mess you created.

Oh, shut up.

He didn't know when he'd developed a bit of a conscience, but it was really starting to piss him off.

"There were other women after her; you were more than happy to make sure I saw you with them all," Sahira said.

This time, he was the one who flinched. What had he done? And why couldn't he open his mouth and fix it?

Because then she would have all the control, and he was a little afraid she might choose to destroy him with it. And even more scared she could.

"That's not what I asked; would it have made a difference?" he demanded.

Red flashed through her eyes as she turned toward him again. "I'm not playing this stupid, pointless game with you! It doesn't matter. There's no way of knowing, and you can't change the past. You made your choices and will make them again once we're free of this realm! For once in your life, could you stop being a selfish asshole and let me out of here!"

"You're right, I am a selfish asshole, and that's why you will *not* feed from the demon or the witch. You're mine, and you better realize it."

When she didn't say anything but stood there staring at him like she didn't recognize him, an uneasy feeling settled over him. He didn't recognize himself either, at least not when it came to her.

Tired of her, tired of this battle between them, and tired of himself, he lowered his hand from the door. He'd never been uncertain about anything in his life.

He'd always taken what he wanted and done what needed to be done. That was who he was, but she made him question everything.

As their gazes continued to hold, he searched for some sign of uncertainty in her eyes, but there was only a cool distance.

"I own you," he said as he stepped away from the door, "and don't forget it."

But as she opened the door, for the first time, Orin questioned if he was wrong and it was *she* who owned *him*.

That possibility infuriated him more.

CHAPTER FIFTY-NINE

THEY SPENT another night on the pub floor before gathering their supplies and heading out as the sun rose. Sahira had gone to sleep ten feet away from Orin and woke to find them in the same places.

He hadn't tried to come to her once she fell asleep, something she was grateful for... or at least that's what she told herself.

After their ridiculous fight in the bathroom, she didn't want to be anywhere near him. But she couldn't deny she missed waking to find herself nestled in his arms.

She longed for a connection to him while also hating him, and it made *everything* so much more difficult. And when she was honest with herself, she could admit she didn't hate him anymore.

She wanted to but couldn't.

Yes, he was an asshole. *No one* could deny that, but even with what he'd said to Elsa, and she knew he meant it, she didn't hate him.

He was more callous than anyone she'd ever met, but there

was some good inside his black heart. Every time she looked at Pip with her battered tail, it confirmed this.

He could have let her die; it would have been easy enough for him to do nothing while she died. He said all they did was irritate him, but he still saved her life.

Not only that, but he hadn't kicked Pip off his shoulder, and she'd slept beside him again last night. The man was such a contradiction, an oddity she couldn't quite put her finger on, but it all came together to create *him*.

And as much as she'd like to choke him most of the time, she wouldn't change him. She'd come to care for him far more than she should have allowed herself to, and it was too late to change that now.

She also had to admit he had a point. They *weren't* together, he'd never made her any promises before or during their first time together, and she hadn't expected him only to be with her. That wasn't how the dark fae worked.

She'd prepared herself to see him with other women, but it hurt so much to watch him with them. Thinking about it caused her to rub her chest as her heart constricted.

It was *her* problem, and she either got over it or didn't. But if she got over it, she'd be opening herself up to him more, and he'd already hurt her. It would only be worse next time.

No, it was best if they kept their distance now because he'd move on once they were free of here and never look back. And she'd be left with only her sorrow for company.

She couldn't allow that. She also wouldn't allow him to *own* her; what a barbaric, asshole thing to say. It didn't matter whether her body reacted to his every touch like he was the puppet master and she was the puppet; *no one* owned her.

Focusing on the wrath those words conjured, she stalked forward, completely ignoring him. Fath shifted on her shoulder but said nothing about her speed walk.

Thankfully, once they were out of town, they no longer had

to climb. Instead, they descended through a mountain passage with black walls so steep and high they were impossible to climb.

She almost wished for the mountains again; at least then she could see around her. With the black walls pressing against them and becoming so close in some places they had to turn sideways to squeeze through them, she saw only rock.

Feeling like a rat in a maze, the air warmed as they descended, but the respite from the cold didn't ease her growing anxiety. The passageway twisted and turned so many times she often lost sight of Orin a few feet ahead of her.

Every time he vanished from view, her heart leapt, and she hurried forward so she could see him again. At one point, the path became so winding she couldn't see him for at least ten minutes, as every time she turned a corner, he'd already gone around a different one.

When she glanced back, she couldn't see Elsa behind her. On her shoulder, Fath sometimes made a small sound of displeasure, but like usual, he didn't speak.

When the sunset came, and they were too tired to continue, they settled into the most wide-open section they could find. From her position, she saw Orin and Elsa, but only one of Zeth's horns.

They were crammed into the passage with barely enough room to stretch their legs across as they leaned against the wall and ate their meager rations. They'd have difficulty fighting it off if something came after them now.

And if something comes from above….

She tipped her head back to stare at the walls well over a hundred feet above. Lifting her spear, she propped it up and held it as she leaned back against the wall, and Fath climbed off her shoulder to join the other brownies in a circle where they slept head to tail.

She could turn sideways to stretch completely out on the

pathway, but then she'd be on top of Orin and Elsa. She preferred being cramped between the two walls.

It took her a while to drift off, and when she woke, her neck bent at an unnatural angle, the rising sun was casting shadows through the passage. She rubbed her eyes and looked at Orin, who had his head tipped back while he stared at the walls surrounding them.

The way he stood with his body tensed made her readjust her spear. It had fallen forward to rest on the wall across from her while she slept. Orin and Zeth had taken the first watch, but when she looked at Elsa, her friend was still sleeping, and she couldn't see if Zeth was awake.

Orin and Zeth had either fallen asleep or decided not to wake them, but that didn't matter. The look on Orin's face did.

"What is it?"

Her question came out as little more than a whisper, but he heard it as he replied, "I think there's something up there."

CHAPTER SIXTY

SAHIRA'S STOMACH CHURNED. "WHY?"

"I heard something."

Sahira gulped as she gazed at the rocks surrounding them. They were sitting ducks down here—something Orin must have also realized because he said, "Wake the others."

As quietly as she could, she grasped Elsa's shoulder and gently shook it. Her friend stirred before sitting straight up; Sahira placed her index finger against her lips, and Elsa nodded before rubbing her eyes.

When Sahira looked past her friend, a bolt of panic ran through her when she saw nothing of Zeth. She pointed behind Elsa, who turned to look before giving her a thumbs-up. Elsa reached out of view, and a second later, Zeth's head poked around the corner.

That was when she heard it too; they all did. Something scratched against the stones above. The skittering sound that followed caused her body to turn cold.

Sahira's head tipped back, and she searched the rocks above. She couldn't see anything there, but the noises continued before abruptly ceasing.

She didn't know if the noise, or lack of it, was worse. At least when it was moving, they had an idea of where it was.

She looked at Orin, who stood with his shoulders back and jaw set. Sensing her attention, his eyes flicked to her, and he jerked his head to the side.

It was time to get out of here. Sahira pulled her blanket off, stuffed her pack, and slid it onto her back as Fath scampered up to sit on her shoulder.

She kept her spear in hand as they started back down the mountain. Whatever was up there didn't attack, but it probably knew this mountain pass far better than them.

Would it be easier for it to attack now, or was there a better area ahead for it to descend on them? Or maybe it was a scout, out to take a look for its friends before reporting back to them.

The hair on Sahira's nape rose as she glanced up, but she still didn't see anything....

Focusing forward, she kept her attention on Orin as she determined to make it out of this alive. Occasionally, a scratch or scuffle on the rocks drew her attention above, but she never saw anything.

Whatever was up there, the scraping made it sound like it had claws that could tear into someone's belly and lay waste to their insides. Her hand tightened on the spear as Orin vanished from view again.

Every muscle in her body tensed to fight or run. She resisted both impulses; she couldn't risk triggering the thing above or rushing into a trap.

She took a deep breath and compelled herself to calm down as they traveled lower and lower through the mountain. Through the small crevice above, the sun's dwindling light faded faster than it would have if they were atop the mountains.

The idea of stopping to rest with that thing tracking them wasn't a happy one, but they had to eat, and eventually, they'd have to sleep. She'd hoped not to experience any more sleepless days and nights after the geyser field, but that might be impossible.

At least they could keep moving here and didn't have to stand completely still. *See, there's a silver lining to something possibly eating you.*

Yay.

As shadows increasingly darkened the walls around them, Orin turned to her and held out his hand. "Candle."

The word was barely more than a whisper as he searched the cliffs above. It had been too quiet for too long up there. She didn't take that as a good sign.

Sahira shrugged off her pack and held it close to her face as she searched for the candle and flint. They only had two left; she possessed one, and Elsa the other.

The two candles were leftovers from their time on the geyser field, and they'd been strict about using them, but she wasn't going to argue with Orin about using them. The sun's rays barely penetrated down here; the moon provided far less illumination.

While pulling the candle from her pack, that thing scraped above them again, and an awful, skittering noise followed. The hair on her nape rose like something was watching her, but if she looked up, nothing would be there.

Sahira steadied her hand as she handed him the candle before removing the flint from her pack. Orin held the candle while she used the flint to light it.

His crow-colored eyes met hers in the glow of the small, dancing flame. Inside, she was a bundle of nerves, but something about his cool, steady gaze calmed her.

His fingers briefly found hers and squeezed before he released her and stepped away. Her eyebrows rose over this display of comfort from *Orin*.

What astounded her more was that after their fight in the bathroom, she welcomed it. He was an asshole, but he was *her* asshole… sort of.

When he turned away, she almost grabbed his arm to hold him back. She didn't want to lose sight of him again, but like with the geysers, their only choice was to continue.

A new scratching sound came from above while another one came from ahead. Sweat broke out on her brow as she realized something had joined whatever was following them this whole time.

She glanced back at Elsa's pale face. There had been a moment when it looked like Elsa might crack and lose it, but she'd recovered since then. However, she looked as unnerved by this as Sahira felt.

Elsa would keep it together out here; she just hoped they both survived as she rounded a corner and her friend disappeared.

CHAPTER SIXTY-ONE

ORIN'S TEETH grated together as the scraping from above grew louder. For a while, he thought the thing might be trying to keep its presence hidden from them and failing, but now that it had a friend, it didn't bother.

The two creatures were either trying to unnerve them, stupid, or convinced they'd win this. He didn't once entertain the notion they might not be seeking to kill them; everything in this realm was lethal.

And these things would soon learn *he* was far more lethal than them. He was tired of all the shit in this forsaken realm, and if that hourglass was any indication, the next town was their last.

Nothing would stop him from getting there.

The shadows dancing across the walls beckoned to him. He could easily slip into them, cloak himself, and continue without the others.

Whatever hunted them wouldn't know he was there. It was an intriguing concept, and he might have entertained it more if it wasn't for one thing… he wouldn't leave Sahira behind.

He could cocoon her in shadows too; he'd done it before, but with everyone spaced apart by the twisting turns of this forsaken passageway, he couldn't cloak them all. Plus, the candle didn't create enough shadows for that.

Besides, Sahira would never leave them behind, even if it meant saving her ass. And Pip, whose fingers dug into his skin as she rode on his shoulder and tensed at every sound, probably wouldn't be happy about leaving Loth behind. He could take Fath with them as he was settled on Sahira's shoulder.

If push came to shove, he'd cloak himself and Sahira and leave the others behind. Fuck them and her opinion on it.

The candle's glow barely illuminated more than a couple of feet in front of him. Normally, he preferred the dark; it was where his kind thrived.

He didn't like it now. There was too much it could hide in this twisty passage.

Something crunched beneath his foot. When Orin stopped to discover what it was, Sahira rounded the corner and walked into him.

Her body bumped his forward a step, and something else crunched beneath his boot. The others hadn't realized he'd stopped either and jostled him twice more before they settled into place.

"What's going on?" Zeth demanded.

"There's something here," Orin answered.

Bending, Pip shifted on him as he lowered the candle. Orin frowned at the dried-out remains beneath his foot.

The thing was an emaciated, dried-out husk with purplish-gray skin. It was in such bad shape he couldn't tell what it was, but with its snout and paws, it looked like some animal.

Leaning down to peer over his shoulder, Sahira made a sound of disgust. "Let's go."

Orin waited until she moved back before rising and starting forward again. He heard her saying to the others, "There's something dead up here; watch where you're walking."

Despite her warning, another crunch filled the air when

someone else stepped on the remains. Orin traveled another fifty feet before something else snapped beneath his foot.

Glancing down, he lowered the candle to reveal another dead creature. This one was in worse shape than the last, as the bones he'd stepped on had crumbled and turned to ash beneath his weight.

Lifting the candle, he spotted another husk ahead. Unease churned inside him; they'd entered the killing grounds of whatever hunted them.

He withdrew his sword as he prepared for an imminent attack. Behind him, the others gathered as close as possible through the twisty mountain while the dead became more abundant with every twist and turn.

The further they got into the passage, the more they uncovered dead creatures enshrouded in a gauzy film that clung to his boots when he stepped in it. Yanking his foot free of the webbing, Orin forged ahead despite knowing what followed them from above.

He never considered turning back but knew death lay ahead.

CHAPTER SIXTY-TWO

SNAP. Crack. Pop.

Orin gritted his teeth against the noise of the breaking bones and crumbling bodies as it drowned out the noises from above. As they progressed through the passage, avoiding the carcasses littering the ground became impossible.

And he wasn't the only one stepping on them, as the others couldn't avoid the remains beneath their feet. The only good thing about this area was, though the walls remained high, the twists and turns in the passage had stopped.

They now walked straight toward whatever nightmare lay ahead, and it was coming fast. After another ten feet, he held his hand up to halt the others.

Sahira stopped behind him; Pip twisted on his shoulder to look at her before turning back. The last crack of bone faded away beneath the demon's feet.

Orin lifted the candle higher; only two inches remained of the cylindrical shape. Wax dripped down to his fingertips, but he no longer felt its heat beneath the coating that had formed.

He suspected the things stalking them had dragged these corpses into the passage so the noise of their passing would hide any sounds made above. He doubted there were only two up there now and would bet his left testicle—which he liked very much—that more had joined the hunt without them knowing.

They were heading deeper into the lair of whatever tracked them, and those things had the advantage. He glanced over Sahira and Elsa's heads to where the demon stood.

Zeth's eyes met his, and in them, Orin saw the same understanding that had come to him a while ago—they'd walked into a trap, but they'd never had a choice. They'd followed the only path from the town to here.

They could have turned back, but none of them would have agreed to do so, and it was too late to retreat now. Plus, he didn't run from anything; he never had and never would.

Except her.

He shifted his attention to Sahira with Fath sitting on her shoulder. As their eyes met, he understood the truth of his realization. He stood in front of her while also running from her and everything she represented, though he still wasn't sure what that was.

And no matter what happened between them, he would get her out of this.

"You should get a protection spell ready," he told her before glancing at Elsa.

Ever since he'd threatened the witch, she'd been doing better and now stood with her shoulders back while glowering at him. He smiled in return.

He was fine with her not liking him; he didn't care about her or her opinion. Sahira was his main concern, which was strange because *he* was always his main concern.

Sure, he worried about his family too, but he had no family here. Unless he counted Cole and Lexi's pending nuptials, which would make him and Sahira relatives in a way, but that didn't count to him.

He'd prefer to keep his future sister-in-law happy by bringing her aunt home, but they weren't blood. And he should still be more concerned about his ass than anyone else's.

The sad truth was that he wasn't.

And he hadn't been for a while now; it's why he went after her when the scarog beetles attacked. It hadn't been because he was playing a game and determined to fuck her. It was because it was *her*.

He hadn't been able to admit that to himself until now. He was a moron and a bigger asshole than he'd realized, as he'd always embraced the label and never denied it.

There were so many things he wanted to say to her and a truth he should reveal. It was all there, ready to pour out, but he couldn't bare himself to her while Fath sat on her shoulder and Elsa glared at him.

This wasn't something for the others; it was for *them*. As multiple scratching and skittering sounds came from above, it became evident it was also something for another time.

Sahira must have sensed something from him as her forehead crinkled and confusion filled her gaze. "Orin?"

He shook his head to clear it. Now wasn't the moment to get all mushy as the noises from above grew louder.

More things hunted them.

"Get that protection spell ready," he said.

Sahira lifted her hands before turning to Elsa. Their heads bent close together, but he couldn't hear what they said over the increasing noise of those things. The creatures were getting anxious for them to continue.

Sahira and Elsa set their spears aside to clasp hands. While he couldn't hear what they said, their power swelled on the air until it vibrated around them and danced through the night.

The currents of it tickled and caused the hair on his arms to rise as something powerful enveloped them. He didn't know how long the spell would last, but it would protect them against whatever lay ahead.

When Sahira released Elsa's hand, turned to him, and nodded, he started forward again. Unable to avoid the desiccated, mummy-wrapped corpses, Orin tried to do as little damage to them as possible as the noises above increased.

Whatever was up there, it wasn't tracking them anymore. It was preparing for an attack while herding them where it wanted them to go.

CHAPTER SIXTY-THREE

SAHIRA KEPT one of her palms facing the ground as she drew energy from the rocks beneath her feet and the walls against her side. The realm teemed with life, and she used its power to help fuel hers while Elsa did the same.

The protection spell would keep them all safe for a bit, but an unrelenting onslaught would eventually break it, and she was certain that was about to come. She tried to control the rapid beat of her heart and the sweat forming on her palms, but she wished these things would get it over with.

The anticipation of the attack was almost as bad as the event. She wiped her palms on her pants as the increasing noises from above caused a trickle of sweat to run down her spine.

As the sun started rising, Orin blew out the candle, slipped it into his pocket, and peeled away the wax on his fingers. Shadows danced around them, but the sun's rays never fully penetrated their crevice.

She tried not to look at the dried husks as they crunched beneath her feet, but sometimes a mushier one would draw her attention, and her stomach would turn at the mangled things. As they progressed through the bodies, they stopped cracking as much of the remains became fresher.

The white filament enshrouding the bodies was the worst as it stuck to her boots and tried to cleave her to the bodies. Sometimes, she'd drag one a few feet before she succeeded in extricating herself.

As the bodies became fresher and the gauze thicker, it also grew stickier. Whatever clung to the dried-out husks was as broken and decayed as the bodies, but not the stuff on these ones.

Ahead of her, Orin struggled to pull his boot free of the webbing clinging to his sole. He finally tore himself free, but the substance adhered to the bottom of his boot, and with every step he took, his foot stuck a little on the rocks.

"Not good," Fath whispered.

The brownie hadn't spoken since they'd entered these winding passages, but now, he'd decided to state the obvious. Sahira refrained from telling him that speaking felt like a way to invite something bad to happen. Considering the bad was already upon them, it was a stupid thing to think.

Unable to avoid it, Sahira got caught in the sticky filament next. Orin clasped her hand and helped pull her free.

She turned to help Elsa, but Zeth grasped her waist and lifted her over the top of the dead thing. He set her down behind Sahira before stomping through the remains that squished beneath his boots.

Sahira winced at the wet, sloppy sound he created; it was far worse than the crackle of bones. This dead thing sounded like its skin was sloughing off beneath the white gauze. She still couldn't tell what any of these things were.

Sahira shuddered before pressing her back against the wall and edging around the next two bodies. They were also the last two bodies as they traveled twenty feet more through the tight confines before the passageway finally opened up.

Inhaling deeply, Sahira stepped out of the tunnel as she

relished the open air around her instead of the walls. That feeling was short-lived as thirty feet away from them, a one-hundred-foot-tall and fifty-foot-wide, intricately woven web blocked their way.

Caught up in the webbing were dozens of filament-encased bundles tucked securely into the strands. Large, black creatures stood over some of those bundles, their front legs working as they sought to encase them deeper into the webbing, or their mandibles worked to drain them of their essence.

Sahira's stomach plummeted as something exploded from above. She looked up in time to see dozens of black bodies leaping from the top of the mountains and over the top of them.

CHAPTER SIXTY-FOUR

THEY HAD NOWHERE to go as the three-foot-high and five-feet-wide spiders descended on them. Some rode air currents down while others shot out webbing that stuck to the wall opposite them. They used it to swing like demonic trapeze artists.

Some spiders hit the protective wall of air she and Elsa had erected. They released squeals of rage as they bounced off and across the ground.

Many rebounded and leapt up again to charge while the others hit or descended to the earth. With every step, the lobster-like claws on their two front legs clicked against the rock or scratched the ground. It was the same scratching, skittering sound they'd heard for a while, but now she knew why.

Some of the spiders clambered back up the walls while others raced forward. She swore the ones above them flew as they drifted on unseen air currents, and a few succeeded in landing on the air bubble instead of bouncing off it.

When they did, she spotted a second, circular mouth in the center of their large, hairy bellies. The razor-sharp teeth within the mouth clicked and clacked as they moved back and forth as it tried to break into the air bubble while sliding off the side of it.

Thousands of bristly black hairs covered the monstrosities. The two mandibles beside their front mouths were more like spikes meant to spear their victims. Two fangs, dripping with a green liquid she assumed was venom, hung down so low they nearly touched the ground when the thing landed.

"Holy shit," Elsa breathed.

"Keep moving," Zeth commanded. "Don't let them swarm us."

The only problem was the spiders blocking the tunnel behind them and a giant web blocking the way forward.

"Head for the web," Orin said.

They all inched toward it as the spiders continued to charge and batter the protective bubble surrounding them. Each one was as ugly and horrific as the one before as their claws struck the air bubble, or they charged headfirst into it while others scampered across.

"How long will this spell last?" Pip asked.

"We can keep it going for a while." Sahira glanced at Elsa, who stared back at her with frightened eyes. "I'm not sure exactly."

She had no doubt Elsa would keep the spell intact as long as possible, but eventually, the spiders would weaken it. Not to mention, exhaustion would get the better of them, and once that happened, the barrier would fall.

For now, strong energy continued to pulse from the ground. That would help them continue to fuel the spell, but they had to devise a way out of this soon.

They were almost to the giant web when Orin stopped walking. If they kept going, the air bubble would get caught in the webbing, trapping them further.

Sahira shifted her attention to the enormous home and death trap the spiders devised. So intricately woven together, the fine, white filaments created strands thicker than her biceps and no more than a few inches apart.

Not even a brownie could slip past without being caught in the spiders' web. More bodies than she'd realized were caught in the webbing as spiders scampered over the strands and descended toward them.

In the top left corner of the web, a massive, black spider was perched low with its legs tucked beneath it. Even though it lay on the web, Sahira could tell it was three times the size of the others.

Its numerous beady, red eyes surveyed them while it sent its children out to destroy them. That thing was so convinced they were already dead that it didn't bother to rise.

Its confidence irritated and unnerved her. She wouldn't be this monster's dinner.

"If I stay inside this air bubble, can I hack at the web through it?" Orin asked.

"No. Once something pierces the bubble, it will collapse," Sahira said.

Orin studied the web before looking at her. "Can you let me out of it while keeping yourself protected?"

Sahira's heart bashed off her rib cage as everything in her protested this statement. "The second you step out of here, those things will be on you. And once you're out there, we won't be able to get the spell around you fast enough to protect you."

"That's not what I asked."

Her mouth was so dry, she could barely speak as he stared at her with his sword raised before him and steely determination etched onto his exquisite features. "They'll swarm you."

"We can't stay here. This protective barrier will fail, and when it does, they'll be on all of us. If I leave here, I can hack through the web and clear a way to the other side."

"They'll follow us over there."

"That will be our next problem, but our first problem is getting *out* of here. We're trapped here; at least over there, we can run."

"Orin—"

"I'm not arguing over this, Sahira. Can you let me out or not?"

She gulped as she shifted from foot to foot and looked at the others. They all stared expectantly back at her. Elsa could answer him, but she knew it had to come from her.

"I can," she whispered.

"Then do it."

CHAPTER SIXTY-FIVE

SAHIRA STARED at Orin in disbelief; she couldn't lower the shield and leave him with those things. They'd swarm over and destroy him.

They crawled all over the shield, looking for a weakness and determined to find it. If he was out there alone, with no one to watch his back....

He doesn't have to be alone out there. Elsa could keep the shield over herself and Zeth while Sahira went out to protect Orin as he cut through the webbing.

All her common sense rebelled against going out there with these things, but she wouldn't leave Orin to face this alone. That would be certain death.

"Can you keep the shield going without me?" she asked Elsa.

"You can't go out there."

"Someone has to watch his back."

"I'll do it," Zeth said.

"You have a family to return to," Sahira reminded him.

"So do you," Orin growled, "and you're not going out there."

She shot an irritated look over her shoulder at him. "You're not going out there alone."

"I just have to cut through the webbing, and then we can all move on together."

Sahira pointed at the things crawling over their shield. "They're not going to let you do that."

"They're not going to have a choice. The longer we stand here and argue about it, the more they'll come."

He was right about that as more of them scampered down from the webbing. She opened her mouth to protest more, but they had to do something to get out of here, and no one had any other suggestions.

He could have his way... for now.

"Fine," she grated through her teeth, "but you better make it quick."

"As you know, that's usually not my way," he told her with a wink, "but your wish is my command."

Despite her terror for him, and the growing number of spiders surrounding them, a smile tugged at Sahira's lips. Only he could be so arrogant at a time like this.

"I'll go with you," Pip said as she removed her tiny dagger from its sheath.

Orin lifted her from his shoulder and set her on the ground. "I don't think so."

"You saved my life; I will fight for yours."

"And I'll move much faster if you're not with me. You're staying."

Pip held her dagger ready for battle, but he ignored her as he shifted his attention back to Sahira. "Let me out."

Reluctantly, Sahira pulled the shield away from him and dropped it in place before her. When he was free of the protection, she rested her hands against the bubble as she gazed at him.

I can't lose him.

The possibility nearly drove her to her knees. He made her crazy, but she'd miss the cocky, manipulative man with a heart bigger than she'd ever considered possible.

Orin lifted his sword over his head before bringing it down on the thick strands of webbing. Much to her horror, it only cut through a little before catching in the sticky filament.

Realizing Orin was free of the protective bubble, the spiders released a gurgling noise before charging him. Orin yanked at the sword a few times before finally breaking it free.

He swung it into the web again before spinning it to face the monstrous beasts. Throwing his hands up, Sahira sensed the swell of his power before a current of air smacked into the two spiders leaping toward him.

Like all dark fae, he could manipulate the elements. The air hit the spiders and flung them back.

When those flying beasts hit the ground, more creatures scrambled across the shield toward Orin. Before she could scream at him to move, Orin pulled the shadows around him and vanished.

Flattening her hands against the shield, her nose nearly touched the protective bubble as she searched for him. The spiders descended on the spot where he once stood.

He couldn't have gotten far; there hadn't been enough time to get around the teeming creatures, but blood didn't erupt, and no screams filled the air, though one remained trapped in her throat.

The power from the shield vibrated against her palms while she struggled to breathe. She'd planned to go out there with him to cover his back, but she couldn't go now.

He'd become part of the shadows, and she had no idea where he'd gone. If she went out there now, she could cause a distraction that might get them killed.

Before coming to the Cursed Realm, she *never* would have considered the possibility Orin might try to save her from these things, but now, he would. She felt that truth in the fabric of her soul.

They drove each other to the brink of madness, but he'd

protect her just as she would him. If she went out there now, he'd come for her, and they'd both die because of it.

So, she stood with her hands against the shield as she tried to figure out where he'd gone and how she could help. The sword remained embedded halfway through the webbing, sticking straight out as the filaments kept it trapped.

It wouldn't take too much more to hack through the web, but it still wouldn't be enough for them to slip through. Maybe the brownies could get through at that point, but no one else.

They'd have to cut through more for that to happen, but they needed to keep cutting to get free or find some other way past the webbing. Staying here wasn't an option.

They were trapped, and Orin was out there with those things. It was only a matter of time before the spiders found him and the shield failed.

Five feet away and closer to Zeth, black blood exploded from a spider. She couldn't see the source of the blow the spider had taken, but she detected a swirl of shadows as the spider squealed.

Blood sprayed from its head as the shifting shadows vanished, and Orin was again undetectable.

CHAPTER SIXTY-SIX

KEEPING TO THE SHADOWS, Orin used his dagger to slice through one spider after another. He slit the throat of one, poked out the eyes of the next, and hacked off the front legs of one scrambling toward him.

He didn't take them out in order but skipped some as he moved. He couldn't give them a clear path as to his location and the direction he was heading.

Even with his bouncing around, the creatures finally got smart and created a circle... around *him*. They couldn't know for sure that they'd trapped him as their feet clicked on the rock and their claws thumped against it.

Instead of going after another spider, he stayed out of the center and stood only a few feet away from one of the hideous beasts as they crept closer to each other to squeeze him in. They were smarter than they looked, which was about as intelligent as dog shit.

The thousands of bristly, black hairs covering the spiders rippled like they were trying to sense air currents. He suspected they were.

He didn't breathe as the one to his right took a couple of

steps forward, and its claw landed only a foot away. The ground shook beneath the blow that left an indent in the rocks.

Keeping the shadows around him, Orin moved steadily forward, with the spiders squeezing him more and more toward the others. They steadily took away what little remained of his space.

He waited until only a few feet remained before crouching and leaping into the air. While he was up there, the spiders moved closer, and pointing his toes down, he fell with the full force of his weight.

When he hit the spider, he slammed its chin into the ground as another reeled back onto its hind legs and jumped. It wasn't the creature leaping at him that caused him to spin sideways and nearly tumble off the one he'd landed on. No, it was the white webbing the thing launched at him that had him twisting awkwardly to avoid the sticky goo ensnaring him.

If they managed to trap him with their webbing, that would be the end. It was too thick and clingy for him to evade its clutches before they started spinning him like the rest of their victims.

This was not going as planned, but what had in this Cursed Realm? Nothing, but he hadn't expected this web-slinging insanity.

Regaining his balance, he ran down the back end of the spider and jumped off. He didn't get away in time to avoid one of the eight-legged freaks swinging out with its claw and slicing open his arm.

His blood spilling free caused them to rear back on their hind legs. Their front ones waved in the air while they made excited, hissing noises before falling simultaneously.

Their claws clattered off the stone as their eager titters filled the air. He kept his hand over the gash as blood welled against his palm and slipped between his fingers.

The spiders moved faster as they tracked his blood.

CHAPTER SIXTY-SEVEN

"WE HAVE TO DO SOMETHING," Sahira gasped as Orin's bright red drops of blood on the black stone became a homing beacon to the spiders hunting him.

She glanced at the web again and the sword jutting out of it. Most of the spiders were focused on their wounded prey, but some remained centered on them. Those spiders were more intent on watching their brethren hunt Orin.

"We need fire," Zeth said.

"These things don't like fire?" Sahira inquired.

"I don't know for sure, but I'm guessing not. They live in these mountains, and I doubt they've seen it before. It might also burn through the webbing."

Sahira's hand went to her sack before she recalled Orin had her candle. She turned to Elsa. "Give me your candle."

"Candles aren't going to do much against these things," Zeth said. "We need something bigger than that to burn, and you have to let me out of here too."

"What about your family?"

"They matter most to me, but I could never look at them

again if I left here a coward. Besides, once they kill the fae, they'll come for us, and it's only a matter of time before they get in here. If I can help hold them off, it will give all of you a chance to live longer and possibly escape."

Sahira's jaw clenched, but she wouldn't argue with him. They had to do something and couldn't leave Orin alone.

"Let him out and give me your candle," she said to Elsa.

"A candle isn't going to help," Elsa said.

"I'll figure out a way to fan the flames higher, and if we're lucky, this thing will burn."

No one said they hadn't been lucky so far; none of them would be here if they had.

"Let him out, and get me the candle," Sahira said.

Fath, Loth, and Pip gathered between her and Elsa as they eyed the demon with sorrow and their tails drooped. Elsa looked helplessly at Sahira before closing her eyes and nodding.

Elsa hadn't been this upset about letting Orin out of the shield, but Sahira understood. She and Pip were the only ones Orin had ever shown any kindness toward; he'd also threatened to kill Elsa, so why should she care if he died?

And Orin was the reason why she wouldn't, but it bothered Sahira more than it should that her heart raced and hands trembled while the others remained completely calm. At any second, the spiders could take Orin down, ending whatever this was between them.

A part of her would break and die if that happened. But while she'd be heartbroken, only she and Pip would mourn his loss in this realm.

"Good luck," Elsa whispered to Zeth.

"Same to you. Get that fire going."

Sahira dropped her sack and knelt on the ground beside it. She removed a shirt and wrapped it around her dagger as Elsa pulled the shield back enough for Zeth to enter the battle.

With his spear in hand, Zeth charged one of the spiders still focused on hunting Orin. His blood trail had stopped, but the spiders had all moved toward where they'd entered this trap. She suspected they had him cornered over there.

Ignoring the staccato rhythm of her heart and the tremble in her hands, she turned as Elsa removed the flint and candle from her sack. She lit the candle and brought it toward the makeshift torch Sahira held.

She'd burn everything in her sack to destroy as many of these things as possible before plunging her dagger through her heart. She'd never let these things take her alive.

She suspected most of their victims were very aware of what was happening to them when they were bound into webbing before being feasted on. She wouldn't be one of them. If she had her way, she'd lose so much blood these things wouldn't be able to turn her into a meal.

Before the flame caught, she looked at Elsa. "Stay here and keep the shield up for you and the brownies."

"I'm not going to hide in here while you guys do all the fighting. There's strength in numbers."

"True." Sahira shifted her attention to the brownies. "You can ride with us. We can't guarantee your safety, but we'll try."

Almost instantly, the three of them grouped together, and Loth and Pip climbed onto Fath's shoulders. "We're going down fighting," Pip said after she rose to the top.

The brownies had little chance against these things, but she understood their desire to die the way they chose.

When Sahira's torch finally caught, she rolled up her sleeve so it wouldn't catch fire too and lifted her torch into the air. Elsa knelt and pulled a shirt from her pack; she removed her dagger from the holster on her hip and wrapped the clothing on the blade.

She held the shirt to Sahira's flame, and it ignited. They

stared at each other for a second before their fingers met, and the shield fell.

They were on their own now with these things, and the spiders would soon realize it.

CHAPTER SIXTY-EIGHT

ORIN HAD SHRUGGED out of his shirt and, with his teeth and hand, cinched it around his bicep to cover the wound. He'd stopped bleeding, but the scent of it was enough to keep these things tracking him, even while enshrouded in shadows.

A roar drew his attention as the demon grabbed one of the spiders by its back legs. Spinning it around, he used it to batter away three of the others.

The force of his hit sent them all flying. Their broken pieces, bouncing across the ground, sent the other ones skittering backward.

Orin wasn't happy the demon had left the bubble but understood it. To some, doing nothing wasn't an option, and the demon was one of those immortals who wouldn't let others fight his battles.

But that meant the witches, or at least Sahira, would soon leave the protection spell behind too. He had to do something about these spiders before that happened.

Though it couldn't know for sure where he was, one of the spiders suddenly charged. Its claws thumped against the earth as it barreled toward him.

Orin leapt back and realized his mistake too late as another came from a different direction. They were working together to try to pin him in.

The first spider hit the wall so hard that the rocks cracked from the impact. This thing was lethal, and if it had another brain somewhere in its hideous body, that organ was now lonely as the spider staggered to its feet, shook its head, and collapsed.

The second spider was a little smarter as it avoided the wall and twisted toward him. Orin threw himself on top of the first, rolled across it, and came up on the other side of the demon.

He couldn't pay attention to Zeth as more spiders scampered across the ground and descended the steep walls. The sound of their skittering feet and clicking claws set his nerves on edge.

He suspected they'd kept the clicking to a minimum while tracking them, but now they were making their presence known and trying to distract them. He refused to let it work.

Orin tuned out the noise as he leapt to his feet and sprinted along the wall toward where he last saw Sahira. The spiders swarming between them blocked his view and made it impossible for him to see her clearly.

When he was free of the spiders trying to entrap him, he sprinted away from the wall and ran down the center of the beasts toward the web. He had to know she was safe, but as he ran, the scent of smoke drifted to him, and his stomach sank.

I have to get to her. If something happens to her….

He couldn't finish the thought as it caused panic to claw at his chest and his ears to ring. He'd fucked up with her; that had never been more abundantly clear than now, but he needed a chance to fix it.

For that to happen, they all had to survive.

He had no idea what was happening to cause the smoke, but it couldn't be good as he suspected it meant Sahira was now exposed to these things too. Trying to avoid the spiders encircling fifty feet ahead, Zeth stumbled into Orin's path.

The demon lifted another spider and smashed it off the ground so hard the legs exploded off it. Another spider crashed into Zeth's leg and nearly knocked him over; with some fancy moves, he avoided going down, but more scampered toward him.

Orin was almost to the demon when a spider launched onto Zeth's back. The demon staggered back as the creature's claws sliced into his shoulders.

The demon bellowed as he crashed into a wall. He leaned forward again and bashed the spider against the mountain. Stones broke free and tumbled around the demon.

Black blood burst from the sides of this thing as Zeth squished it against the rocks. The other spiders screeched as they swarmed toward the demon.

He should run around the demon and leave him to deal with these things while he went for Sahira. It was what *all* his instincts told him to do... except *one*.

He had no idea where that one, traitorous, far-too-kind-for-him instinct came from or how it clamored louder than *all* the others, but it screamed at him to help.

What about Sahira?

As he thought it, the spiders parted enough to give him a glimpse of her. For some reason, the monsters were holding back from her. He had no idea what she'd done to establish that, probably conjured another spell, but for now, she was safe.

That might not last, and if he helped Zeth, it could spell her demise. But he didn't have to help for long; the demon could take care of himself, and if he couldn't free himself after Orin's assistance, so be it.

Lowering his shoulder, Orin crashed into a spider and sent it flying into another one of its brethren. Alerted to his presence, another spun toward him and lifted its claw.

Orin grasped the claw and bent downward and up, pulling it toward the spider's middle. He caught the edge of the mouth in its belly and yanked upward.

The spider shrieked as it reeled backward, slicing itself open further with its movements. Orin ducked the next claw flying toward his head as he climbed the back of another spider.

The thousands of bristly black hairs covering it were prickly against his palms and made them itch, but he ignored the discomfort as he lifted his dagger and jammed it into the thing's skull. The spider sank its fangs into Zeth's shoulder a second before he stabbed it.

Spider legs kicked and spasmed as Zeth gripped its head and pried its fangs from his shoulder before flipping it to the side. Orin rode the spider to the ground before jumping off.

When more spiders swarmed them, he grasped the demon, yanked him back, and drew the shadows around them.

It wasn't much of a disguise considering the spiders knew where Zeth stood. He shoved the demon's head down and pointed for him to go low as the spiders charged.

There wasn't much room between the spiders' abdomens and the ground to crawl under, but these creatures wouldn't expect them to be closer to the ground. It could give them a chance to get out of this.

Orin plastered himself against the cool rock and between the legs of one spider as it crawled over him. Lifting his dagger, he drove it straight through the spider's heart.

When the creature started screaming, he braced his legs on the ground, lifted it, and threw the thing at the wall. As the others came for him, he rolled away from the crush pushing toward the wall.

When he rose again, Zeth was standing beside him. While separated by the spiders, the shadows had fallen away from the demon, but Orin drew them around Zeth again as the scent of smoke intensified.

When the spiders released a screech and spun toward the web, Orin knew he didn't have to worry about himself or the demon anymore. The spiders had become fixated on a new enemy... Sahira.

No! Orin wanted to get to and protect her, but the spiders had formed a wall between them.

CHAPTER SIXTY-NINE

SAHIRA PLACED the flames of her makeshift torch to the strands of webbing while holding her palm near the fire. Focused on the blaze, its heat warmed her cheeks and hand as the power in the flames, the air, and the earth beneath her feet fueled her abilities.

"Flames of fire soar ever higher. Let the air bring you there."

Lifting her palm, she pushed the fire upward as her powers and air increased the flames. Smoke choked the air as fire flowed over the webbing, crackled across the thick filaments, and covered the strands until she couldn't see what lay beneath the blaze.

The noise grew so overwhelming that, only a few feet away from her, Sahira couldn't hear what Elsa recited before she lifted her hand too. More flames surged across the webbing and up the towering structure.

Buried beneath the flames and smoke, Sahira couldn't tell if the fire affected the web. She hoped the loud crackling meant the fire was devouring this thing while sparks rained around her.

As the inferno climbed higher, the spiders started their awful, hissing scream again. She didn't have to see the creatures to know they were now the focus of their fury.

The flames on her shirt started sputtering; there wasn't much material left to fuel the fire. Taking a deep breath and working to keep her hand steady, she lifted the shirt she'd draped over her shoulder in preparation for this.

It was the last shirt she had with her for this trip. Once it went up in flames, she'd have only the shirt on her back to get her through the rest of the way, but she'd burn it too, if necessary.

Biting her lip, Sahira braced herself for what she had to do. *This is going to hurt.*

With that knowledge blazing through her mind, she didn't hesitate before wrapping the newest shirt around the dagger. The fire leapt and danced as it sought to engulf the clothing. She was careful not to smother the flames while also giving them a chance to set the new shirt ablaze.

Unable to keep her hand from the flames, blisters bubbled across her skin as her flesh peeled away and sloughed to the side. When her skin crackled beneath the heat, she gritted her teeth to keep from crying out as the fire devoured more than her clothes.

Sweat beaded her forehead before sliding into her eyes. The beads of it hanging on her lashes made the world a little blurry as her entire body trembled from the onslaught of damage she continued to inflict on it.

She yanked her hand away when she finally finished adding new kindling to the flames. She couldn't look at the burnt mess she created as her teeth pulsed in rhythm with the blisters pulsating on her hand.

It felt like something had chewed her hand to the bone, and all the skin peeled away, but if there was pain, then she still had nerve endings. She wasn't sure how much longer she'd have them as she had two pairs of pants to burn too.

"We have a problem!" Pip called, her small voice barely carrying over the crackle of the flames.

The urgency in the brownie's voice caused the hair on Sahira's nape to rise, but she kept her focus on the fire. With her palm near the flames, she repeated the spell and lifted her hand for air to fuel the fire.

When she finished, she looked back toward the spiders. Her stomach plummeted into her toes as, in unison, those monsters crept toward them.

The brownies backed toward her and Elsa as the creatures closed in on them. Pip extended her dagger as her expression became one of steely determination. Those spiders could destroy the tiny immortals with one swipe of their claws, but none of them backed down.

Dozens of red, beady eyes shone with rage, and hunger pulsated from the creatures as drops of venom, or whatever it was, plopped onto the ground. Their claws clicked against the stony ground when they clambered closer.

That incessant clicking hammered into her head until her right eye twitched with each bang. The fire reflecting in their eyes created bursts of orange in their red depths, but amid the flames, she spotted herself in some of the shiny orbs.

Sahira yearned to back away from the death creeping toward them, but the fiery web at her back blocked her retreat. They had no choice but to stand and fight against these things as her shirt clung to her while sweat poured down her nape.

When the spiders were only fifteen feet away, their steps slowed. Their claws stopped clicking as some of their heads tilted up, and ashes fell around them.

Sahira's hand constricted around her dagger, but she didn't pull the torch away from the web. If they came any closer, she would require a weapon and might have to remove her blade from the fire.

Their hesitation told her they didn't like the blaze or didn't know what it was. It could be a powerful weapon against them, but she still hesitated to remove her shirt from the conflagration.

Glancing up again, she blinked away the sweat coating her

lashes as she used her good hand to block the sparks from falling onto her face. But it wasn't just sparks drifting around her anymore….

Sahira's heart leapt when she realized parts of the web were also floating through the air as burning filaments descended to earth. Most disintegrated before hitting the ground, but some fell at her feet and onto her.

She slapped the burning pieces of the shirt she wore before they set fire to it. She held back tears when the fine filament disintegrated beneath her hands. *Finally,* something was going somewhat right for them.

Glancing at the burning web, she tried to see how much damage it had sustained, but it was impossible to tell with the fire raging above. It was falling apart; she was sure of it, but how long it would take to collapse remained a mystery.

The clatter of Orin's sword breaking free and hitting the ground was confirmation of this. And as the spiders continued to hang back, she realized they had a new weapon against them.

If they didn't come to the fire, she would bring it to them.

CHAPTER SEVENTY

"Elsa, keep your flames on the web!" she shouted to be heard over the increasing cacophony of the fire.

"I will!"

Sahira pulled her makeshift torch away from the webbing. She ignored the throbbing in her hand and the inward scream of her soul as it protested what she was about to do... again.

Removing one of the two pants still draped over her shoulder, she placed them over the flames rising from her dagger. Her brutalized skin sizzled more as her old blisters burst while new ones formed.

She left enough room to ensure she didn't smother the flames before encircling the pant legs around the dagger. It took a couple of seconds for the clothing to catch. In those heartbeats, the spiders crept a little closer but stopped when the pants started burning too.

The throbbing in her hand intensified from this fresh onslaught of fire, but she ignored it as she ran toward the spiders with her dagger aimed out as sparks and webbing cascaded around her. She didn't pause to think she could be running toward her death; she only sought to buy Elsa more time to destroy more of the web.

Some held their ground as she rushed toward the spiders, but most backed away from the flames. She was almost to the creatures when one of them collapsed and black blood exploded from its head.

The shadows melted away to reveal Orin kneeling on the creature's head. He yanked his dagger free.

Orin stabbed the dying spider again and rode it to the ground before jumping off. Before she could blink, he enshrouded himself in shadows again and disappeared.

To her right, Zeth grabbed one of the creatures by its back legs, lifted it off the ground, and bashed it down. Distracted by the deadly threat of Orin and Zeth, the spiders didn't pay as much attention to her.

When the spider closest to her shifted its attention to Zeth, Sahira lunged toward it. She had no idea what would happen and had a good chance of getting eviscerated, but she had to know if they could use fire as a weapon against these things.

Before the spider could see the flames coming, she pressed the burning pants against its side. A popping sound issued from its flesh, and the spider released a piercing shriek that caused her to wince as it rebounded in her ears.

Its scream grew louder when the thousands of black hairs covering it erupted into flames that raced around its body. Those hairs acted like a propellant that soon engulfed the creature in fire.

Unprepared for how fast the flames caught on it, Sahira gawked as the spider scurried away with a trail of fire whipping off its ass. Its claws clicked while it ran toward the web; it collapsed before arriving at it.

With hope and excitement pulsing through her, Sahira raced toward the next spider. It wheeled backward to evade the torch she thrust at it, but the creature wasn't fast enough.

Its screams, and those of its friends scampering out of the way, filled the air while it tried to get away from the blaze encasing it. Sahira spun toward the other spiders who had originally crept closer to her; they all backed away as they prepared to flee.

They had these things on the run, and she wouldn't let up. Smiling grimly, Sahira advanced on the spiders as they retreated.

In their haste to evade her, some crashed into each other and staggered back. Their united front vanished as death approached, and Elsa's flames spread higher through the web.

The heat of the fire and the light surrounding them grew when the flames spread across the web. Shadows danced over the land as the blaze crisscrossed the intricate pattern; thick filaments collapsed and floated around them.

Instead of being hunted, they were the hunters as the spiders sought to flee. Some managed to scamper into the shadows and up the smooth face of the cliffs. Their claws dug into the rocks as they easily hoisted themselves up.

Some failed to get away as they fell beneath Orin and Zeth's wrath. The shadows faded, and Orin materialized as he darted between two spiders; he sliced their legs out from under them while Zeth kicked the claw off another.

Removing the last pair of pants from her shoulder, Sahira draped them over her dagger and pleaded with Hecate for it to be enough to destroy more of these things.

When she stuck her hand back over the fire, what little remained of her flesh peeled away to expose the muscle and ligament beneath. Some of the throbbing in her hand eased as the fire finally destroyed her nerves.

She'd burned herself so badly she'd stopped feeling the flames devouring her. It also made moving the pants around more difficult as the sensation of the material against her fingers was gone.

Trying to control her frustration over her awkward movements, Sahira worked to get the pants in place. She didn't know if the lack of pain was better or worse, but once she started to heal, it would hurt like a bitch... *if* she got the opportunity to heal.

Finally succeeding in getting the pants to catch fire, she charged at the spiders, slowed by Orin and Zeth or their own inability to get out of the way in time. With a scream born of murderous intent, she ran at the creatures.

Swinging the flaming dagger, she caught one in the side and then another. It didn't take much to get these fuckers to burn, and she relished watching them do so.

She'd always been a nature lover and caretaker for all creatures. As a witch, she had a close bond with all living things, from plants to insects.

She'd always gone out of her way not to kill or harm things, but she felt no regret as first one spider, then another, erupted into flames. Some of the spiders she set on fire managed to scamper back into the web. Once there, they spread the fire further as their flames devoured their home.

When some smoke cleared from the already burnt areas, she saw the conflagration had moved well beyond Elsa's fire. With the smaller spiders spreading the flames across the web, it was only a matter of time before the blaze reached the big bitch in the upper corner.

Sahira smiled over this as another spider tried and failed to escape her wrath. It reeled back onto its hind legs, exposing the hideous mouth beneath. As it did, Sahira jammed the flames into the gaping maw.

The spider flipped over; its feet kicked in the air, and its claws swung wildly while it tried to right itself, but it was too late. She set another one on fire before the flames at the end of her dagger started sputtering.

She didn't have much time before she lost her best weapon

against these things. Sensing this, a couple of creatures slowed in their backward retreat.

"We can get through the webbing!" Elsa shouted.

Sahira turned toward her as the enormous, mommy spider leapt from the web. The earth shook when it hit the ground and rocks tumbled free of the cliffs. They rattled and pinged off the walls as they fell.

CHAPTER SEVENTY-ONE

THE GROUND QUAKED beneath Orin's feet when the big bitch of a spider landed. The big twat was so ugly she made all the others look like beauty queens.

It rose to its full height, which was at least ten feet tall. The hooked claws on its front legs were easily three feet long; it tapped one off the ground as it gazed at each of them, trying to decide who to go after first.

Its gaze focused on Sahira as she held her sputtering flame before her and backed toward the disintegrating web. The reflection of fire shining in its eyes made it look like a blaze was inside them.

Its fangs nearly touched the ground as its claw click, click, clicked in a steady rhythm against the rocks. If Zeth's sluggish movements and increasingly green hue to his black skin were any indication, the liquid beads dripping from those fangs were poison filled.

Finally free of the spiders surrounding him, the demon staggered toward Orin before falling to a knee. He bent his head and rested his fist on the ground before lifting his gaze to Orin's.

In his yellow eyes, Orin saw the truth; Zeth didn't expect to leave here alive. He didn't know how to feel about that as he drew the shadows around him.

When Orin first arrived in the Cursed Realm, he was indifferent to the demon, who mostly kept to himself. But when Sahira arrived, he saw the demon as competition for her and disliked the man.

When he learned she'd fed from Zeth, Orin wanted to kill the demon but didn't because he couldn't let his emotions gain control of him like that. He wasn't a *lycan*.

He'd often envisioned tearing the demon's head off, but once Sahira told him Zeth was married with a child, and they never had sex, he'd come to see the demon as an ally in this land. He was strong, powerful, determined to escape, and would help Orin get Sahira through this.

Unlike many of his brethren, Zeth remained more level-headed, probably because he had a wife and child to return to. He wasn't brash, irrational, and prone to violence.

Orin respected this more-controlled aspect of the demon as the dark fae were often more reserved and in control of their emotions. He'd always been completely rational... until the witch.

She'd rattled him, and while he didn't like it, he couldn't deny she'd changed something inside him. His gaze flicked to Sahira as her flames dwindled while the fire behind her raged.

The spiders maintained their distance as she backed toward the burning web. Her fire might be going out, but the web was building into an inferno that scared the rest of the monsters.

He could leave the demon behind; it was his right to do so, survival of the fittest and all. He'd always put his life above most others, but he hesitated to leave Zeth.

Before Sahira, he wouldn't have thought twice about letting the demon die. Now, a conscience, that he'd never known he possessed, raised its ugly head and started sputtering nonsense about saving the man.

What the fuck?

He wasn't sure if this new development was good or bad, but he didn't like it. And because of it, he would have to risk his life to help another, so it must be bad.

But there was Sahira, and she would be upset if he left the demon to die. However, conscience or not, ally or not, he'd throw the demon aside to save her.

He didn't have to worry, as Sahira had moved close enough to the burning web that the spiders stayed far away from her. She could also use those flames against the big bitch if she tried anything.

Sahira was as safe as she could get in this place, and the spiders were closing in on the demon. He was going to have to save Zeth's ass again.

With the shadows encased securely around him, Orin raced toward Zeth as a spider shot some webbing at him. It hit the demon in the side.

Zeth grasped the filament and tried to tear it free, but he was too weak, or it was too strong. The demon's razor-sharp claws should cut through the webbing; the fact they didn't, confirmed the demon's weakness as the spider started dragging Zeth toward it.

Adjusting his hold on his dagger, Orin sprinted faster and jumped onto the spider's back before it could pull Zeth beneath it. He plunged his blade into the tail end of the thing's ass and sliced across it.

With deft movements, he cut away the spider's ability to make more of the sticky web while freeing Zeth. He didn't bother finishing off the thing as the other spiders closed in on them.

He had to get the demon away from here and closer to the flames where he would be safer from the spiders looking to eat him. Sliding off the spider, he sprinted toward Zeth as another creature, encased in fire, raced past them. Its piercing screams alerted Orin that things had become far quieter since most of the spiders retreated.

The flames continued to roar, but the spider's screams subsided while they watched their home and relatives burn. Some of them hovered feet away from the demon, but most had retreated toward the cliffs and that big bitch.

Orin kept the shadows around him as he skidded to a halt beside the demon. By the time he reached the man, Zeth had gotten to his knees. With his head bent forward, sweat dripped from Zeth's brow to plop on the ground.

He looked like death, and when he slumped to the side, Orin thought he might be.

CHAPTER SEVENTY-TWO

STEPPING on the web still connected to the demon's side, Orin used his dagger to separate Zeth from the spider's ass. The webbing clung to his boot, refusing to come free until he kicked off his boot and yanked his dagger free of the sticky substance.

Once they were free, he slid his arm under the demon's and lifted him off the ground. The man was a heavy, dead weight as he leaned against Orin's side. His weight pulled on Orin's wounded arm, but he didn't say anything or release him like he should.

Orin ignored the flare of discomfort from his injury as, shifting his hold on the demon, he draped Zeth's arm around his shoulders before drawing the shadows around them. Zeth's feet dragged across the ground as Orin ran toward Sahira and Elsa.

Why am I doing this? Orin pondered as Zeth's weight pulled at his shoulders. If the spiders started swarming again, or mama web-slinger decided to charge Sahira, he'd drop the demon.

He told himself this, but as Zeth hindered his progress, he kept dragging him. Orin cursed himself and his conscience as a newfound weakness that might get him killed if he wasn't careful.

As he ran, the coldness of the rocks seeped through his sock, but it did nothing to cool him as the conflagration heated the night. Sweat dripped from his brow, slid down his face, and cleaved his clothes to him while he raced toward the blaze.

Standing before the fire, Sahira and Elsa came in and out of sight as smoke choked the air around them. When Sahira vanished from view again, his heart lurched, and he pushed himself faster.

I have to get to her.

The sparks bouncing off his flesh left welts where they burned him. They singed his clothes and skin and smoldered longer than he would have liked before going out, but with one arm around the demon and his other hand gripping the dagger, he couldn't slap away the sparks.

When he made it to the two witches, he briefly let the shadows fall. Sahira and Elsa took startled steps back as he exposed himself and the demon to them.

At their feet, the brownies thrust out their tiny swords before realizing it was him. They lowered their weapons and dismantled their tower.

Sahira's mouth parted as hope and relief burned in her eyes. She stretched a hand toward him before letting it fall to her side.

Her customary bun had come loose to dangle against her nape, and hair clung to her sweaty, flushed cheeks. Despite the soot and sweat covering Sahira's face, she was still incredibly beautiful, and he had to get her out of here.

"Come closer," he commanded as he shifted his hold on the demon and bent to retrieve his sword from where it had fallen.

Pip climbed swiftly up to sit on his shoulder while the other two found a perch on Elsa and Sahira. When they all gathered closer to him, he pulled the shadows around them.

He glanced back at the spiders gathered away from the flames and close to the cliffs. Some had perched like they were about to spring off the cliffs and come after them, but none moved.

He didn't know how long the fire would keep them away. He'd prefer to go after that giant one and kill it before they left, as he had a feeling the rest would fall or scatter once it was dead, but they had to get the demon out of here.

They also couldn't take the chance the fire would burn out before he succeeded in destroying that monstrous beast. Or that he was wrong and, even with her gone, the others would be more vicious.

He hated retreating while leaving any enemies standing but didn't have a choice. They had to go before the fire burned out, and these ugly, eight-legged beasts followed them.

If the creatures decided to pursue them, they should lose what remained of the spiders if he kept them all cloaked in shadows. Orin didn't know how likely pursuit was, considering they'd destroyed the spiders' home and many of their friends; they'd probably think twice before coming after them, but if they did, they would pay.

Sahira draped the demon's other arm around her shoulders and winced before lifting her chin. Orin frowned over her reaction and looked down to see the destruction of her hand.

An unexpected, hot rage rushed through him, and he almost released the demon to charge the massive spider. He'd gut that bitch alive and hack off each of her legs for this.

But as he contemplated it, the momentary lack of control slipped away, and the calculating reasoning of the dark fae returned. He'd put her in more danger if he ran back at that thing and took the shadows with him.

Yes, he'd love to hack that monster to pieces and savor watching it fall, but it was far more important to get Sahira out of here. Inhaling and exhaling slowly, he managed to further subdue his fury before turning toward the web.

Thuds vibrated the ground as the bodies of the spiders'

victims started falling from the web and hitting the earth. Some might still be alive, but Orin wasn't stopping to check.

Locked securely in the shadows, nothing could see them, but they all saw each other. Together, the seven of them jogged beneath the burning web as bits of it rained down on them while fiery strands of webbing floated to the ground.

He ignored the burning sting of the sparks and filament against his nape while they ran as fast as they could beneath the inferno and away from the monsters seeking to eat them.

CHAPTER SEVENTY-THREE

THEY'D ONLY GONE a couple of miles before Sahira said, "We have to stop."

"We can't," Orin said from between his teeth.

With the demon draped around his shoulders and Zeth's increasing inability to help maneuver him, it was difficult for Orin to look back, but he knew they hadn't traveled far enough to stop safely.

"We have to," she insisted. "Orin…."

The pleading in her voice caught his attention; Sahira didn't grovel for anything. His hand squeezed Zeth's increasingly cooler wrist before he looked at her.

The second their eyes met, he knew he'd made a bad choice. The pleading and desperation in her gaze tugged at a heart once cold as ice; she'd thawed parts of it.

And those parts were leading to bad decisions.

"We have to do something about the poison," she said.

He released the shadows obscuring them. They were far enough away from the spiders not to need them anymore, but he'd like to get a lot farther… soon.

"I don't think we can do anything," he told her.

When her jaw set and her eyes narrowed, he inwardly groaned. They didn't have time for this fight, and it was one he wouldn't win if she decided to refuse to move... which she did five seconds later when she planted her feet on the ground like a recalcitrant horse.

Jerked to a halt, Zeth hung awkwardly between them. Orin considered pulling him like a wishbone to see if Sahira would cave, but he hadn't risked his ass for the demon to rip him in two now.

He glowered at Sahira as he released Zeth and helped the demon sag to the ground. When he stretched out his wounded arm, the skin around it pulled a little, but the gash was already healing, and it had stopped bleeding.

"If you can't do anything by the time I'm back, we're leaving," he stated.

Sahira chose to ignore him as she knelt at Zeth's side. The demon wouldn't make it, but she wasn't ready to hear the truth.

And when the demon died, which was likely coming soon, they'd have to stop again to get rid of the body. He'd discovered a bit of a conscience but wasn't about to carry a dead body with them.

She'd fight it, and she would lose. No way was he letting the dead get in his way.

Orin turned to study the terrain they'd covered since fleeing the spiders. The area between the mountains remained much wider here than before they encountered the spiders' giant web.

The mountains faded as their black rock became interspersed with more flat land and dirt. Trees and grass were also sprouting up more often.

The trees were small and sparse, but unlike the ones in Belda's town with their barren limbs, these had red leaves on them. Orin didn't take this sign of life as a good one; he'd been here too long to believe anything good about this place, but he appreciated not having to climb mountains or being squished between them anymore.

What little remained of the mountains wasn't big enough to hide the spiders that could be stalking them, but he didn't trust the monsters to have given up the hunt. They'd torched their home and slaughtered some of their kin, friends, or whatever they were.

That big bitch had been pissed, but it didn't seem they were following. Perhaps fear, and the need to repair their home, had kept them at bay; he wasn't taking the chance it hadn't.

Those things could be back there somewhere, waiting for their chance to attack again.

"I'll be back." He nudged Pip with his finger. "You should get down."

She yawned as she scrambled from his shoulder and settled on the ground. Before anyone could ask where he was going, he encased himself in shadows and ran down the path.

As he sprinted, the mountains rose to surround him again. They weren't anywhere near as thick or obstructive as they were before they encountered the spiders, but they blocked his view more.

He kept his breathing steady while running so he could hear the slightest hint of claws or legs scraping against rock. His gaze ran over the stones rising from the earth to tower over him, but no shadows shifted or stirred up there.

He traversed a mile before slowing to a stop. If the spiders had decided to track them, they would be at this point by now.

He searched the rocks while straining to hear anything to indicate the spiders had pursued them. He didn't know if that bitch's need for vengeance would propel the spiders to follow or if the fire would keep them away.

Those monsters had probably never encountered an adversary who caused them any damage before. He doubted they knew how to handle it.

Those spiders were apex predators, but even apex predators hesitated when encountering something bigger and worse. And he would do much worse if those things followed.

But, for now, the spiders had decided to stay away. And if they did regroup and hunt them, they now had trees and more kindling to make the bastards regret their piss-poor choice.

Satisfied they would have a break from the spiders, he turned and raced back toward the others. They had some time, but not much; he'd learned this realm didn't give much of a reprieve when it came to the things that could kill them.

They had to get moving *now*. It would take some doing to get Sahira and the others to leave Zeth behind, but he'd make it happen.

When he was only a hundred feet away, he rounded a bend in the path, and the others came back into view. They all remained at Zeth's side as Sahira leaned over him.

It wasn't until he was nearly on top of them that he realized Sahira had her mouth against Zeth's neck. The white-hot poker of fury stabbing into his stomach and twisting deeper made him forget all about the discomforts of his body as he focused solely on *them*.

CHAPTER SEVENTY-FOUR

SAHIRA LEANED AWAY from the demon and spat something out before bending over Zeth again. She wasn't feeding on the demon; there was nothing intimate in her actions, but jealousy battered Orin like rapid punches to the gut.

The breathing he'd kept steady while running became labored and hectic when he forgot to concentrate on it. His nails dug into his palms as he stalked toward her, determined to yank her away from the demon.

He started to yell at her to stop when she lifted her mouth from the demon's neck and spat yellow bile across the ground. *She's sucking the poison from him.*

Orin halted a few feet away from them. He tried to get control of the tumult of emotions battering him but didn't know where to start or how to handle this influx.

Did he tear her away and drag her from the man? She'd hate him, he had no doubt, and she'd fight him every step of the way, but when she bent to sink her fangs into the demon's vein again, everything inside him spun.

He was a *dark fae*. His emotions didn't rule him… but that was no longer true.

They *did* rule him when it came to *her*.

She'd brought out more emotion in him than anyone else before, including his family, and as much as he hated it, he couldn't stop it. When it came to her, he was as explosive as the lycans, a breed he'd always disdained for their volatile temperaments.

What has she done to me? But while he lamented what he was becoming, concern rose to the forefront of the tumult assaulting him.

"What are you doing?" he demanded. "That could poison *you*."

Sahira glanced at him. "It needs to be injected into your bloodstream for that."

"You *can't* know that."

She couldn't know it, but she chose to ignore his words as she bent her mouth to Zeth's neck and bit deep. When he stepped toward her, she held up a hand.

Their gazes locked as she tried to draw the poison from Zeth. If he yanked her away from the demon, that would be the end.

He'd done some pretty shitty things to her, but they could still fight and fuck. If he tried to take her from her friend, he'd sever whatever strange connection simmered between them for good.

And as much as he hated what he was becoming, what *she* was turning him into, he couldn't do that. It would probably be best for them both if he did, but he refused to lose her.

But she doesn't know what's good for her and needs to be protected. She could be poisoning herself right now.

Still, he didn't move as she spat more venom across the ground. While he watched, a truth rose inside him.

He was many things, but a liar wasn't one of them, and he was finally seeing things for what they were. Sure, he liked to play games and twist things to his benefit, but he was always honest with himself.

It wasn't only the possibility of poisoning herself that concerned him; he didn't want her doing this because he didn't like her touching the demon. She really was *his*.

The horrible, newly awakened emotion of jealousy rattled him again as it took him to darker places than he'd ever been before, and he'd been to some *really* sinister places. It clawed at his insides while Sahira worked to rid Zeth of the poison ravaging his system.

With his nails digging back the flesh from his palms and blood welling inside his closed hands, he recalled his words to her in the bathroom. *What does it matter who I fuck?*

He'd demanded an answer to his question, all while knowing she never had sex with the demon. She'd revealed her truth to him, but he'd kept his to himself.

She didn't know he'd never been with the nymph or anyone else since she arrived in the Cursed Realm. He'd demanded an answer from her for something that hadn't happened, and she'd refused to give him what he sought... confirmation she might care for him too.

But she had no way of knowing that's what he sought, and maybe she hadn't replied how he wanted because she didn't know how to put it into words... like him. But standing here, he was given his answer as to why she cared about the nymph and those other women.

This horrible, useless, acidic rot of an emotion clawing at his insides over something as innocent as her trying to save the demon was *why* it mattered. If she'd experienced a quarter of this jealousy churning within her when she saw him with the nymph, no wonder she wouldn't let it go.

Am I actually empathizing with someone else?

What is wrong *with me? What did she* do *to me?*

But he couldn't deny it anymore. She meant something to him, he cared for her, and she was *his*, except... for her to be so, then he would have to...

What? What would he have to do or *become*?

Orin didn't know the answer and had no idea how to navigate any of this. Thrown into a stormy ocean, he was clawing at the water, trying to break free of the surface so he could breathe again, but on the verge of drowning.

One thing was certain; he wasn't a quitter. He'd get through this just as he had everything else in his life.

He'd survived his father's death... a death caused by *his* actions. That guilt and heartbreak would never leave him, but he'd learned how to handle them, mostly by trying not to think about it.

He'd endured the loss of his brothers and the severing of his relationship with Cole and Brokk until they mended those bridges. *This* uncertainty was nothing compared to all those things.

But what if seeing me with those other women didn't make her feel like this? What if this is just me?

This unfamiliar doubt plaguing him caused his teeth to grind together as some of the welling blood dripped from his palms to hit the ground. She *had* to have felt this too; she wouldn't still be so angry and bitter about his actions with those women if she hadn't.

And he would have to tell her the truth. He inwardly groaned while rebelling against the prospect of revealing so much to her.

He didn't owe her, or anyone else, any explanations... but he did.

Even he could admit that. If seeing this made him want to bash the demon's face in with his one remaining boot, what would he do if he saw her sitting on another man's lap?

The idea of it caused more blood to hit the ground. He had no doubt he'd kill that man.

Sahira spat out more poison as Elsa dug through her pack with one hand. When she removed her jar of salve, he saw she'd badly burned one of her hands too.

As she fumbled to remove the top, Orin knelt and took it from her. After he opened it, Pip dipped her hand into the salve and scooped out a small glob.

Her brown eyes met his as she nodded to Sahira. "I'll take care of Elsa; you help Sahira."

Orin dipped his fingers into the cool, white cream. Turning, he shoved aside his jealousy as Sahira sucked more poison from Zeth.

He tenderly clasped her hand and tried not to wince at the lack of skin covering the red, swollen, and burnt muscles beneath his palms. Ever so carefully, he dabbed on the salve.

Their eyes briefly met when she lifted her head from Zeth's throat again. Confusion and sadness shone in her gaze before she turned away and spat more venom across the ground.

CHAPTER SEVENTY-FIVE

ZETH'S HEAD REMAINED BOWED, but he was walking better since Sahira sucked as much of the venom as she could from him. By the end, she was spitting blood instead of yellow bile across the stones.

Venom still mixed a little with his blood, but she couldn't weaken him further by taking more, and she had to hope she'd gotten out enough for his body to fight off the rest. Zeth still leaned heavily on her and Orin but was lifting his feet again, and the green hue had faded from his black skin.

The sun was setting on the open field of grass and trees they walked through when the faint outline of something came into view. She studied the vague images against the pink and orange twilight sky as she tried to ascertain if it was real or not.

Clasping Zeth's wrist tighter, Sahira looked around him to Orin. His eyes remained straight ahead as his shoulders bent beneath Zeth's weight.

She wasn't entirely sure who she was looking at anymore when it came to him. Despite her every intention not to analyze or look too deep into it, she kept seeing the care in his gaze while he tenderly applied the salve to her hand.

He'd been so gentle and nurturing, two things she never believed Orin could be, but there he was, taking care of her. And not only that, but he'd done it without any quips or innuendo that she now owed him.

He hadn't issued any smart remarks that would have ruined the moment. It probably would have been better for her if he had because she felt her heart softening toward him again.

This man was such a dangerous enigma, but he kept drawing her back in with his contradictory and infuriating ways. It might be what ended up destroying her.

Lifting her hand, she studied the healing flesh. It throbbed with every beat of her heart, which meant the nerve endings were healing.

More pain was soon to come as it healed further, but the reddened flesh forming over her damaged muscles looked healthier than the charred remnants attached to her before. She recalled Maverick, with his crisp-fried body and the agony he must have endured after surviving the fire.

She'd only badly burned one hand; his entire body had been burnt to a crisp. But he was doing well now... or at least he was the last time she saw him. He and everyone she loved could all be dead now.

Sahira pulled herself from thoughts of her friends and loved ones. Getting lost in the sorrow of being separated from them wouldn't help. She had to remain focused on trying to escape and surviving.

Lowering her hand, she glanced at Orin again. She resisted a smile as she took in his handsome profile and the determination etching his features.

It was treacherous to start feeling anything other than wariness and dislike for him, but he had a way of battering her defenses into little more than rubble. He also had a way of making them become a brick wall... like by declaring she was his in a bathroom.

Asshole.

As the word crossed her mind, she knew it wasn't entirely true. Yes, he was a jerk; *no one* would deny that, but he was also changing, or at least he seemed to be.

She could also be trying to see something in him that wasn't there. However, his actions said something was different about him.

Instead of leaving Zeth, he'd returned to help a man he disliked. He could have easily left Zeth to die; she was sure he'd left many others behind to save his ass, but he hadn't left the demon.

Why?

She wasn't sure about the answer. He'd left the safety of the pub behind to help her against the scarog beetles, but he felt a sense of family duty toward her and also trying to have sex with her at the time.

Orin had been determined to win that game of his and couldn't screw someone who was dead. He'd won and moved on, yet he continued to help her.

She could attribute that to his sense of duty to family, and she was also the only one who would feed him by screwing him out here, but he didn't have *any* of those reasons for saving Zeth.

She couldn't be certain, but something about the Cursed Realm was changing Orin. Yes, he'd told Elsa he'd kill her, and Sahira had no doubt he would do it to survive, but Orin also told *her* that he'd choose her life over anyone else's.

She was beginning to think that might be true.

It wasn't something she would have believed possible a few short weeks ago; she did now. He was still cold-hearted and always would be, at least on some level, but something had changed with him.

Being trapped in the Cursed Realm hadn't humbled him. She didn't think anything could *ever* do that, but the changes in him were taking shape and becoming more prevalent. She couldn't deny it anymore.

She didn't know what it meant for him or *them,* but she couldn't deny how much she'd come to care for him. Yes, he enraged her, and there were days when she loathed him more than she'd ever believed it possible to hate someone, but there were also times, like now, when she stood on the precipice of falling in love with him.

If this continued, it would result in a broken heart for her; she was sure of it. But despite her determination to keep him at a distance, he'd broken through her barriers. And she'd come to care for him more than any other man who'd walked through her life.

How can that be possible?

Feelings were never really involved in any of her past dealings with men. She liked some of them and spent more time with them, but most were simply a fling, and she was okay with that.

She was immortal; she had plenty of time to find someone to love… if she ever decided to do so. Until then, she was content to keep the party going, or at least until Lexi entered her life.

Things changed for the better after that, but the party aspect of her life screeched to a halt. She could continue the party now, but after helping to raise Lexi, it was far from a priority.

Sahira was sure the same couldn't be said for Orin. He was far from ready to stop his fast-paced, bed-hopping lifestyle; he'd proven that to her with the nymph and the other women who followed.

Sahira glanced at her burnt hand as she recalled his tender touch. At the time, she couldn't feel his fingers moving against her, but she'd seen the care he took.

He doesn't do that with other women.

So what?

It was true; he wasn't like that with other women, even Elsa said so, but what did it matter? So what if he was kinder and more protective of her; he was also manipulative and content to screw any willing woman who crossed his path.

What a messed-up, soul-sucking relationship this was. *Relationship? Are you insane?*

With a shake of her head, she tried to clear her mind of the treacherous notion they could ever be anything more than what they were. She could see herself waiting at home while he went out to do *anyone* else because he would never be faithful.

A life like that would destroy her. No matter how much she'd come to care for him, it could never happen; she wouldn't survive it.

She had no idea what he was becoming or who she was anymore, but she was certain of that much. She also might be stressing about nothing, because she might not have long to live.

There's looking on the bright side of things.

CHAPTER SEVENTY-SIX

FOCUSING her attention on the sun setting behind what she could now tell were distant buildings, Sahira decided not to think about Orin anymore tonight. They had something else to face now.

It was warmer here, and the layers she'd piled on in the mountains now caused her to sweat, but she didn't stop to remove any. She'd far prefer to wait until they knew what lay ahead.

Tall grass brushed her waist and fingertips while they walked. The plant's sweet scent filled her nostrils as it swayed in the breeze drifting across the land. The whispered rustle of the tall blades, while their feathered ends brushed each other, reminded her of waves coasting onto the shore.

Longing pierced her heart as she recalled the peaceful sense of being connected to *all* living things while standing at the sea's edge. She *never* wanted to sit on a sandy beach again but yearned for those waves while the seagulls cawed and the sun glinted off the water.

But that was another place and another time, one she hoped to return to. With a sigh, she focused on the buildings again.

She was still too far away to get a good look at the structures, but she already knew what they were—the same seven structures that formed Belda's town, the brownies' town, and the last one they traveled through.

The sun had nearly set when they arrived at the edge of town and her suspicions were confirmed. Unlike the other places they'd encountered, more tall grass choked the roadway and surrounded the buildings here.

The structures were all located in the same places as the ones in the other towns. Except for the whisper of the wind and the rustle of grass, no noise could be heard, and like all the other places, no wild animals stirred.

Maybe there would be some rodents or something else in the buildings, but the sky remained free of birds, and the small trees didn't house any creatures. She doubted that would change once they got a chance to explore.

As they climbed to the pub's porch, their feet thudded on the steps. The door creaked when Elsa opened it to reveal a completely barren room. There wasn't even a bar in this place.

Sahira frowned as she took in their sparse surroundings. Instead of chandeliers, only a single bulb dangled from the ceiling.

It lit up when Elsa flicked the switch to reveal the thin coat of dust on the floor and walls. The place wasn't filthy, but it could use a cleaning. However, it was far better than sleeping on the ground, out in the open, with Hecate only knew what hunting them.

A single pair of booted prints also tracked their way around the building. The burnt immortal had been here too, but she didn't see any other signs of life.

They stopped in the middle of the floor, and she and Orin lowered Zeth to the ground. The demon sat with his head bent and his hands on his knees.

Sahira rested her hand on his shoulder. "Are you okay?"

"I'm fine, just tired."

Sahira had managed to get most of the poison out of his system but wished she had some dandelions or milk thistle to make a detox tea for him. She'd never seen either of those things in this realm.

"I can take a look around town and see if there's any herbs we can use for a detoxifying tea," she told him.

Orin's eyes narrowed on her; he looked ready to protest, but before he could, Zeth spoke.

"There won't be anything like that here." Zeth waved a hand at the empty pub. "There's grass, but I doubt we'll find much more."

"We don't know that."

"We don't know what we'll find here, but the sun has set, the spiders might still be hunting us, and there could be many things out there looking to destroy us. Don't risk going out there for me. After some rest, I'll feel great again tomorrow."

Sahira debated this as he lifted his head to look at her. He still looked a little greener than normal, but his skin tone was far better, and more life shone in his yellow eyes than a few hours ago.

He *was* doing better, but if that changed, she would go out to see what this town had to offer... if anything.

"It's time to lock this place down," Orin said.

Sahira squeezed Zeth's shoulder before releasing it. She paused to try to open a portal, which again proved useless, before striding to the stairs.

If her hourglass theory was correct, then this should be the last town, and getting out of the Cursed Realm should loom on the horizon, but she wasn't surprised when the portal didn't open. She wasn't even disappointed; she just *existed* in this place now.

She glanced toward the alcove and the symbol but wasn't in the mood to see what was etched into the wall. There was plenty of time to deal with it later.

Her feet were silent on the steps as she ascended to the second floor while Elsa and Orin shuttered the windows and doors downstairs. She went through all the rooms above, closing the shutters and securing them in place with the metal bars.

All the bedrooms here were as barren as the pub below, even her room, which she entered last. Her gaze fell on the trap door hidden perfectly in the center of the floor.

She should check it too, but all she wanted was a shower, to ensure Zeth was okay, and some sleep. The trapdoor would be there in the morning.

She cast a protective spell over the door and, retreating from the room, hurried on toward the bathroom. Much to her dismay, when she turned on the sink, the pipes didn't rattle or thump as unused water surged into them.

Nothing came out of them. Shoulders slumped, and feeling more than a little defeated, Sahira checked the shower to discover the same thing. This town had far less to offer them than any of the others.

Sahira retreated to the balcony and walked along it before descending to the pub. Zeth slept on the floor with a blanket tucked around him.

Lying on his chest, Loth lifted his head to look at her. "His heartbeat is steady. I'll let you know if that changes."

"Thank you," Sahira whispered.

Feeling like she was dragging herself across the ground, she walked to where Orin and Elsa stood in the alcove to the downstairs bathrooms. Orin leaned against the doorway with his arms crossed over his chest as he stared at the symbol. Pip remained on his shoulder.

Before her eyes landed on it, Sahira knew she wouldn't like what she was about to see. The set of Orin's jaw and the irritation he radiated told her that much.

CHAPTER SEVENTY-SEVEN

WHEN SAHIRA ENTERED THE DOORWAY, her gaze fell on the symbol etched into the wall across from her. To either side of the symbol was a bathroom, but she didn't have much hope they'd have water.

This symbol was different than the last one. The figure eight remained, but all the arrows had been removed, and the bottom of the hourglass was completely shaded while the top half was once again empty.

Beside the symbol, the final arrow had joined the two arrows from the previous towns. In the center of the X the first two arrows formed, the last arrow stood straight out. It was the bull's-eye in the middle of the X.

"There's no doubt it's an hourglass now," Orin said.

Sahira shook her head as she tried to understand what was happening. "But what does it mean? There's nothing here, and I still can't open a portal." She tried to transport, but that failed too. "Or transport. What are we supposed to find here?"

She tried to keep the frustration from her voice but couldn't stop it from rising as she finished speaking. It took everything she had not to start beating on the walls while tearing the symbol from them.

"Who knows," Orin said. "These symbols have been nothing but a mindfuck since the beginning."

"We still haven't searched the town," Elsa said. "There could be something here. We'll find out in the morning."

If the spiders don't catch up to us first. Sahira kept that possibility to herself. They already had enough depressing shit to deal with; she wasn't adding to the pile.

"There's no water here either," she said. "At least not in this building."

"We know," Orin said. "We already checked these bathrooms."

Without replying, Sahira retreated to the main room. She shrugged off her spear and sack before setting them on the floor.

Sitting beside them, she used her good hand to dig into her pack and removed her last full water bottle. The others were already empty.

Removing the protective rag wrapped around the bottle, she used her teeth to uncork it before taking a sip and setting it on the floor. She placed the cork on top and slapped it down with her good hand.

Orin sat beside her and dug into his pack. He brought out a water bottle and held it out to her. "You need more than that."

She waved the bottle away. "I'm fine."

"You were close to that fire, and your hand is badly burned; you need more hydration."

"We all do, but there isn't any around here."

"There isn't any *in here*; there could be more outside the building. The grass is growing, which means this place gets rain. There could be a stream behind the buildings, like in Belda's town. We'll find out tomorrow."

"That stream wasn't in the last town. I doubt it exists here."

"Then we'll wait for it to rain. Either way, it doesn't matter; you need more water than that. Now, drink."

He uncorked the bottle and waved it at her. She stared at the bottle and then at him as she realized he was taking care of her again... and doing something he probably wouldn't do for anyone else.

Don't let it get to your head.

But it was too late. It was already in her head and her soul. She didn't understand this man or what was between them, and probably never would, but she couldn't resist him either.

She wanted to tell him to save his water, but her parched throat and chapped lips kept the words trapped. Slowly, she grabbed the bottle, tipped it back, and took a sip.

He started to protest when she held it out to him, but she spoke instead. "I'm not drinking any more, so arguing over this is pointless."

"Stubborn woman."

"You're far more stubborn than me."

"I'm the one putting the water away."

She chuckled because he had a point there. Cradling her wounded hand in her lap, she watched as he removed a blanket from his sack and spread it across the floor.

When he grabbed her bag and pulled it close to him, she started to protest as he dipped his hand inside. It was an invasion of her privacy and space, but she didn't have any arguments left in her.

He removed her blanket and gestured for her to climb onto his. Exhausted and desperate for sleep, Sahira crawled onto it and lay down.

When he draped the blanket over her, she sighed as a feeling of contentment stole through her. She said nothing when he curled up behind her and draped his arm over her waist.

Secure in the warmth and strength he exuded, Sahira closed

her eyes as a feeling of rightness spread through her. This man would most likely tear her heart out, but she couldn't deny it already belonged to him.

CHAPTER SEVENTY-EIGHT

When Sahira stirred early the next morning, Orin let her slip from his arms to rise and pad toward the bathroom. He lay there, listening as the door shut and debating what to do.

After seeing her yesterday with Zeth, he knew he had to tell her there hadn't been anyone but *her* since she arrived in this realm. She deserved that much.

She probably deserved more, but he didn't have that in him. Instead, he could give her this.

It was time.

Pushing himself up, he maneuvered around the demon, whose chest rose and fell steadily. Sound asleep on top of him, Loth snored as he rose and fell in rhythm with Zeth's breaths.

Orin's hands fisted as he made his way toward the alcove; he could do this. He *would* do this, even if he dreaded every second of opening himself in such a way.

He refused to look at the symbol when he stepped into the alcove. It would just piss him off, and he had to remain focused.

A few seconds later, the bathroom door opened and Sahira slipped her small bar of soap into her pocket as she emerged.

They didn't have water, but the soap they brought was at least something.

She came to an abrupt stop when she spotted him. Seeing her like this threw him back to another time of her emerging from a different bathroom in another town.

That encounter hadn't gone well, but things would be different this time. He already knew the answer to the question he asked her before.

Clasping her elbow, he guided her into the other bathroom. They'd designated the one she was in as the pee room, and he wasn't about to talk to her in there.

"I already told you that I'm not having sex in a bathroom," Sahira said as he pushed the door open and guided her inside.

He had to stop cornering her in bathrooms, but he couldn't do this in the main pub area, where they could wake the others. *There's always upstairs.*

Orin discarded the option almost immediately. He wanted this over and done with.

He'd never considered himself a coward. He'd run into countless battles and never hesitated to face anyone trying to kill him, but he was afraid that if he waited to do this, he never would.

Why is telling this woman this one *revelation the most difficult thing I've ever done?*

He had no idea, but his heart raced, his palms were sweaty, and he suddenly felt like he was back on a dragon, soaring over the land and about to fall off. He'd despised riding that dragon.

This was worse.

"I'm not here to have sex with you; I'm just here to talk," he told her.

He turned on the light as he shut the door behind him. Sahira retreated a few steps into the room, where she stood with her arms crossed over her chest. "About what?"

He opened his mouth to speak, but the words stuck in his

throat as they had so many times before. She deserved to know the truth, but the revelation would make him so vulnerable to her. He was more terrified of that than a field full of wendigos and berserkers.

What am I opening myself up to here? How is she going to react to this?

Not good.

He didn't have to be a mind reader to know that, but he also refused to be a coward who continued to hide this from her. He took a deep breath as she gazed at him with warmth and curiosity in her beautiful, amber eyes. The unexpected warmth in her eyes was about to vanish.

"There's been no one else," he stated.

He'd expected the words to come out in a rush, but they were calm and controlled. And once they were out, a weight lifted from his chest. He hadn't known he was carrying that weight until it vanished.

Confusion replaced the tenderness in her gaze. "No one else for what?"

"I haven't been with any other women since you entered the Cursed Realm."

Her brow furrowed as her confusion grew. "I don't understand."

He wasn't surprised by this. "You're the only woman I've had sex with since you arrived here."

She lowered her head and rubbed her temples as she spoke. "I saw you with that nymph, and a parade of other women, after we had sex."

"I didn't fuck them."

"You licked beer off her chest!"

When he shrugged, her nostrils flared. She looked ready to skin him alive, but that wouldn't stop him from making this clear to her.

"And that was all I did with her," he said.

"What are you telling me?"

"I wanted to see how you'd react to seeing me with her; it didn't seem to bother you."

"How I'd *react*?" she sputtered as red flashed through her eyes. "How I'd react!"

He realized he'd said the wrong thing but didn't know what words would make it better. In all his many years and countless experiences, opening up like *this* was a first for him.

He was good at getting women into his bed and making them *very* happy there; what to do with them after wasn't something he'd ever cared about or experienced. That was clear here as he did all the wrong things.

CHAPTER SEVENTY-NINE

"WHAT WAS I supposed to do, charge across the room and pull her off you? Fight her? Or maybe I should have punched *you* in the face like you deserved! Tell me, Orin"—she stomped toward him and thrust her finger into his chest—"what was I supposed to do? Make a fool of myself in front of everyone?

"What would have been the purpose of that? To prove something to *you*? When you, with *your* actions, proved to *me* that you had moved on. When you'd *proved* to me you were exactly what you'd always claimed to be... a dark fae who doesn't care about anyone except himself and his family."

He grasped her finger in the hopes that connecting with her would calm her; it only inflamed her further as she ripped her hand away. "I'm so sick of you and your games! Are you even telling me the truth now?"

"Why would I lie about this?"

"Why! Why? Because that's all you do! Why would you try to make me think you were screwing all those other women? Because you like fucking with me, and this could be another one of your *stupid* games. Who knows how your brain works!"

"Sahira—"

"I can't look at you right now."

She followed this up by bowing her head and shaking it. When she spoke again, her tone was more defeated. "Why are you telling me this?"

"Because you deserve to know."

He realized tears coated her lashes when she met his gaze and blinked rapidly. Hating the sight of those tears and the fact *he* was the cause of them, he took a step toward her. He sought to comfort her but had no idea how to do so.

What have I done?

Telling her was the right choice, but it never should have come to this. He should have told her sooner or better yet... *I never should have set these events into motion in the first place.*

He shouldn't have tried instigating her with that nymph and the other women. He should have been honest with her... and himself.

Whatever this was between them was different than anything he'd ever experienced, and he was completely in over his head. Because of that, he was messing this up when he wanted to make it *right*.

Orin ached to draw her closer and clasp her against his chest, but when he reached for her, she threw out her hand and stumbled back a few steps. "Don't touch me!"

His arms fell limply back to his sides as he tried to explain it to her; it was difficult to do when he didn't understand it. "When I saw you sucking poison out of Zeth, I realized why the idea of me with other women bothered you so much."

Had he really said that? He ran a hand through his hair, tugging at the ends of it as he realized how much he was opening himself up to her.

What am I doing?

But now that he'd started, he couldn't stop. "I understood why you couldn't let the idea of me sleeping with another woman go."

He understood the meaning of someone looking spitting mad as she glowered at him. He was still screwing this up, and his mind spun as he tried to figure out how to fix it, but, with a sinking sensation, he realized he might have messed up too badly to repair it.

"I'm glad you *understand* this because I don't," she retorted. "I don't know why you keep doing these things to me. I'm not a game! I'm a woman, an immortal with *feelings,* and you think I'm a toy you can play with whenever you want a laugh."

"That's not true. I don't find any of this funny."

Those were the truest words he'd ever uttered. This situation was the least humorous thing he'd ever done, and he was nearly gutted and killed by a wendigo during the final battle against the Lord.

"I needed you to know the truth, Sahira."

"Why? What do you expect to happen between us now? What did you think the truth was going to do?"

He tried to form a response but didn't have one. He'd asked himself the same question before coming here and still had no idea. "I don't know."

"You. Don't. Know. Well, that's fantastic, Orin. Is this just another game? Because we both know you love screwing with my head. You're worse than those symbols."

Feeling helpless and hating it, he reached for her again, but she retreated until she nearly collided with the opposite wall. "Don't touch me. Don't... don't... don't do *anything*. You keep not knowing because I can't... I don't... I *won't* do this with you anymore."

"What do you *want* from me?" he demanded with far more anger than he'd anticipated as her words caused his patience to fray. Not having complete control of his emotions was maddening, but she pushed his buttons more than he'd ever believed possible. The idea of losing her terrified him more than anything else in his life.

Concentrating on his breathing, he asked in a much calmer voice, "What do you want me to do?"

"*No*! This isn't on me. This is on *you*! *You* have to decide what *you* want, but just so you know, I won't sit around and wait for you to figure it out. This is *your* shit to deal with, Orin, not mine."

"Sahira—"

"I don't know if you're telling me the truth about this or lying to me again."

She shook her head before focusing her bright red eyes on him.

"I've never lied to you," he said.

Her lips curved into a snarl that revealed her elongated fangs before she stalked toward him again. "What would you call it when you have a nymph draped all over you and other women parading in and out of your arms the day after we slept together? What was all that, if not one. Big. Lie?"

"A misdirection, but not a lie."

She gawked at him before snorting in disbelief. "You're way more fucked up than I ever realized. I don't know if all dark fae are like you or if it's just *you*, but I refuse to be your punching bag anymore."

With that, she lowered her shoulder, shoved it into his chest, and pushed him back. She stormed over to the door and flung it open.

He didn't try to stop her as he gazed helplessly after her until the door closed again. Rage boiled up inside him and spilled over in a torrent he couldn't control.

Grasping the sink, he tore it from the wall, lifted it over his head, and smashed it down. Porcelain shattered around his feet and scattered to the corners of the room.

The breaking sink didn't appease his wrath but enflamed it as he punched and tore at the wall. His fists battered the plaster and wood until pieces of it littered the ground at his feet.

He hit the wood and plaster so often that his knuckles split open and streaks of blood splattered the wall. It dripped onto the ground, marking it as much as the debris he sent flying.

Turning, he kicked the toilet so hard with his booted foot that he tore it from the floor. It skittered a foot across the ground before crashing into the wall and stopping.

Some of his wrath disintegrated as he stood with his shoulders heaving while trying to control himself. He'd never done anything like this, but as he glanced around the ruined room, with all the holes in the walls, he saw how much control he'd lost.

Running a hand through his sweaty hair, he tugged at the ends as blood ran down his wrist and arm before spilling onto the floor. What had he done, and not just with the room, but also with *her*?

He'd never meant to hurt her, but he had. And their conversation had gone so much worse than he anticipated. He'd known she wouldn't start jumping for joy when he told her the truth and would most likely be annoyed with him, but he hadn't expected so much fury.

For someone who's been with countless women, you're clueless.

He hadn't considered it a possibility until Sahira, but it was true. He had no idea what to do with a woman outside a bed, and all this had completely proven it.

At least she knew the truth about there not being any other women. He had no idea what she'd do with that truth or what would come of it, but if one of them died, at least she would have this knowledge.

This had all blown up in his face, but he felt better knowing that. Even if she hated him forever—and he would ensure that didn't happen—he'd done the right thing.

Normally, doing the right thing wasn't something he cared about, and plenty of times, he'd done the completely *wrong* thing to suit his needs, but this time, he was glad for his annoying, new conscience. She was incensed with him, and he was happy about it.

He would figure this out; no matter what it took, he'd make things right with her.

CHAPTER EIGHTY

BY THE TIME EVERYONE WOKE, Sahira still wasn't talking to him. No one noticed, as the demon was doing much better, and they'd all focused on him.

Zeth's gait was still stiff and his skin color duller, but the green hue was gone from his face. He moved on his own as they searched the town.

No one had gone into the bathroom he'd trashed yet either, and when he emerged, they'd woken up but wisely chosen not to comment on the noise. Sahira must have heard him but kept her nose in the air and ignored him.

Orin hadn't expected much from this town and wasn't disappointed. With his eyes on the sky as they walked through the settlement, he searched for some sign of life amid all the endless blue... there was none.

He missed crows. He hadn't realized how much he enjoyed the sound of their caws, their black feathers shining in the sun, or their talons gripping his arm as he sent or received a letter from them. The barren sky was another reminder of everything he'd lost when he became trapped in this realm.

Like the pub, the other buildings in town were empty. If he

336   BRENDA K DAVIES

hadn't known what they were supposed to be, it would have been difficult to figure it out.

Even the stable, though it retained its rectangular shape and sliding doors, was barren of anything inside. No walls had been erected to form stalls.

Despite their emptiness, every structure still contained a symbol; each symbol was the same as the one in the pub. Orin scowled at the final one in the mercantile before turning and walking out the door. He hated those things as much as this realm.

Besides the pub, the library was the only other building with footprints inside. Their crispy, immortal friend hadn't explored any other structures but had been here too.

After the buildings, they investigated the surrounding land-scape. He wasn't surprised that no stream flowed behind the buildings and there wasn't a lake.

They wouldn't get any water from this place, which meant they might be screwed. He didn't regret giving Sahira his water last night; he wished she'd taken more because she wouldn't now that they knew for sure there wasn't any water here.

The grass and trees proved it rained here, or he assumed these things required water to survive. For all he knew, they thrived on the blood of their victims, but since the plants weren't trying to eat him—yet—he would rule that out... until one chomped on his arm.

The sun had passed its zenith in the sky and was starting to descend when they returned to the pub. There wasn't anything left to see in this town; they'd traversed every inch of it and discovered nothing of use.

As they set out their meager rations on the floor, he knew they had no choice but to continue past this town and see what lay ahead. They could stay for a few days and hope for some rain to refresh their water supply, but since they hadn't encountered anything they could hunt, they'd run out of food soon.

They had enough food to get them through tonight and tomorrow, but it would be almost impossible to stretch it beyond that timeframe, especially since he knew Sahira would give the demon some of her rations. While he nibbled at his stale, rock-hard bread, he studied the defeat on the other's faces.

It didn't feel right to move on from here, not with those symbols and a big X with an arrow in the center marking *this* town, but they'd found nothing to indicate a reason to stay. At one time, there might have been something here, and that was what the symbols were trying to show, but that time must have passed... along with whoever etched the marks into the walls.

Maybe it was time to return to Belda's town. The idea of admitting defeat caused his teeth to grind, but defeat was better than death.

But is it? Is this realm any kind of life?

His gaze settled on Sahira, and a pang tugged at his heart. Maybe, if it was just him, he'd keep going until he dropped, but it wasn't just him.

He couldn't watch her slowly die in this shithole of a realm. But did they continue or return to Belda's town?

He had no idea how they would make it back through the spiders and across the geyser field without any food, but continuing into nothing could mean certain death. The symbols, and the emptiness of these buildings, seemed to indicate this was the last town. They had no idea what lay beyond here.

When the others finished eating, Sahira rose and wiped her hands on her pants. "Excuse me."

No one spoke as she retreated up the stairs and into the bathroom. He didn't question why she didn't use the bathroom down here; there were some things he was better off not knowing.

Plus, he'd probably get his head ripped off if he tried talking to her again. When she wasn't outright ignoring him, he could feel her glaring daggers into the side of his head. She might try to kill him while he slept tonight.

He smiled at the possibility; at least she'd get close enough so he could touch her again. Though he hoped she would, he wasn't counting on her sleeping beside him again tonight.

When she emerged from the bathroom a minute later, he frowned as she glanced over the balcony railing before slipping into the room she'd resided in at Belda's. He'd assumed she checked the trapdoor last night but was pretty sure that's where she headed now.

Orin finished the last of his bread and leaned back to place his palms on the floor while he crossed his long legs before him. "We can wait for rain or leave here tomorrow."

"Do we have any other choices?" Pip asked.

"I think we've run out of those," Zeth said, and Orin agreed as Elsa nodded.

CHAPTER EIGHTY-ONE

After removing her protective spell, Sahira's fingers skimmed the floor as she searched for the seam to the trapdoor. It was so flawlessly put together that, even knowing it was there, she had difficulty locating it.

Finally, her fingers found it, and she lifted the wood away to reveal the stone steps descending to the hidden room. The rich scent of earth and the mineral aroma of stone enveloped her as she climbed down and stepped off the last stair.

With the shutters above closed, barely any light filtered into the room, but she knew it well enough to find the rock that opened the hidden door. With ease, she crossed the small space to the back wall.

The stones were cool against her fingertips as she ran them across the surface. It took her a minute, but eventually, she located the correct rock and pushed it.

With a tiny click, the door swung open to reveal the space behind the pub and the tall grass swaying in the breeze...

Except, it didn't.

She so fully expected to see the field of grass she'd seen while surveying the town that it took her a few seconds to realize it wasn't there. She'd stood behind this building earlier and knew grass crowded the back of the pub, but the door didn't reveal a meadow.

Instead, it opened onto another stone staircase. The steps descended into a darkness so complete she could only see the first two.

At the top of the stairs, one on each of the rickety banisters running along the rocky walls, were two skulls of immortals.

Shit.

The empty, black eye sockets of the skulls stared at her. Their teeth-filled jaws were set in a smile that sent goose bumps across her flesh.

One of them had pointy teeth that could easily shred the flesh from someone. She almost recoiled from their hideousness, but shock kept her riveted as she gazed from one unseeing skull to the other.

But are they unseeing?

The hair on her nape rose at the possibility of someone or some*thing* using those eye sockets to watch her. With enough magic, it wasn't impossible.

She almost slammed the door shut before stopping herself. She didn't understand what was happening or what this *was*, but these stairs were *finally* something new to explore, even if they creeped her out.

Are they real?

The idea she could be hallucinating this wasn't impossible. She was functioning on little sleep, food, or water. Her mind might be seeing something that wasn't there to give her a reprieve from the hopelessness of their situation and *Orin.*

That asshole.

Her teeth ground together as her rage over his earlier revelation momentarily doused her amazement. It had been hours since he'd told her what she could only assume was the truth, and she still had no idea what to make of what he'd said or how to process it.

She still wasn't sure if he'd been telling the truth, lying to her, or starting some new, fucked-up game. Whatever the answer, she refused to be his pawn anymore.

She wanted to believe him though. He didn't have a reason to lie to her about it except to screw with her more, but there had been a strange vulnerability in his eyes and a lack of confidence she'd never seen from him before.

Orin knew how to be many things and was quite capable of screwing with people until they went insane, but he wasn't good at being vulnerable or faking it. That had been something new with him, something she'd never seen before.

And he was so thin before we had sex the first time in the Barren Lands.

There was no faking that. She hadn't realized it then, but if he had been sleeping with all those women, he would have looked healthier out here for longer than he did.

He'd gone for a while without sex when she first entered the Cursed Realm, and he hadn't looked that bad. The time between when he would have been with the last woman and when they had sex in the Barrens Lands was about the same, which meant he was most likely telling the truth, but she still couldn't deal with it.

He was so screwed up in the head, and she couldn't wait around until he figured it out... if he ever did. After getting to know him better, she knew there was a good possibility he wouldn't.

The man was a complete idiot, and her dumb ass had gone and fallen for him. She'd kick herself in the ass for that for the rest of her life, but she had to live to do so, and escaping this place was a good way to guarantee life... or to ensure her death because these stairs looked as inviting as a steel trap. However, with no food and water here, they didn't have many options.

But is it real?

She squinted her eyes closed and rubbed them before opening them again. The stairs and skulls didn't vanish. They continued staring at her as those stairs beckoned with the promise of freedom or death.

With those skulls, death was probably more likely. They didn't exactly scream a welcome to anyone who saw them unless that's what the smiles were supposed to do. And if that was the case, whoever was behind these stairs had failed in their intentions.

When she rested her fingers against the white banister, the smooth coolness of it confirmed this wasn't a hallucination. She grasped the railing before the knowledge of what it was sunk in.

Sahira yanked her hand away from the femur and wiped her palm on her pants as she realized that connected bones comprised the entire banister. No matter how hard she rubbed, she couldn't rid herself of the feel of those things.

Stepping back, she grasped the door to close it while she went to get the others but hesitated before shutting it. What if she closed it and opened it again to discover the stairs had vanished?

What if I leave it open and something comes out to attack us while I'm gone?

After the scarog beetles and those spiders, that possibility decided it for her, and Sahira closed the door. She'd hate herself forever if she'd shut the door on their only chance of escape, but she wouldn't take any chances of something evil coming out of there to eat them while she was gone.

Turning, she sprinted up the stairs and back to the others.

CHAPTER EIGHTY-TWO

"WHAT IS IT?" Elsa inquired as she peered down the stone steps into the secret room below.

"A hidden room," Sahira answered. "In the wall below is another door that opens into the area behind the pub. There's one just like it in Belda's pub. It's how Radagast got into my room to attack me and where Orin and I hid after we fled the scarog beetles."

"Shit," Loth murmured as the three brownies leaned over the hole.

Elsa lifted her head to stare at Sahira with confusion and distress. "You've known about this the whole time?"

"Yes. I've checked it in every town we've gone through."

"I slept in this room when I first arrived in the Cursed Realm," Zeth said as he stared at the room in disbelief. "And I never knew it existed."

"*Belda* didn't know it existed until we showed her," Orin said.

"Why didn't you tell us about this?" Elsa demanded. "We've slept in the pub with you throughout all these towns. What if something had entered through this door while we were sleeping?"

"I placed a protection spell over it in every town we've gone through. It would have alerted us if someone tried to enter through here," Sahira said.

"You still should have told us but didn't trust us enough."

Sahira hated the sadness in her friend's tone and eyes, but she couldn't do anything about it. She probably should have told them; they were all still alive because they'd relied on each other to get through this. They were more than friends now; they were family… even Orin… sort of.

"I'm sorry." She rested her hand over Elsa's shoulder and squeezed. "I trust you; I do. After what happened with Radagast, I didn't want anyone else to know about this… except Belda and Orin."

Zeth lifted his head, and his eyes narrowed on Orin. "*You* knew about this?"

"Of course. I was there the night Radagast tried to kill her, and I wouldn't tell anyone else about it."

Zeth studied him with a furrowed brow until he glanced at Sahira; his forehead smoothed as understanding descended over him. Sahira didn't know what that understanding was, but when Zeth looked at Orin again, they held each other's gazes until Zeth nodded.

"I don't blame you," Zeth said.

Sahira had no idea what kind of an exchange they'd shared, and she didn't care. They had more things to worry about.

"Why are we getting to learn about it now?" Elsa demanded.

"Because something is different," Sahira said.

She ignored Orin's questioning look; he didn't deserve any answers. Lifting her chin, she descended into the darkness.

With her knees knocking a little, she crossed the room to the back wall and ran her trembling fingers over the rocks while she searched for the right stone. When she found it again, her hand stilled on it.

"This door should open onto the field behind the pub," she said as she pressed the rock.

Holding her breath, Sahira chewed her bottom lip while she waited for the door to open. For all she knew, what she'd seen before had vanished and now the field lay beyond.

She'd look like an idiot, and they'd all probably hate her for closing the door on their possible freedom, but she'd done what she believed was right. There was also the awful possibility she really *had* hallucinated it.

Except, when the door swung open, the skulls and bone-lined stairs greeted her. Her breath exploded from her as she stopped biting her lip. Relief and dread roared to the forefront while she gazed at the laughing skulls.

CHAPTER EIGHTY-THREE

"WHAT THE FUCK?" Orin whispered.

"Where do they go?" Pip inquired.

"I have no idea," Sahira said. "I've never seen this before. It's *never* been there before. This is all new."

"There's finally a difference in the realm," Loth murmured.

"Do we go down there?" Elsa inquired.

None of them spoke as they pondered this question, but Fath finally answered. "We don't have a choice. We *must* see where this difference leads."

He never spoke much, but he was right.

"It looks like it leads to Hell," Elsa said.

"This whole place is Hell," Orin said. "It's time to see what else it can throw at us."

When Sahira stepped forward, Orin grasped her wrist. She tried to snatch her arm away, but he held firm, and her body betrayed her by reacting to his touch.

If she was a cat, she might have purred as small sparks arced from his body and into hers while her pulse accelerated. He deserved to be kicked so hard that his nuts went up inside him, but her traitorous body still yearned for him.

Life was a cruel, treacherous bitch.

"I'll go first," he said.

"You will?" Pip squeaked from his shoulder.

"Yes."

Sahira started to argue but stopped; she was *so* tired of fighting with him. Besides, maybe he wouldn't make her so miserable if he died.

A sharp stab to her heart and an influx of panic at the thought of it happening told her she was wrong about that, and she hated being wrong.

She waved her hand at the door. "Go ahead."

He quirked an eyebrow as he released her wrist. "I'll go first, you can follow, and Elsa and the demon will bring up the rear."

Sahira didn't respond or tell him not to go, though the words were on the tip of her tongue. They *had* to do this.

Her heart thundered, and while a part of her contemplated shoving him down the stairs, she almost stopped him when he stepped onto the first stair. She fisted her hands to keep from doing so when the darkness enveloped him.

Silently, and half certain they were walking to their deaths, she fell in behind him with Fath on her shoulder. She didn't even descend one step before Orin vanished into the dark.

She glanced back as she sought some light, but it was already gone, and while they had their packs and weapons, their candles were lost during their battle with the spiders.

When she turned forward again, she still couldn't see Orin or Pip. Adrenaline pulsed through her as her fingers grazed the banister; she hated touching the atrocious thing, but she used it to keep herself oriented in the dark. It wasn't working that well.

She had no idea where they were or what lay ahead of them. Every part of her longed to return to the light, but she forced one foot in front of the other.

As she descended, the air grew chillier and the minerally tang of the rocks increased. At least it didn't smell like death.

Their steps were nearly noiseless on the stone stairs, but occasionally one of their boots scraped along them. When a small thud came from ahead, her heart leapt into her throat as she worried something had happened to Orin.

"The stairs twist to the right down here," Orin said.

His voice was a relief, and she realized his hand must have collided with a wall or something. She wanted to ask if he was okay but didn't dare speak as her fingers skimmed the banister while she followed it through the twist in the steps.

The stones encasing them like a tomb made hearing anything beyond a few feet difficult. Fath shifted on her shoulder but didn't speak; none of them did. What was there to say?

They all knew they were thinking the same thing. One way or another, this could be an end to them... or this realm. Despite the possibility of freedom, only trepidation thrummed through her.

After another fifty stairs, they took a turn, descended some more, turned, and climbed down some more before a dim light became visible at the bottom of the steps. At first, she wasn't sure the glow was there, but then Orin's head and shoulders started coming into view.

Not far ahead of him, the stairs ended in smooth, compressed dirt. Orin stepped off the last stair and moved forward enough so they could move out of the stairwell to fan out around him.

When she saw what lay ahead, Sahira's jaw dropped.

A town full of dozens of two and three-story buildings lay before them. All those buildings were turned so their windows faced the stairs, even the houses on the side streets spreading out to their left and right.

Sahira had no idea where the dim glow came from, but it hung behind the town. It wasn't the sun, as they remained underground, but that unknown glow cast a silhouette behind the buildings.

Each of the houses had lights on within them. Those lights

also weren't bright, but they revealed enough for her to see into all the open windows as no drapes or blinds obscured the view.

Nothing moved within the town or inside those homes as an aura of emptiness enshrouded everything. An air of expectation hung over them while they waited for something to happen.

As she concluded they'd only discovered more *nothing*, like they'd been pulled by magical strings, shadowy figures slid simultaneously into the windows.

The figures filled every single one of the hundred or so glass panes. They didn't move, wave, or do a thing but stand there and look out.

Sahira bit back a gasp as beside her Elsa jumped, and Fath almost tumbled off her shoulder. They were all different sizes, but the radiance behind the town didn't reveal any other features or details about the shadowy figures staring at them.

Then the figures all slid to the side, disappearing from the windows as suddenly as they arrived.

Sahira's heart raced as a rush of adrenaline told her to run, but her feet remained planted while she waited for the doors to open and the figures to rush out. Once again, nothing stirred, and the town settled into complete stillness.

What is going on?

She didn't dare voice the question; introducing noise into this land of silence seemed sacrilegious and a good way to unleash a horde of monsters on them.

Beside her, Orin's hand twitched, and his fingers found hers. She should jerk her hand away; she was still completely pissed at him, but she couldn't turn him away.

She needed this connection as his fingers slid perfectly between hers. Gulping, she tried to wet her suddenly parched throat and met his gaze.

She had no idea what lay ahead or what would happen to them now, but she suspected they'd finally find answers. Before then, this realm, and Orin's games, might destroy them both.

However, when his fingers tightened around hers, she couldn't turn him away as they walked into this new unknown together.

~

Read on for an excerpt from *Gilded Curses*, Book 9 in the series, or download now and continue reading: brendakdavies.com/GCwb

~

Stay in touch on updates, sales, and new releases by joining to the mailing list: brendakdavies.com/ESBKDNews

Visit the Erica Stevens/Brenda K. Davies Book Club on Facebook for exclusive giveaways and all things book related. Come join the fun: brendakdavies.com/ESBKDBookClub

As THEY CREPT through the town, Sahira's eyes darted from one building to another. Every part of her tensed for an attack. Her muscles ached, her heart galloped, and she didn't realize she'd clenched her teeth until her jaw started hurting.

Her hand remained entwined with Orin's. The warmth of it helped bolster her confidence even as she prepared to face down whatever monster came for them.

And she did not doubt that something was coming soon. There were no other options. She'd spent enough time in the Cursed Realm and the Barren Lands to know that nothing was ever simple or easy.

They hadn't made it this far for something else not to try to kill them too.

She glanced at Orin's profile as his crow-black eyes searched the town. His hair was the same color as his eyes. It had grown since she first met him and now curled against the collar of his black fae tunic. The tips of his pointed ears, a feature of all fae, dark and light alike, poked out of his hair.

His slightly pointed chin jutted out as anger radiated from

him and crackled against her skin. She almost felt bad for whatever awaited them in this strange town... *almost*. Because, at this point, she'd gladly gut, behead, or choke to death anything or anyone who came at them.

She'd had *way* more than enough of all this shit.

Sitting on Orin's shoulder, Pip hefted her spear and held it at the ready as what remained of her burnt tail stuck up in the air. The brownie's face showed no fear as she glowered at the buildings.

Like all brownies, she wore some form of brown clothes. Instead of a dress like some of the other females in the town they'd left far behind wore, Pip wore pants and a baggy shirt.

If she stood, she'd be about six inches tall, which was the average for her kind. Like all brownies, she had a mouse-like face, pointy nose, big front teeth, a tail, and whiskers.

Pip's friend, Fath, sat on Sahira's shoulder. He was far quieter than his companions, but Loth and Pip were both silent now. This wasn't a place where one sang songs as Pip loved to do or talked about the scenery as Loth did.

Loth perched on Elsa's shoulder. They'd started this journey with four of the small creatures but lost Gior on the geyser field. Sahira hoped they could get the three remaining ones out of here and back home, where they belonged.

She hoped she could get *herself* out of this too.

Maybe, once free, they could find a way to help all those they'd left behind. But first, they had to survive this awful place and everything it still had to throw at them.

When the shadowy figures inside the homes slid simultaneously into the window again, Sahira jumped a little as her fingers tightened on Orin's. She knew they were there, she'd seen them before, but she still wasn't prepared to have them all appear in that same creepy way again.

Whatever they were hadn't attacked yet, but she *hated* them even more than the spiders. At least they knew what to expect from the spiders; she had no idea what was happening here.

Orin's thumb stroked her hand as he sought to soothe her. She wasn't sure how long she'd been trapped here anymore; the days had all blurred into one, especially once they entered the Barren Lands. But two or three months ago, if anyone told her she'd willingly hold hands with Orin, she would have laughed in their faces.

Now, not only was she willingly holding hands with him, but she'd also had sex with him and sort of grown to like him... when he wasn't being a complete, obtuse asshole.

That wasn't very often.

And he'd reinforced his complete idiocy when he confessed to her, in a bathroom, that *she* was the only woman he'd had sex with since she entered the Cursed Realm. All the other women he'd paraded in front of her after they first had sex were nothing but another way to mess with her head, hurt her, and keep her on her toes.

It was then that she realized just how fucked in the head Orin was. She'd vowed *never* to let him in again, but she couldn't release his hand despite still being furious with him. No matter how messed up he was—and it was *huge*—she needed him.

The weird thing was, she believed he needed her too.

However, they could sort through the convoluted mess of their relationship later—or not, if something ate them first— but for now they had to concentrate on escaping this place and the horrors it harbored.

They had to be closer to finding answers and getting free. They just had to be.

And if they weren't, she might finally spiral out of control and lose her mind. Maybe the Cursed Realms were meant to be a place designed to break them, make them fall, and die a slow, miserable death full of despair and loneliness.

There you go, always looking at the bright side. But it was hard to look at the bright side of anything when everything seemed to be one endless maze of horrors.

~

As noiselessly as they appeared, the shadowy figures vanished from the windows again.

"What are those things?" Elsa whispered.

No one answered her. Whatever they were, they didn't appear dangerous as they hadn't all rushed out to attack. But they were in those homes, working as one strange unit and keeping an eye on *them*.

A shiver ran down Sahira's back as they all edged past the second set of buildings and moved deeper into the town. Around the bend, the road remained hardpacked dirt, and the buildings remained turned so the front door and windows were all at an angle to the street, allowing for more windows to look down on it.

All the curtains were open and dim light filled the windows, but no lamps or light fixtures hung in or stood near them. Most of the buildings were wood and painted in different shades of pale yellows, blues, reds, and greens. A few brick buildings also mixed with the others, but not many.

In this area, side roads branched off from the main one. They led through more houses angled so she could see the front doors and into their windows.

Although they didn't discuss it, no one tried to venture down one. They all stayed on the main road but would venture onto those roads once they finished here.

It was also only a matter of time before they had to enter one of the homes and discover what the shadowy figures were, but no one suggested doing so… yet.

When the shadowy figures slid into the windows again, Sahira couldn't stop herself from jumping *again*. She cursed herself for being an idiot. She'd faced far worse in this Cursed Realm and should be used to those awful things by now, but they still surprised her.

Probably because there was no rhyme or reason to their movements; they were just there and gone. This time, she counted the seconds until they vanished again; fifteen passed.

From the time they disappeared, she counted again. She was up to ninety when the entities reemerged; they stuck around for thirty seconds before retreating.

"I didn't think it was possible to hate anything more than those fucking spiders, but this place is starting to vie for first," Zeth growled.

Sahira didn't look at the demon as she counted while searching the windows. She was up to over two minutes when they reemerged. No, there definitely wasn't any rhyme or reason to these things... other than making life miserable.

When they vanished again, Orin's fingers squeezed hers before releasing her hand. "Fuck this," he growled. "Stay here."

Before she knew what he intended, he stormed away. Sahira lurched forward to stop him, but he was already too far gone, and her hands fell away into nothing as he stalked toward one of the homes.

Elsa grasped her arm, holding her in place as Orin grabbed the knob and twisted. Sahira wasn't surprised to learn the door was unlocked as it swung open with a creak.

"Wait!" Sahira called.

But Orin pulled his sword from his sheath and charged inside.

∾

Download *Gilded Curses* and continue reading now:
brendakdavies.com/GCwb

∾

Stay in touch on updates, sales, and new releases by joining to the mailing list: brendakdavies.com/ESBKDNews

Visit the Erica Stevens/Brenda K. Davies Book Club on Facebook for exclusive giveaways and all things book related. Come join the fun: brendakdavies.com/ESBKDBookClub

FIND THE AUTHOR

Brenda K. Davies Mailing List:
brendakdavies.com/News

Facebook: brendakdavies.com/BKDfb

Brenda K. Davies Book Club:
brendakdavies.com/BKDBooks

Instagram: brendakdavies.com/BKDInsta
Twitter: brendakdavies.com/BKDTweet
Website: www.brendakdavies.com

ALSO FROM THE AUTHOR

Books written under the pen name
Brenda K. Davies

The Vampire Awakenings Series

Awakened (Book 1)

Destined (Book 2)

Untamed (Book 3)

Enraptured (Book 4)

Undone (Book 5)

Fractured (Book 6)

Ravaged (Book 7)

Consumed (Book 8)

Unforeseen (Book 9)

Forsaken (Book 10)

Relentless (Book 11)

Legacy (Book 12)

The Alliance Series

Eternally Bound (Book 1)

Bound by Vengeance (Book 2)

Bound by Darkness (Book 3)

Bound by Passion (Book 4)

Bound by Torment (Book 5)

Bound by Danger (Book 6)

Bound by Deception (Book 7)

Bound by Fate (Book 8)

Bound by Blood (Book 9)

Bound by Love (Book 10)

The Road to Hell Series

Good Intentions (Book 1)

Carved (Book 2)

The Road (Book 3)

Into Hell (Book 4)

Hell on Earth (Book 5)

Into the Abyss (Book 6)

Kiss of Death (Book 7)

Edge of the Darkness (Book 8)

The Shadow Realms

Shadows of Fire (Book 1)

Shadows of Discovery (Book 2)

Shadows of Betrayal (Book 3)

Shadows of Fury (Book 4)

Shadows of Destiny (Book 5)

Shadows of Light (Book 6)

Wicked Curses (Book 7)

Sinful Curses (Book 8)

Gilded Curses (Book 9)

Whispers of Ruin (Book 10)

Secrets of Ruin (Book 11)

Tempest of Shadows

A Tempest of Shadows (Book 1)

A Tempest of Thieves (Book 2)

A Tempest of Revelations (Book 3)

A Tempest of Intrigue (Book 4)

A Tempest of Chaos (Book 5)

Historical Romance

A Stolen Heart

Books written under the pen name

Erica Stevens

The Coven Series

Nightmares (Book 1)

The Maze (Book 2)

Dream Walker (Book 3)

The Captive Series

Captured (Book 1)

Renegade (Book 2)

Refugee (Book 3)

Salvation (Book 4)

Redemption (Book 5)

Vengeance (Book 6)

Unbound (Book 7)

Broken (Book 8 - Prequel)

The Kindred Series

Kindred (Book 1)

Ashes (Book 2)

Kindled (Book 3)

Inferno (Book 4)

Phoenix Rising (Book 5)

The Fire & Ice Series

Frost Burn (Book 1)

Arctic Fire (Book 2)

Scorched Ice (Book 3)

The Ravening Series

The Ravening (Book 1)

Taken Over (Book 2)

Reclamation (Book 3)

The Survivor Chronicles

The Upheaval (Book 1)

The Divide (Book 2)

The Forsaken (Book 3)

The Risen (Book 4)

ABOUT THE AUTHOR

Brenda K. Davies is the USA Today Bestselling author of the Vampire Awakening Series, Alliance Series, Road to Hell Series, Hell on Earth Series, The Shadow Realms Series, A Tempest of Shadows Series, and historical romantic fiction. She also writes under the pen name, Erica Stevens. When not out with friends and family, she can be found at home with her husband, son, and pets.